Also by Erin Zarro

Fey Touched series:

Fey Touched
Grave Touched
Ever Touched
Sun Touched (online serial)

Reaper Girl Chronicles:

Reaper Girl

Horror collection:

In Flames

Poetry chapbooks

Life as a Moving Target
Without Wings

Fireborn

ERIN ZARRO

Printed in the United States of America

First printing, 2018

ISBN-13: 9781983249082

A Turtleduck Press release
http://www.turtleduckpress.com

Cover design © Molly Phipps (We Got You Covered Design)
Interior design © Kit Campbell
Author photo © Karen Conroy

Except Love. She's real. □

Author website: http://www.erinzarro.com

Chapter 1

I USED TO BE A Grim Reaper.

Now, I was human.

But as I was discovering, I had yet to get the hang of it.

My husband Rick and I were watching the television. A show called "Survivor."

"I don't really understand," I said. "There aren't any people in the back of the television. Where are they?"

"They tape the show onto film and then broadcast it from a building in town. Sometimes even farther away," Rick said, squeezing my hand.

It still made no sense. "Tape? Like the sticky stuff we use to put things together?"

Rick chuckled. "No, no, Leliel. It's film. It records what they say and do. Kind of like a camera, except they can move around and the camera captures it."

I sort of understood cameras.

"Why are they talking and gossiping when they should be making sure they have food for dinner?" I asked, frustrated. "This show makes no sense! If I were there, I'd start working on dinner. And maybe making my dwelling warmer."

"That's how this show works. See, they are worried about food, but they are also worried about alliances. Alliances help them survive longer on the show. You'll see. It's cool."

I'd have to take his word for it.

A half hour later, after the people-not-in-the-back-of-the-television made fish for dinner and several of them fought over who should get the most, two people wandered off to kiss—again, not worried about shelter when it started getting windy—and then some guy gathered them together and they voted to get rid of someone, and then it was over.

It wasn't "cool." It wasn't even fun.

"I'm not sure I like this show, Rick. It's too strange," I said. "Are there any shows that make sense?"

Rick chuckled. "This is what's called 'reality TV.' Real people doing real things. It's not made up ahead of time. People love this crap. And while it's kind of stupid, it's interesting."

"I guess," I said, shrugging. "But that's kind of like life. Too much, you know? Don't you watch the television to escape from real life?"

Rick pushed a button on the "remote control," which I understood to be the thing that controlled the television. "Most of the time. But not always."

The picture changed to a "game show." Rick had explained that people played games and it was broadcast to the television. At any rate, I didn't understand what the people were supposed to do.

Rick must have noticed my confused look. "The player spins the wheel, and where it lands determines certain things. And see that grid there? The player has to guess what it says. They pick letters, and if the letters are in any of the words, they are displayed. But they have to buy vowels."

"Huh?"

"They use the money they have from spinning the wheel," Rick explained. "You'll see."

I lay against Rick's shoulder and watched as the one player kept spinning the wheel and got more and more money but could not guess the phrase.

I was about to comment on that when my stomach twisted, and I got goosebumps. In my mind's eye I saw flames. Flames leaping, flames destroying. A human-shaped figure sat in the middle of it all, not moving.

This was no natural death. It was in a house. And somewhere close. I could almost feel the flames on my own skin.

Clearly I hadn't had enough sleep last night.

I rubbed my eyes.

"Leliel?" Rick's voice jolted me out of my trance.

I glanced at him, still seeing the flames.

Rick squeezed my hand again. "What's wrong? You look pale."

"I'm seeing a fire and a person sitting in the middle of it," I said, swallowing hard. "I think it might be a suicide. Something's not right. We should—" I shut my mouth. I was human now, like Rick, and we needed to live like normal people. The Underworld and reaping souls were behind me.

But something called to me, waiting for an answer.

THE NEXT DAY, I was making dinner. Rick wasn't home from work yet. Love, our hellcat, twined around my legs and nuzzled me. She was from the Underworld. Hellcats were the fiercest cats around, but Rick had somehow tamed her. When we left the Underworld, we took her with us.

"I'll feed you once I get this casserole in," I said, hooking an errant strand of hair behind my ear. I'd just learned what casseroles were and I was anxious to try one. It was simple, with chicken, mayonnaise, cheese, and broccoli. So many yummy foods! We didn't have half of this when I was alive three hundred years ago before I became a Reaper.

I placed the casserole in the oven, then went into the cabinet for Love's food. As I opened the can—I was learning to *hate* can openers because they were so hard to use—a chill went up my spine. And an overwhelming sense that something was wrong again.

I set the can down. "Give me two minutes, okay?"

With a feeling of dread, I sat down on the couch and closed my eyes.

In my mind's eye, I saw flames again. And a human figure curled into a ball. Unnatural, just like the last one. Anger. Sadness.

Another suicide? In forty-eight hours?

I blinked, and it was gone.

Something was wrong. I couldn't put my finger on it. But it didn't follow the natural course of things. The two humans apparently dead before their time…in the most horrific way possible.

I knew. Because I'd died in a fire, too.

I stood and paced, trying to expend my nervous energy. "What's wrong? Why are they dying? And why two fires? I can't…it's not right." I headed back into the kitchen and grabbed the can of food. "We should help. No, we shouldn't." I spooned the food into Love's bowl, wrinkling my nose at the smell. "Here you go." I put it on the floor next to her water bowl. She dove in, not even looking at me. She only had eyes for chicken pâté or whatever that stuff was.

"We can't help. We're just regular people," I muttered, checking the casserole. I wasn't sure what I was checking for. It had only been in there—oh, no. I'd forgotten to set the timer!

We didn't have timers way back when.

How long had it been? I set the timer, hoping I was at least close. I didn't want a burnt dinner.

Burnt dinner…which reminded me about the fires.

I was sure the police had been notified and were working on it.

Yes, but…

But what?

Was I imagining this? Was I so bored being a housewife that I'd made this up?

Could there have been two suicides by fire? Did these things happen all the time?

No, something inside me said. *You know what to do.*

"I'm not a Reaper anymore." Love looked up at me, ears perked forward. "I don't have the responsibility. I'm human now." Love gave me a skeptical look. "Really, Love. We're normal people with normal lives and that's that."

I KNEW RICK was trying to make me feel good when he dug into the burnt casserole with enthusiasm. I'd apparently screwed up the cook time. Damn. When would I get the hang of things?

I poked at mine. "You don't have to eat it. We can order…what's it called?"

"Takeout," Rick said in between bites. He looked up at me. "It's not *that* bad. Some parts aren't even burnt." He took another big bite.

I winced. "Yeah, but it's mostly burnt—"

"It's okay, Leliel," Rick said. "Really."

I shrugged. If he wanted to eat it, I guess I'd give it a shot. I speared some of it on my fork and put it into my mouth. I chewed. It wasn't too bad. After I'd swallowed, I said, "There's been another fire. I'm beginning to believe something is horribly wrong."

Rick fed Love an unburnt piece of chicken. "What do you mean?"

How could I explain it? "It isn't natural, what's happening. Those people weren't supposed to die."

Rick's expression was one of concern. "Well, death by fire isn't natural. It's unfortunate, but—"

"That's not it," I said, setting my fork down and leaning forward. "It's not natural, yes. But it's more than that. It wasn't their time."

Rick's eyes widened. "Does this have to do with the fires?" He met and held my gaze. I knew that whatever my answer was, he'd still love and support me. Even if I sounded stark raving mad.

"Yeah, it does." I shrugged, not sure how to go on.

Rick laid his hand on mine. "Whatever's happening, we'll get through it."

"I know." I forced myself to smile. "But I am human now, and I need to put all of that behind me."

"That's one way to do it," Rick said, stroking my thumb and palm. "Or we could try to see what's going on. See if…if we could help."

"The police are working on it, I'm sure," I said, but even that didn't make me feel better. This something, whatever it was, was beyond the police. But I didn't tell Rick. One thing at a time.

Rick nodded. "True."

"I'd be stupid to get involved with death stuff again." I took another bite of my casserole.

"Yeah. We need normalcy," Rick said, taking a sip of his soda. "This is your one chance at living a normal life."

I nodded firmly. "Then that's it. We're not going to get involved. We'll feel bad for those deaths, but it's not our concern." I lifted my soda glass up. "What matters is you and me and Love."

We clinked glasses.

"And what lies ahead of us, not behind us," Rick said.

"Hear, hear," I said, giggling as Love chose that very moment to hop onto our table and try to eat my casserole.

She ate a lot of it.

See? She liked it, too.

What a relief.

"I CAN'T STOP thinking about those deaths."

Rick and I were in the car on our way to the veterinarian—an animal doctor—which was what normal cat owners did. Rick figured that Love looked pretty normal, with the exception of her razor-sharp claws and glowing eyes. She managed to dim them for now, and I hoped they'd stay dimmed. Or else we'd have lots of questions to answer.

I had been wondering how her general health was. Whether living outside the Underworld had caused any permanent effects. It didn't seem that way, but what did I know? I was still impressed with indoor plumbing and telephones.

Rick glanced at me. "Are you are still being called?" He made a turn to the right.

I shrugged. "I don't know. It's just…I want to fix it."

"You can't fix death, as extraordinary as you are." He flashed me a grin.

"I don't mean it that way," I said, watching the scenery pass by. "I meant…change it…no, that's not it." I sighed. "This is tough to explain. I want to stop the suicides from happening."

Rick stopped at a red light. "So you do want to help?"

"I feel like I should, you know? But this life means that I get to be normal again, and I don't want to be involved with death anymore. I can't decide." My chest constricted. What I didn't tell him was the wrongness that had been poking at me like a blade since the two suicides. Wrongness that needed to be righted.

Rick made the car go again and pulled into the parking lot of the veterinarian's office. Love let out a pissed-off meow and a growl, just in case we couldn't tell that she was mad about riding to an unknown, weird place in what amounted to a cage.

I was pretty sure that if it were me in there, I'd be mad, too.

Rick turned the car off and opened the door. "Let me carry her, okay? She's heavy."

"That's fine." I got out of the car and looked at the place that would hopefully take good care of Love. She was our child.

Rick opened the back and retrieved our pissed-off hellcat. "I'm wondering if you should just do something. Get it out of your system."

I nodded. "Maybe. But what can I do? I'm not—" We passed a couple who were leaving the veterinarian. The woman carried a cage with a squawking bird in it. "I'm no longer extraordinary," I said softly.

"Then that solves the problem," Rick said as he opened the door for me. "If you aren't what you were, you can't help, right?"

Love growled again.

"Relax, baby. We're almost there," I said in what I hoped was a soothing voice. I'd never had kids. Or cats, for that matter. So I was guessing. "But what about how I am feeling? I can't stand it."

We walked into the veterinarian's office. It was a brightly decorated, happy kind of place with pictures of animals on all four blue-painted walls. A large, long desk stood prominently in the center of the room. There were several other doors.

A large dog barked at us, and its owner said apologetically, "She's friendly. Doesn't bite. Sorry if she scared you."

Another cat in a cage hissed when I passed it. Love hissed back.

The room bore the smell of several different animals. I wrinkled my nose and wondered if I should breathe through my mouth for the duration.

Rick went to the desk and talked briefly to one of the women there. She looked young, with glasses and a colorful outfit that looked to be a sort of uniform. Rick filled out some paperwork, then picked up Miss Grumpy and led me to some seats closer to the doors and away from the animals.

"So, um...what are we going to do?" Rick said softly. That was one of the things I loved most about him. We were a team. Whatever I did, I always had his full support. And I would do the same for him.

I stuck a finger into the cage and wiggled it. Love pounced on it, giving me her idea of love bites, which were like little needles. I let her get her aggression out on me for a bit. Maybe she'd wear herself out. "I don't know. I *want* this life, Rick. I really do."

Rick touched my cheek with a fingertip. "I know that. We've had an amazing life so far."

"It's only been a few months," I said with a chuckle. "We have a long way to go yet."

"The best few months of my life."

I smiled. "You are such a romantic."

"But don't tell the guys at the bike shop. It'll ruin my tough-guy image."

A woman opened the door closest to us and stepped into the room. "Love?" She glanced at the papers in her hand. "Feline?"

We both stood.

What was the protocol? Let her take Love? Then what?

"That's us," Rick said, jolting me from my thoughts.

We walked over to the woman. She led us into another smaller, very bright and cheery room with more pictures of animals.

Rick set Love on the counter.

"You can let her out as soon as I leave and the door is closed." She made a notation on a piece of paper. "I can tell she's not a happy kitty."

I glanced at Rick, one eyebrow arched. He chuckled.

The woman left the room, closing the door behind her.

Rick opened the cage. "Freedom!"

Love shot out and jumped down onto the floor. She made two whole circuits of the perimeter, then stopped and curled up, probably exhausted.

And I realized that all this turmoil was exhausting—and I was tired of my indecision. I had to help. Whatever the cost.

The veterinarian bustled in and introduced herself as Dr. Sutto. She examined our poor hellcat and did do the most unspeakable thing ever—a thermometer up her butt—and then squeezed and touched and prodded her. Love's eyes glowed a few times, but Dr. Sutto didn't notice. Love hissed at her several times, then went to batting her with a paw when she got close.

"It's going to be okay," I told Love, giving her a scratch behind her ears. "We just want you healthy."

Love let out a yowl, which was probably the hellcat equivalent of "Screw you, Mom."

"It looks like she's fine, but I'd like to take some blood to make sure she's good there," Dr. Sutto said. "Has she had her shots? Heartworm pills?"

Rick looked mystified. "New cat owners here. Can you explain that?"

Dr. Sutto was patient as she explained everything. We agreed to the blood test—with more apologies to Love—and also agreed to the heartworm pills.

She could be immune. But who wanted to take that chance? She was basically a normal cat with, most likely, normal cat issues.

So we ended up leaving there three hundred dollars poorer, with an angry feline in a cage, and a box of pills we might or might not need.

Progress.

As we were getting into the car, I said, "I have to fix this."

"The suicides?" Rick asked.

"Yes. Someone has to. And I guess it's me." I buckled myself in.

"Are you sure? This is pulling you back to your Reaper life." Rick made a turn to the left.

"I think we should. I'm feeling these things for a reason," I replied. Damn. I'd thought I could have a normal life. And now...it wasn't going to happen.

Love let out a mournful cry, as if she agreed.

Apparently the party was just getting started.

Yay.

FIRE, BURNING beneath my eyelids.

It woke me from sleep and beckoned me to follow it into the night. Hellfire! The feeling was back again and stronger.

"Leliel, what..." Rick murmured, still mostly asleep.

I got out of bed and started getting dressed. Love meowed plaintively, and I stopped and petted her a few times.

But the fire—I had to get to the fire. It was so *wrong*—

I had to investigate. Because that was what you did when you were mostly human and felt weird things and needed to set things to rights.

I switched on the lamp on my night table.

"Leliel?" Rick's eyes opened and squinted at me. "What are...what are you doing? Is it morning yet?"

Who'd be crazy enough to get out of bed and get dressed at two-thirty in the morning? Me, of course. The feeling wasn't going away; in fact, it intensified—again—and filled my veins.

"There's something wrong." I slid on my shoes and reached for my jacket. "I have to go."

And then I saw it.

A young man. Port wine stain on his left elbow. Appendix scar on his abdomen. His mother had thought it was indigestion, and he had nearly died. How did I suddenly just know that?

He was sitting in a small room on a recliner. The recliner was old, with frayed edges. The room was warm and welcoming. Not a place of death.

He was on fire, flames reaching high, engulfing his body. His skin turned black; his fingers and toes fused together.

He was screaming, his flesh melting, his hair disintegrating.

Someone whispered one word: "Vengeance."

"Oh, no," I whispered. "I need to go…"

Rick sat up. His longish hair was sticking out every which way. "I'm going with you."

I headed for the bedroom door. "I can't wait. I have to—"

He grabbed my hand. It grounded me, brought me out of my haze. "Please tell me what's wrong."

I took a breath, then exhaled. "There's a fire. That way." I pointed. "I just saw a young man being burned to death. I have to do something."

"Oh, baby." He got out of bed and wrapped his arms around me. "You had another vision?"

I pulled away. "Yes. I don't understand, but something is telling me to go to him."

"To save him, maybe?" Rick started getting dressed, too.

I shook my head. "No, we're too late. But I still need to go there. There's something important about it."

Rick threw on his shirt and grabbed his keys. "Whatever it is, it must be huge."

"For me to suddenly start having visions?" I asked. "Maybe."

"Do you think it's connected to the Underworld or His Highness?" Rick asked, his eyes narrowed. "Because that might make sense."

His Highness was the king of the Underworld. And my former boss. I opened the door. "I'd say so. It's clear that he isn't through with me yet.

THE AREA SMELLED of fire. But the house hadn't burnt to the ground. It appeared that the fire had been somewhat contained.

We'd found the location using my ability, whatever it was. It had led us right there.

Several confused-looking police officers milled around outside.

"Excuse me?" I said, suddenly feeling shy. I didn't belong here…but I was meant to be here.

One of the police officers looked my way. "Can I help you?" he asked sharply.

I took a breath, smelled smoke, and let it out. "Um, I'm here to talk to a relative of the…the deceased."

"We were hoping to help," Rick put in. "We, uh, saw the commotion here and, uh—"

"I'm not sure what you *can* do," the police officer said. "But we're about done here so I guess it can't hurt." He started to walk away, shaking his head.

"What happened?" I said.

He turned around, his eyes distant. "What looks to be suicide. But…for someone to set himself on fire…" He shook his head again. "It doesn't make sense. And it's our job to make it make sense, and…" A shrug. "To be determined, I guess."

And then he was gone, disappearing into the house.

Rick glanced at me. "I guess we go in?"

I took his hand in mine. "Yep."

We went inside, into a foyer that looked like it belonged in someone's castle.

And then we followed the police officer into the room where it happened.

It used to be a lovely room. The brocade curtains were singed. The shelves were oak now stained black. The carpet—the parts that the fire had not touched—was a pretty cream color. Vases of flowers were placed strategically around the room, bringing a hint of color into it. One of the flowers, a red rose, was singed.

The recliner was there, but it looked more like a burnt hunk of wood and fabric that anything else.

A woman with a tear-streaked face—presumably the mother of the deceased—stood talking to a police officer. She had the look of someone whose plug had been pulled from reality.

Several police officers were already present.

"Are you sure we should be here?" Rick asked me. He lagged a bit behind me as I headed toward the woman.

Something wasn't quite right about this.

I glanced over my shoulder at him. "I'm positive."

Rick caught up to me, gripping my elbow. "But it was a suicide—"

"No, it wasn't," I whispered, tasting bile and ash. I wanted nothing more than to get out of here, go back to my little apartment and little cat and my husband and being human.

But the visions wouldn't let me. These odd feelings that didn't make sense were going to drive me insane if I did nothing.

"This is a private residence," one of the police officers said once he caught sight of me. Hellfire. Busted in the first five minutes. Way to go. "I'm going to have to ask you to leave."

I gave him a tight smile. "I'm not here to cause any trouble. I just need to speak with the mother of the deceased. For like, five minutes."

"If you're with the press—"

"She isn't," Rick put in, holding his hands up. "You have my word."

The police officer seemed to be warring with himself, his brow puckered and his teeth clenched. "I don't understand why you're here, but I'll allow it. If I find out you were here under false pretenses, there'll be a jail cell with your name on it."

I crossed my chest. I'd seen people do that on the television. "I promise. I am not here under false pretenses."

"And what is your name, ma'am? For my records?" He took out a pen and small notepad, his eyes searching for something. It made me feel wrong in my skin.

"Leliel Ashton," I said, drawing myself tall. I wasn't doing anything wrong.

"Rick Ashton, her better half," Rick said with a smile.

"All right, then. Five minutes," the police officer said, and left to talk to another police officer. I could feel his weird smarmy eyes on me, though.

"Let's do this," Rick murmured. "Before he changes his mind."

"Right," I said with a sigh. "Why do I feel like a criminal? Or a reporter? I'm none of those things, but I feel wrong."

"It's okay," Rick said, taking my hand in his. It was solid, warm, and alive.

This was not a suicide.

We came to the mother and I almost lost my nerve. Her face...the pain in her eyes...

"Excuse us?" Rick said. "We, uh, wanted to give you our condolences. I lost my daughter to leukemia, and I know how much—"

The woman's face distorted in anger, her hands clenched into fists. "Who are you and why are you in my home?"

I inclined my head to her, hoping to look less guilty than I felt. But I needed to talk to her, because something was very wrong here. "I wanted to discuss something with you."

"There's nothing to discuss," the woman said. "My son is dead. He took his own life—"

Another flash.

An overwhelming feeling of being out of control. Of being controlled by something—or someone— other than myself.

Pain. But not my pain...someone...else's.

Flames. Purging. Vengeance.

"Leliel?" Rick asked. "What's going on? Is something wrong?"

"Who are you people?" the woman asked. She called out to the police officers, "Hey! Get these people—"

I resurfaced long enough to protest. "No! Please! Just let me explain—"

"Crap, the police guy is headed this way," Rick muttered. To the mother, he said, "Look, I know you don't know us and you have no reason to trust us, but my wife is—she's psychic and she's—I think she knows something about your son's passing. Please let her talk to you."

"Need some help over here?" The police officer was giving us a dirty look. What a jerk.

"Not yet," the woman said, squaring her shoulders. "I will listen to what she has to say. Then you can remove them from my property."

Another flash. I closed my eyes.

A voice that filled every part of me. A strong compulsion.

Had this happened before he died?

"Please. We'll go as soon as Leliel tells you what she knows," Rick said.

I opened my eyes. "What's your name, ma'am? I'd feel better—"

"Aimee Chandler," the woman said. "I used to be a fashion model back in the day."

I arched a brow. Hmm, her face was devoid of wrinkles, and she had long eyelashes. Her hair was brown and shiny and impeccably styled in a bun at her nape. Yeah, I could believe it.

"I bet," Rick said, and I jabbed his ribs.

"Hey, just sayin'," he said. "You know I only have eyes for you. Hell, I brought you back from being—" He seemed to realize where we were and stopped. "Anyway, I am... currently making a fool of myself. Carry on."

Ms. Chandler chuckled softly. "You two seem like you're so much in love. I wish I'd had that with my ex-husband."

I decided not to ask. I had to get to the point quickly or be kicked out. "Ms. Chandler, as my husband said, I have some unusual abilities. I had a vision. I believe it was about your son. And I'm getting flashes of things. I think these were things that were happening just before he died."

Ms. Chandler's face paled even more, giving her a chalky kind of look. Not so pretty now. But death and grief weren't pretty things. "How—how do you know this?"

"She's learning about these things as she goes," Rick said.

I decided that Rick's idea of calling me a psychic might actually work better than telling her the truth.

"Hellfire, I'm going to come out and say it," I said, giving Ms. Chandler a searching gaze. "And you can decide if I'm right or wrong, okay?"

Why'd His Highness have to curse me with this crap? Why couldn't I just be normal?

Rick glanced at me, and his expression said, *Go for it. You can do this.*

Ms. Chandler nodded, hugging herself. "Fine. What is it?"

The words stuck in my throat. "I'm psychic. I feel this stuff so vividly that I can't imagine it not being true. I'm sorry."

"I guess I can—maybe it's true," Ms. Chandler said softly, her eyes distant. "If you're psychic, it would make sense you would know things, I guess." She lifted one shoulder in a shrug. "If I were to believe in such things." And there was the mask—the polished, perfect, fashion model with her distant looks and artificial life. She used it to bury her feelings. Specifically, her devastation over losing her son.

And I was about to smash everything into splinters.

Why me?

I took a breath. "The short version of the story...I'm getting the distinct impression that your son didn't do this of his own free will. He was...forced," I said. Nausea churned my stomach, and the room spun. Was I really hurting this poor woman?

"That's impossible. He left a note. And a card," Ms. Chandler said tightly, mask firmly in place. "Let me get it. You'll understand when you see it, Mrs. Ashton."

She left, head held high, and I felt defeated.

Rick put his arm around my shoulders. "What if it's wrong? We're torturing this poor woman."

"It's right," I said. "I feel it deep inside. For whatever reason, I have been chosen to figure out the truth."

I watched the police officers as they did…whatever police officers did. The officer from earlier was eyeing me again, and I stopped watching them.

"That police officer is watching us really closely," I said. "We should probably try to wrap this up before he throws us out."

"Good idea," Rick said, taking my hand and squeezing it.

I grinned. He always had a way of making me smile.

"Here, look at this," Ms. Chandler said from behind us, startling me. She held out a piece of paper. I took it.

Another flash.

Hand cramping. Trying to stop the movement of the pen. Concentrating. Fighting. *Don't want to do this...*

I blinked, and the letters on the paper resolved into words.

Not many.

Dear Mother,

I can't take it anymore. I have to leave. I know you'll be sad but I'm in a better place. Love, Freddie.

It was so...canned. I mean, that was what you'd expect someone to write as a suicide note. Something told me it wasn't Freddie. It was someone else. It was why he'd fought it, but ultimately lost.

I handed the paper back to Ms. Chandler. "He wrote it, yes, but he was forced into it. There's no feeling in this at all. Anyone could have written it."

"Feeling?" Ms. Chandler squeaked. "He said he couldn't take it anymore—"

"Couldn't take what anymore, Ms. Chandler?" I asked. I was on the razor's edge of being kicked out, but it was important she know this. Too important.

Her brow furrowed. "I don't...know."

"Exactly. Because he was never suicidal to begin with," I said.

"Did he present any of the signs?" Rick asked. "Loss of interest in things he liked to do, withdrawing from the world, stuff like that?"

Ms. Chandler studied her impeccable high heels. "No, I don't believe he did."

"You said there was a card?" I prompted. "A greeting card?" Now that was just plain weird.

"Oh, yes," she replied, distracted. "It's here, in my sweater pocket." She reached in and took it out. "It's one of those Tarot fortune-telling card things. Freddie wasn't into that."

Another point in my favor. I knew about the Tarot. I'd known girls who were into it back before I became a Reaper, always trying to figure out their futures. Never quite worked the way they wanted, though. Over the years, I'd done readings, primarily for insight. "Which one is it?"

She showed it to us.

Two of Cups. The soulmate card.

"Okay, translation," Rick said, breaking into my thoughts.

Why would he leave the Two of Cups at the scene? Had he been in love with someone?

"Was he in a relationship?" I asked. To Rick, I said, "It's the soulmate card. Usually..." I broke off, the gerbils in my head spinning their wheels.

"None that I am aware of," Ms. Chandler replied. "He had girlfriends, but I never let him get serious. He was too young."

"How old was he?" Rick asked.

"Twenty." Ms. Chandler pursed her lips. "He was going to school to be a lawyer."

"Where did he go to school, ma'am? If I may ask?" Rick said.

Ms. Chandler's eyes glistened with tears. "Amsburg Law School." She took out a handkerchief and dabbed her eyes. "But...how could he have not done this to himself?" Her lower lip trembled, and she sniffed.

"I don't know, but I'm going to find out. Your son was murdered."

"THERE'S ABSOLUTELY no way he was murdered, Mrs. Ashton," Ms. Chandler said, taking a sip of coffee. We were seated in her impeccably clean and cheery dining room, resplendent in gold and cream. Everything was in its proper place, and there was no clutter anywhere.

And there wasn't any life, either.

I set my coffee mug down, the sound ringing in the tense air. I met Ms. Chandler's gaze squarely. "Everything points to Fred not doing this of his own free will. Which is murder."

"But who would kill him?" Another sip, her fingers trembling.

"Did he have any enemies? Any problems with anyone?" Rick asked, squeezing my hand underneath the table. He kept me centered, focused. He also kept me from running away.

Ms. Chandler shook her head. "Absolutely not. He was well liked by everyone."

"No one is well liked by absolutely everyone," I said before I could stop myself. Smart. Really smart. "I mean, people are funny sometimes. Maybe he never told you about it?"

"Freddie told me everything," Ms. Chandler said, her nose in the air. How dare we question the sanctity of her relationship with *Freddie*? Hell.

"Young men are weird," Rick put in. He was drinking water. Filtered, naturally, because how could Ms. Chandler put impure water into her body or anyone else's? "They don't always tell their parents everything. I know I didn't when I was that age."

"What happened to your husband?" I asked.

Ms. Chandler looked down at her coffee. "Ex-husband. He's not here. We divorced years ago."

"Did Fred have any contact with him?" I asked, hoping I sounded reasonable and casual.

"Yes, of course. They saw each other every other weekend and every other holiday." Ms. Chandler sounded defensive. "What does that have to do with this?"

I shrugged. "Just a thought."

"Tell her about your vision." Rick nudged me. "But leave out the specifics. I don't think Ms. Chandler wants to hear that."

I wasn't sure I should go there. The vision had terrified me. "I... don't know."

Rick took a sip of water. "It'll help."

"Do tell," Ms. Chandler said.

"Okay, fine." I picked up a mini cake with a complicated French name but didn't eat it. I still tasted ash. "I saw…he was burning alive. He was sitting on an old recliner. And he...screamed…"

"Go on," Ms. Chandler said. "What else?"

I swallowed hard. "A voice kept whispering something to him. One word. *Vengeance*."

"And this is why you think he was killed? Because of something you think you saw? How do you know it was even my son?"

I knew she'd ask that, because it was a logical question. "Did Fred have a port wine stain birthmark on his left elbow?"

Ms. Chandler paled. She tried taking a sip of coffee, but her hand shook too much. "Yes, he had one."

"And an appendix scar on his abdomen? He had it done when he was five, correct? Almost died because you thought it was indigestion?"

Ms. Chandler made a wheezing sound, and then her head hit the table, spilling the coffee. Brown stained her lovely cream tablecloth. I watched it make its way to us.

She had fainted.

"WE ARE GOING to investigate this," the same police officer who'd threatened us said. His name was Officer Bailey, and he hated us on sight, apparently. "While it appears to be a suicide, we still have to look into things."

The police were still outside, and I just had to open my mouth.

"What about the Tarot card?" I said. "It's weird, right?"

"We will determine what is weird and what isn't," Officer Bailey snapped, his face turning red. "Don't tell us how to do our jobs."

I blinked. "I understand, sir. I just...none of this makes sense to me."

"We will figure it out," Officer Bailey said, his voice a bit less snappy. "Most of us have been doing this for many years."

He was so going to hate me. "Maybe I can help. I'm psychic—"

Officer Bailey rolled his eyes, stopping me cold. "We don't use psychics, ma'am. We use *science*. Something called forensics."

Great. Just another way I was different from them. He clearly thought I was some weirdo who didn't know anything about life. And...I didn't.

"Well, anyway, even if you weren't a psychic, we do not let civilians into investigations. Have a nice day." And he was gone, the subject closed

I knew that I was right.

Now I just needed to prove it.

Chapter 2

THE NEXT DAY, Ms. Chandler asked me and Rick to come over and discuss the findings of the police. My stomach clenched painfully with anxiety as we walked into her living room, bright with cream walls and pink curtains. The sofas were velvet with a flowered pattern that perfectly complemented everything. A shelf stood against one wall, holding books and assorted knickknacks. All gold, pink, and cream.

Ms. Chandler settled into the love seat and gestured for us to sit on the sofa. She asked her maid— seriously? —to bring us "drinks and some light snacks."

Talk about putting on airs.

I fought with myself not to roll my eyes or storm out of there. I had never felt so outclassed in my three centuries of life as a Grim Reaper and in the few months of my new mortal life. What was she trying to prove?

"The police found no evidence of murder. Unofficially. They are still investigating, however," Ms. Chandler said once we were given coffee and water and those mini cakes again. "Regardless of what they find, I would appreciate it if you would lay this matter to rest."

I popped one of the cakes into my mouth, chewing thoughtfully. The irony of her turn of phrase wasn't lost on me. "Why? Don't you want to know the truth?"

Ms. Chandler blinked at me. "And I suppose you are the ones to find it, not the police?"

"Leliel would be an asset to this investigation," Rick said. "Even though according to Officer Bailey, they don't use psychics. Maybe we could persuade them."

Ms. Chandler frowned. "No. I do not want you involved."

"Because a psychic can't solve a murder case?" I asked, taking a sip of coffee. It burned my tongue.

"I would appreciate it if you'd leave this alone. Forget about this supposed murder," Ms. Chandler said. Her coffee cup shook a bit. Was she nervous? "You're not the police. You're just...regular people."

Regular people? I stood, my heart racing. "I am psychic, and apparently I have a connection to the dead. Can you sit there and tell me you have no doubts whatsoever about your son's passing?"

Rick stood and gripped my elbow. "Leliel, maybe we should go."

"Not until I have an answer," I said. I couldn't believe that Ms. Chandler believed the police so strongly that she wouldn't at least let me continue to investigate. "His death wasn't part of the natural order. Something is really wrong here."

Ms. Chandler set her coffee mug down with agonizing slowness. She stood, her lips pursed in a thin line. "I would like you to leave before I call the police and have you forcibly removed."

I nodded. "Fine, but if you decide you have any unanswered questions, you know where to find me." I arched a brow. "I live where the regular people do. It's been fun." I turned to leave but bumped into Rick. "We can go now, honey."

Rick took my hands in his. "Are you gonna just give up?"

I gave him a look that said *hell no*. "Of course. Ms. Chandler thinks I can't be of help. So, we're not needed here."

Rick sighed. "Okay." He glanced at Ms. Chandler, whose hands were twisted together. "Thank you for hearing us out. We're leaving now."

And we left.

IT WAS SILENT ON the drive home, Rick and I both lost in our own heads. The sun was just beginning to set, staining the sky gold and mauve tones.

"You know she believes you, right?" Rick asked, jolting me to the here and now. "She's afraid of something."

"Maybe she's afraid of the truth," I said, watching the trees and cars pass by. "Maybe she knows something."

"That's possible." Rick made a turn to the left. "But what could she possibly know?"

I shrugged. "Maybe Fred had enemies. Maybe this whole business is too distasteful for her. A lot of people shy away from murder." I thought of the Tarot card. "The soulmate card? It's too weird, especially since he didn't have a girlfriend."

"But was he in love with someone?" Rick asked as he pulled into the parking lot of the apartment complex. He turned off the car and turned to me. "Did I mention how amazing you are? How brave? How perfect?"

My heart did a slow somersault. "Thanks. Sometimes I don't feel brave."

Rick put his hand on my cheek. "You're the bravest woman I've ever known. You're after a murderer. What's next?"

"I don't know. But we'll do this together," I said, taking his hand in mine. "Something has to pop. I just feel it." We walked hand-in-hand to our apartment.

It was an older apartment complex, on the top floor in a corner. We liked being secluded, and Love enjoyed roaming around.

Heh, regular people. Maybe we were, deep down.

"We should talk to Fred's professors, and maybe even his classmates, too," Rick suggested as he set the table for dinner.

"That's a great idea."

Rick looked up the telephone number to the college and was even able to find the right department for me.

A few minutes later, I had a face full of cat fur and my cellular telephone to my ear. I still didn't quite get the idea of telephones, let alone cellular telephones. But they were useful for sure. Easier than writing letters and waiting weeks for an answer.

"Yes, I'd like to come by and ask some questions," I told the woman on the other end. She was one of Fred's professors at Amsburg Law School. "I'm not with the police or press—"

"I'm not sure I can allow that," the woman said, her voice deep. "I knew Fred personally. I can say with one hundred percent confidence that he was very popular. No one had cause to murder him. It's ludicrous."

"I'd feel better talking in person." I scratched Love behind her ears, trying to remain calm. This wasn't the time to get upset. "I just need a few minutes of your time. I promise it won't be long."

A sigh. "Okay, come down tomorrow morning. Nine o'clock. I start class promptly at nine fifteen. You must be gone by then."

I smiled. "Fantastic. See you tomorrow."

"See you then," the woman said, and hung up.

I set my telephone down and gently moved Love away from my dinner plate. "Well, it's a start, right?"

Rick turned to face me, holding a platter of pot roast. It smelled amazing. "Better than where we were ten minutes ago." He set the platter down between us. "This is my mother's special recipe. Try it."

Love jumped onto my lap, and I tried to serve myself while trying not to get tangled in cat paws and tail. It was a struggle, but I managed. "I bet it's amazing."

Rick smiled. "I hope so." He bowed his head in prayer, and I did the same. "Thank you to the universe for bringing Leliel, Love, and me together. Please keep us close in each other's hearts for as long as we remain on this earth. Amen."

It was an odd type of prayer, to the universe, but we were odd people. I used to thank His Highness, too, but stopped after a while. Didn't want him to get a swelled head.

I took my first bite of Rick's pot roast. Favors and spices exploded on my tongue, and it was good. Very good.

I was pretty sure I had died.

Okay, I hadn't actually died. But it sure as hell felt amazing.

"I love it," I said.

Rick took my free hand in his. "Thank you, Leliel. It means a lot to me. Cooking is...well, not very manly."

"Well, I don't need a manly man," I said, spearing another piece of amazing on my fork. "I just need you, Rick." I took a bite, chewed, and met his gaze. "I just wish I was a proper wife to you."

Rick's fork clattered on the plate. "You are a proper wife to me."

I shook my head. He didn't understand. "A proper wife would be cleaning the apartment and having your babies."

Love nuzzled my ankle.

Which made me laugh. Without a shred of humor.

"I suck as a wife." I threw my napkin onto the table. Pushed my plate away. I'd been raised to be a housewife. That was what all women were three hundred years ago. I was clearly a failure. "You shouldn't be—"

"Leliel." Rick came around to my side of the table and knelt in front of me, taking my face in his gentle hands. For a former biker guy, they were at odds with his looks but it felt like my secret. "You are the perfect wife for me. Maybe unconventional, maybe not the best cook..." He trailed off, and I felt my face flush. My first few attempts had ended in charred ruins and burnt pasta. Who burns freaking pasta? I got lucky with the casserole, apparently. It was at least edible. "But I chose you. And those things make you all the more special to me."

My heart damn near melted. It surprised me every time, as my heart used to be a black, shriveled thing. Now...it was different.

Love meowed.

I reached down and petted her again.

"Do you understand how much I love you? I can't even put it into words. Just that you're you...and that makes you the perfect wife for me." We kissed, soft, gentle, loving kisses.

I was with an amazing man who loved me for me.

"You are the perfect husband for me," I said between kisses. "You make me want to be a better person. You make me want to love more."

"Of course," Rick said, kissing me on the nose. "Now what do you say we finish this dinner and then have dessert?"

The twinkle in his eye told me exactly what dessert was going to be.

WHILE RICK AND I were watching the game show with the big wheel—Wheel of Luck or something—someone knocked on our door.

Since I wasn't understanding the game, and was sure I wasn't about to, I got up and looked into the peephole. A distorted view of our neighbor, Detective David Landis, stared back at me.

I opened the door. "David! What a surprise. Come on in."

David lived a few doors down from us. I wondered what he needed at such a late hour.

"Pardon the intrusion," the detective said. "I just got off work. I was hoping to discuss something with you two."

"Sure," I said. "Would you like something to drink? Water, soda, liqueur?"

David chuckled. "With the day I've had…liqueur sounds great. But I shouldn't have any. Soda's good, whatever you have."

Rick went into the kitchen.

I gestured toward the sofa. "Have a seat."

The detective sat, and Love approached him. She nuzzled his ankle and sat on the floor next to him. I was curious as to what he wanted to discuss with us. Rick popped out of the kitchen with three cans of soda in his hands. He distributed them, then sat down next to me on the love seat.

David opened his soda can and took a long swallow. "So, here's the thing. We've had three suicides back-to-back, all with Tarot cards left at the scene. The first two were female, Mary Lakefield and Summer Jordan. And then Fred Chandler. We're in the process of investigating them. I heard an interesting rumor at the station."

"And what was that?" I asked.

"That you offered your services as a psychic to one of my colleagues," David said. It was hard to tell how he felt about it. His expression was neutral, and his body was relaxed.

I exchanged a glance with Rick. Rick gave me a slight nod.

"Yes, I did," I said.

"I can't believe I'm asking you this, but do you have any information to impart?"

I remembered all three visions, and a shiver went up my spine. "I believe I saw all three. The deaths weren't natural."

"What do you mean exactly?"

"It wasn't their time to die." I took a sip of soda, watching the detective's reaction.

"That would be consistent with suicide," David said. "The evidence points to suicide. But the Tarot cards suggest foul play."

I nodded. "We—uh—went over there—"

"You visited someone having to do with this?" The detective's face was carefully blank, but I could tell he was interested.

"We did," Rick replied after a pause. "Leliel had a strong feeling that we needed to be at the scene of the third one. So we went."

"How did you even figure out where the house was? Your psychic ability?" Another sip of soda.

I nodded. "Yes. And Ms. Chandler told us about the Two of Cups. And, uh, she wanted me to not get involved."

"Maybe she knows something?" David pulled out a notepad and a pen and made a note. "I'll talk to her again, see if I can find out anything." He made another note. "Do you know about Tarot cards? The ones left at the first two were..." He flipped through his notepad. "Ah. The Fool and The Ten of Swords."

Love meowed and came over to where I was sitting. She jumped up onto the love seat and squeezed herself between Rick and me. I put my hand on her head, scratching between her ears.

"As a matter of fact, I do. I have done readings. First, the Two of Cups is considered to be the 'soulmate card.'"

"Explain that," the detective said, his eyes widening slightly.

"Usually it points to a romantic relationship. One that has a deeper connection. And..." I took Rick's hand in mine, causing Love to yip in protest. "Shush. I asked Ms. Chandler if Fred had a girlfriend and she said no. That he was too busy with school. But...what if he did have a girlfriend? Or a boyfriend? And he just wasn't telling his mother?"

"Anything is possible," David said. "What about the others?"

I thought about it. "The Fool is basically a beginning, a new journey. The Ten of Swords is an unexpected disaster, and an ending. It's the Death card of the Minor Arcana. But it's not pointing to death at all."

David's eyes narrowed. "What if the killer is telling a story? The Fool is the beginning, and The Ten of Swords points to the first suicide. Mary Lakefield. Assuming this is all murder."

"So what's your next step?" Rick asked.

"We need to take another look at the evidence. Talk to the parents of the deceased, see if they were depressed or something like that. I will keep you posted."

Another shiver went up my spine, and I had the impression of feminine energy. "I believe there are more coming. And the next victim will be another woman."

THE AMSBURG LAW School was small, having only five large buildings with a bridge between two. The buildings were brick and nondescript, built in a horseshoe shape with a common area in the middle, where students perched on concrete benches. Some sat on the ground, studying or reading a book. Others gossiped and talked about classes and professors.

So this was what college looked like.

I'd never gone to college. In my brief first lifetime, it just wasn't done if you were a woman. But times had changed. There were a ton of women here, of all races and ages, and it stung a bit. If I'd been born later, maybe I would have had the chance.

"This is nice," Rick said. "I never considered going to college. I'm not smart enough."

I frowned. "Of course you're smart enough. I never even had the chance." I glanced wistfully at the students gathered, trying not to let my emotions hijack me. I was a lot more emotional now that I had Rick and Love. Before, I'd been an empty shell, going through the motions. Once you've reaped one soul, you've reaped them all. Forever.

Rick nudged me gently. "You have the opportunity now."

I stopped dead, and Rick almost crashed into me. Several pairs of eyes came to rest on us. I lowered my voice. "Um, it's a great idea, really, but how? I don't officially exist."

Rick's brow furrowed. "Well, I'm just saying...if you want to go to college, we could find a way to do it. If you wanted to."

Hope slowly unfurled inside me. "Yeah, maybe. But what would I do?"

Rick swept his hand in an expansive gesture. "Anything, milady."

"Anything?" I asked skeptically. "I'm not really that smart, and—"

Rick took hold of my shoulders, his gaze intense. "Anything, Leliel. We'll make it happen. Together."

My eyes stung with tears. I blinked them away. "Okay. We'll talk about it later."

"So where are we headed?"

I consulted my notes. "Building E, room five-thirty-six." I checked my watch. "Getting close to nine."

"Let's see..." Rick spun around, studying the buildings. "It's that one." He pointed to the building that just so happened to be the farthest from where we stood. Not a million miles, but it felt like that.

I hadn't slept well, again, so I was sleepy and frankly not energetic at all.

Rick grabbed my hand. "Let's go."

We walked in silence, in the brisk, cool air of autumn. The trees had turned, and birds flew overhead. The sun peeked out of clouds to drench us in golden, hazy light.

College, I thought. Who would have thunk it? Me, in college? Suuuure. But maybe it was possible. Maybe I could do something.

Something to do with helping people. I'd never quite shaken off my many years as a Reaper. It still called to me, and it felt right.

Rick approached the building and opened the door. "After you, Leliel."

My heart lurched. Something felt wrong again.

But I crossed the threshold, inhaling the musty scent of old buildings. The walls were white stained yellow, with windows that needed a good washing. To each side of us was a long hall with rooms on each side. Low talking and murmurs filled the silence. Some of the doors were closed.

"So...what's the room number again?"

"Five-thirty-six," I said, taking note of the room numbers. "Even's on your side, and it looks like they are going up as you go." Unease made me sluggish, and a headache started in my temples.

"Leliel." Startled, I stopped. Rick was watching me with one of those uh-oh-something's-wrong-and-you're-not-telling-me looks. "Tell me what's going on. You don't look like you want to be here at all."

"I'm sleepy," I said.

"Right, and I'm Superman. Come on, out with it."

"Who's Superman?" I asked.

"He's a superhero who saves people," Rick replied. "He even flies."

"Really?" I asked. "Sounds cool. How does he fly?"

"What isn't cool is that you're changing the subject on me."

"We're going to be late," I protested. "It's almost nine."

"It can wait a second. You're more important," Rick said, squeezing my forearm.

I guess I had to talk if I wanted to get there on time. *Men*. I drew in a deep breath and let it out. "Okay, fine. I feel wrongness around here. Off kilter. It's kind of freaking me out."

"Kind of?" Rick arched a brow. "You look like you're on the verge of a mental breakdown. What exactly feels wrong?"

I threw my arms up. "I don't know. Let's keep walking." I started forward, and Rick fell into step beside me, all protective and concerned. He took my hand in his, and I felt a bit calmer. "It's in the air or something. Nothing overt...just a feeling."

"Any more visions?"

"No, but I didn't sleep well. Nerves, I guess." I shrugged. "It's up here." I led the way to what looked to be the last room on that side. The door was closed. I stepped forward and knocked, bracing myself for more weirdness.

Nothing happened.

I knocked again. And again.

"Maybe she forgot," I said. My nerves were busy chasing each other in my insides. Playing hide and seek. Playing chicken. Having a three-legged race—

"You must be Leliel and Rick," a female voice said behind us. "It is Leliel, right?"

I turned to face the owner of that voice, and almost gasped.

She was...wow. Dressed in a bright, floral dress that almost blinded me, with several beaded necklaces, and beaded bracelets dangling from each wrist. Her hair was done in many small braids, starting from the front of her head and running to the very back. A ruby ring caught the light and flared red. But...she radiated badness. Like I'd swallowed something sour and evil. My skin crawled with invisible bugs. The hairs on the back of my neck stood up. Could she be the wrongness I'd been sensing since I walked in?

"Hello," Rick said. "You have it right. You must be Professor Everson?" He put his hand out and they shook.

I had to say something, or she'd think I was being rude. "A pleasure to meet you." We shook hands, and hers felt oily and unclean, even though it looked fine. I fought the urge to wipe my hand on my jeans.

She slid past us and unlocked the door, opening it and stepping into the room. We followed silently.

My mind was a whirlwind of impressions: the room was clean but bore signs of age like the hallway. The light was too bright and the silence was starting to gnaw on me.

"So... you wanted to discuss Fred Chandler, correct?" Professor Everson asked.

Rick and I exchanged a glance. His said, *say something*. "Yes. We just wanted to get some information about him. If he has any enemies, what things are like here, that sort of thing."

Professor Everson sat down at a large, ornate desk and sighed. "Well, as I mentioned yesterday, he had no enemies. He was well liked and did exceptionally well in my class, as well as the others. I asked around and his other professors said the same thing."

So why did I feel so strange? Was I imagining things?

Students started to file in. Some of them gave us curious looks while others were downright hostile, elbowing both Rick and me aside. I pitied their lack of manners.

One student, a guy with a long beard, stared at me. Almost daring me to do something. What the hell?

"Well, as you can see, it's almost time—"

"Professor Everson," I said softly, moving closer to the desk. "Why is that guy staring at me? Why is everyone so rude?"

Professor Everson blinked at me. Glanced at the bearded, staring guy, then back to me. "I don't know. Maybe because it's rare that anyone visits us?"

"Anyone" meaning normal, not-brilliant people.

"Can we talk to a few of them? Just for a few minutes?"

The professor checked her watch. "Two people, five minutes. And then you leave."

"Thank you," Rick said, pulling me toward him. Under his breath, he whispered, "Are you sure you want to do this?"

I fought the urge to glance back at the guy who I knew was still staring at me. I could feel the weight of his gaze. "Yes, I do. Starting with him." I turned and met his gaze without flinching, standing straight and tall.

Rick tensed. "He looks like he could eat you for breakfast."

I fought the churning in my gut and the sense that I was about to do something horribly stupid. "It's okay. I'll be fine."

Rick let go of me with a sigh. "Remember, you're mortal now."

"He's not going to hurt me. Not with so many witnesses," I whispered, then started toward the guy, every step loud and ominous to my ears. I swallowed hard, reminding myself that we needed to find out about Fred's murder. For justice…and the terrible feeling that he shouldn't be dead. I couldn't let fear get in the way of answers.

I stopped in front of the guy, who wore a flannel shirt and had blue eyes. His meaty hands were on his desk. His books sat on one side.

He wasn't smiling.

Now I really felt the wrongness, the oily feel of evil.

No fear, I reminded myself.

"Hi, I'm Leliel, and this is my husband, Rick." He did not move, did not acknowledge us at all. "We're here to investigate the death of your classmate, Fred Chandler." I kept talking, but my nerves were making me jumpy. "Um, did you know him well?"

Finally, the guy blinked and said, "No, not really. He was one of the brats."

"What does that mean exactly?" I asked.

The guy looked around him, at his fellow students who were talking to each other, some studying. One was frantically writing something, which was probably an essay or test at the last minute. His gaze came back to mine, and he shrugged. "They think they're better than everyone else. Rich parents. Multimillion-dollar trust funds. Want for nothing. They're posers. They don't want to be lawyers to help people. They want the prestige, or to follow in the family tradition. They don't care."

"I take it you have personal experience with them?" Rick asked.

"Oh yeah. I used to be one of them."

This was interesting. "So, did you uh, leave the group or something?"

The guy, who still hadn't given us his name, frowned. "I was disinherited by my folks. I'm here on a scholarship and a ton of loans. I don't fit in with them anymore."

Rick was watching students on the other side of the room. He turned back to me. "I think we may have a problem."

What the hell?

Everyone on the opposite side was staring at us. Hostile. Pissed off. With a bunch of you-don't-belong-here and this-isn't-your business looks on their faces.

But, why? I figured I might as well go all in. Stupid or smart, take your pick. Hellfire. I turned to face the others. "What's going on?"

"I don't understand," Professor Everson said. "Class, please cooperate with our guests. They are trying to help." She glanced at us with an apologetic look. "Sorry about that. They're nervous because they are about to take a major exam."

I wasn't sure I believed that, but okay.

A thin guy with short-cropped black hair frowned at me. "We should ask you the same question. Who are you and why are you here?" He gave me a blatant look over from my shoes to the top of my head. "You're obviously not students."

"We're not." My voice came out tense. This asshole pushed every button inside me and then some. "Professor Everson gave us permission to be here. We wanted to ask you a few questions."

"Oh?" a blonde girl asked. "What kind?"

"Questions concerning Fred Chandler. Did any of you know him well?" Rick asked, his hands clenched. Nice to know I wasn't the only one with issues.

"I knew him very well," the blonde said, fiddling with her pen. "We used to date."

"Were you dating when he passed?" I asked, my heartbeat kicking into high gear. Maybe we'd get a decent lead out of this.

"Nope. We broke up five months ago. Then he started dating Sam."

I arched a brow. "Sam as in..."

"Samantha. He was straight. Not that it matters," the black-haired guy put in. He didn't look up at me. "Sam died a few months ago."

It was like being hit by lightning, this knowledge. Could it be that simple? "Were they having any problems? How did she die?"

The blonde girl crossed her arms in front of her chest, her glare daring me to do something. "Don't know. It's a bit of a mystery."

Rick and I exchanged looks. Coupled with the evil feeling I felt, and her body language—she'd shut right down after being open just seconds ago—I had no choice but to believe she was lying. Or withholding information. "How can you not know how your classmate died?"

"That's enough," Professor Everson cut in. "I gave you five extra minutes. This discussion is over."

"What?" Rick asked, aghast. "We're trying to get information on Fred's murder—"

"Fred wasn't murdered," said another girl, who sat in the back and looked about twelve. "He committed suicide. Probably because of Sam."

I looked her straight in the eyes, not believing it for a second. "Why would he kill himself over Sam?"

"The police claim suicide. There was a note and everything," the twelve-year-old snapped. "Why investigate this? You're wasting your time."

"How do you know all of this? The police haven't released any information on it yet," Rick said, his eyes narrowing.

That was a valid point.

"I have a relative on the force. He told me," the girl said quickly. "He says they are closing the case. So why pursue this?"

David had specifically said that they were still investigating all three suicides. But I decided to keep that to myself.

"I see things a bit differently." I stepped forward, trying to look as in control as I could when everything was crumbling to pieces. It wasn't easy. "I'm trying to find out the truth about what happened to your classmate. Don't you want to know? To have justice? You guys are going to be lawyers. Doesn't any of this interest you on some level?"

"Leliel," Rick murmured. "I think we're done here."

Another girl in the back caught my eye. Her lips quivered, and her face was red. And were those tears in her eyes?

I went to her, trying not to appear intimidating. "Hey…are you all right? You look really upset."

She just shook her head. Her lips moved, but nothing came out.

"Don't even bother," said the bearded guy. "She never talks. She was friends with Sam."

Oh.

"I'm sorry for your loss," I said. "I—uh—lost loved ones. And I know how painful it can be."

One tear slid down her cheek, and she wiped it away with an angry motion.

"Anyway..." It was time to wrap this up. Clearly, she wasn't going to talk to me. "Take care." I moved back to the front of the room, anger boiling in my veins. "I can't believe that no one else cares." I felt deflated and pointless. "I can't believe you'd just believe the first theory the police came across. There's more to this, I swear."

"Enough. One more word from you and I will call security," Professor Everson snapped, giving me a hard look. "You've disrupted my class enough. Time to go."

I held up my hands in a surrendering gesture. "Okay. Thanks for your time. Anyone who wants to talk, here's our number." I turned to Rick. "What is our number?" Rick rattled it off, and I noted that several students took it down. It figured. The second girl in the back did take it down, so I felt a bit better. "Have a nice day."

Rick took my hand and led me out of the room. Everything spun and blurred together. My head...

I somehow got farther down the hallway and the—whatever it was—brought me to my knees. I put two fingers on each temple and breathed deep.

"Leliel?" Rick sounded as if he were a continent away.

Hellfire.

A flash.

Fire. Leaping flames. Distorted voices.

A woman.

Hanging from...something.

Laughter.

Flames.

Engulfing the woman.

Screams.

Screams.

Screams.

Oh, my head was going to freaking explode—

I screamed.

Chapter 3

EONS LATER, I opened my eyes.

I was home, Love was cuddled next to me in the living room, purring away, and Rick looked gutted.

"Leliel, how are you feeling?" He knelt beside me, tucking a few errant strands of hair behind my ear. "You had an....episode. You screamed a lot."

I put my head in my hands. It still throbbed. "I—I don't know. I had another vision."

"Professor Everson was pushing me to call an ambulance," Rick said. "But I refused. Told her that you have epilepsy. It was the only thing I could think of that sounded remotely normal."

I snorted. "The operative word being 'normal,'" I said, lying back against the two fluffy pillows that Rick had probably put there. I laid a hand on Love's head. She nuzzled me. "We're nowhere near normal, you know."

Rick sat down next to me, taking my hand in his. "Tell me about the vision."

I didn't want to even think of it, much less talk about it, but this was Rick, my husband, and this was all my doing. I let out a huff of air. "I saw someone hung up, and flames. And heard her screams. They were—inhuman. Her pain must have been immense. She didn't—didn't die right away. She suffered."

"She's at peace now," Rick murmured, squeezing my hand. "But who was she?"

I shook my head. "I don't know. I don't even know if she died recently or years ago. But that hallway...it triggered something."

"She was a student."

"Yeah, I think so. But I don't know anything else about her." I ground my teeth together. It was so fickle, this ability of mine. It only gave me pieces of the whole, and not enough to figure out where they all fit. But there was one thing in common.

"If she died from fire, and Fred and the first two died from fire—"

"They have to be connected somehow," Rick finished for me. "Do you think hers was a suicide?"

"No. I'm positive. There were others there. Laughter. Like it was some kind of joke." And burning to death was one of the worst ways to go. I knew from experience. I'd died in a fire and had lost my mother and baby brother. "Wait a sec. Fred's girlfriend Sam died recently. Could that have been her?"

Rick's eyes widened. "I wonder. It would explain why everyone was so cagey. They knew something. They just wouldn't tell us."

"And, it would explain how that one girl knew. I don't believe her story about having a relative who's a cop." Rick nodded. "If it was the brats that did it, I could see that happening. Maybe Sam wasn't from a wealthy family or something."

"Maybe."

"Does this bother you at all?" Rick's eyes were two beacons of light that kept me from the brink of insanity. As long as I had him, I'd be okay.

"It does bring back memories, not going to lie." Love nuzzled my hand again, then licked it. "My…death was over pretty quickly, which was a mercy. The pain...I can't even describe it in words. If you can just imagine the worst pain ever, that'll be enough."

"I got a taste of it during the Trial by Fire. Not fun," Rick said, his expression solemn. "I think you might need to consider letting this go, Leliel. It's hurting you."

Was he insane? "No, I can't let this go. Fred was murdered, and so was this girl. And maybe the first two as well. I need to know who did it. I need to give them justice. I need…I need for deaths to be natural. These aren't. I think that's why I'm having visions. Their souls aren't at peace, and won't be, until I solve this."

Rick stood and shifted from foot to foot. "I just can't stand what this is doing to you."

I reached out to him, and he gently helped me upright. The room spun, but I needed to be on equal footing. I looked up at him, my lips twisting in remembered pain. "But I have this ability for a reason—"

"Maybe His Highness is torturing you because you're no longer a Reaper."

His Highness was the King of the Underworld and when I was a Reaper, he'd been my boss. We'd made a deal—I was turned human so I could be with Rick. I'd believed that that was the end of it.

But maybe it wasn't.

I mock-swatted Rick. "Yeah, okay. Like he's getting his jollies off watching me bumble my way through this." I thought about it for a second. He could be really sadistic when he felt like it. "Maybe. We need to find out more about this girl. Which means we have to go back to the school. Today."

"Leliel, you need to rest." Rick took my hands in his. "I can't let you run yourself ragged. We can wait till tomorrow."

My eyes widened. "And give the murderer time to kill again? Absolutely not."

Rick let out a sigh, and gave me a resigned, forlorn look. I appreciated his concern, but I needed to keep moving. I couldn't dwell on my own death or these visions. He said, "Okay, fine. But will you at least get some food and drink into you, and see if you can shake the dizziness?"

Oops, I guess I wasn't able to hide that. "Deal."

So we ate. Beef and chicken tacos, most of mine going to Love, who loved anything Mexican. Rick even made these custard things called flan, which were yummy.

"I didn't know you could cook so well," I said after I'd eaten the last bite of Rick's serving of flan. I'd inhaled mine already. "Maybe I should make you cook from now on."

"This is the one of the few things I can do right," Rick said, his mouth quirking in a half-smile. "Everything else comes out awful. Honest."

"Well, maybe once a week we can have tacos and flan." I fed Love a piece of a taco shell. "I could get used to being cooked for, waited on hand and foot."

"More drink?" Rick asked, leaning over and brushing his lips over mine. "I have more margarita mix..."

"Nah, need a clear head." I stood, now energized. "Let's get going."

"Are you sure you're okay?" Rick took the dirty plates and bowls into the kitchen.

I followed him, restless. Ready to blow this thing wide open. Love followed me, meowing plaintively. "We can do dishes later."

Rick spun to face me. "I'd rather do them now, give you a chance to relax." He went back to the dishes. Turned on the faucet and went to town, the smell of dish soap filling the air.

I leaned on my elbows, brushing Rick's as he scrubbed the pot he'd made the meat in. "Relax? I can't sit on my butt and—"

"Leliel, you're vibrating, you're so damn fidgety. We'll get there, I promise. But you need to chill."

"I don't want to chill," I murmured. "I want to find this horrible person and let the justice system do its thing. And stop more unnatural deaths. Too bad we couldn't take him down into the Underworld." I laughed mirthlessly. "That'd be a trip and a half."

Rick glanced at me sidelong. "Can you get back into the Underworld?"

"Hell, no. I lost access when I became human."

"Human plus, you mean." Rick held out a plate and a dish towel. I took it, feigning grumpiness, but it was easy, relaxed, and so mundane that it made me smile. We did this every night. It took me away from the horror of the murder for a bit.

Before another vision hijacked my brain.

"So..." I said softly, setting the now-dry plate on the counter. "You haven't had anything odd happen to you, have you?"

Rick glanced at me, eyes wide. "Not at all. I'm still one hundred percent human. Would've been cool to get some kind of ability, but alas..." He shrugged.

"Well, usually humans who do enter the Underworld, and especially those who complete Trials and are given their souls back, usually end up with something. The Underworld leaves its mark on you."

Rick stilled, the scrubber falling from his hand. "Uh—no, nothing. Really."

I moved closer to Rick, taking his free hand in mine. "We're bonded. And you're not being honest with me, are you?"

Silence, heavy and damning.

Love meowed as if to say, *please don't fight.*

I picked her up. "Look at this face and try to lie to it."

Rick chuckled, scratching Love underneath her chin. He sighed heavily. "Okay, fine. I didn't want you to worry about me with all this crap going on. But..."

"But what?" I met his gaze, held it. No judgment.

"I felt it. What he felt. What the girl felt." He closed his eyes. "It—I couldn't—it was—"

I pulled him closer with Love between us, who twitched her tail and whined. "Hellfire, Rick, that had to be torture for you. How did I miss this?"

"You didn't."

"No." I slashed the air with my hand. "You had to be hurting while I was having my episode. How'd you mask it?"

He shrugged. "Probably because my first priority was you."

"But the pain..." We hugged, and I nuzzled his cheek like Love did sometimes. "Please, next time, tell me, okay? I can't bear the idea of you hurting and me not being there to help."

"I will. I'm sorry. I didn't think it was that big a thing. I didn't even connect it to the Underworld." He shuddered. "I guess it *did* mark me."

"Marked us both," I corrected him. "Come on, let's finish these and get rolling. I'm sufficiently chilled now." And not just relaxed. The idea of Rick enduring such pain without my knowledge chilled me down to my marrow.

I needed to protect him. Keep him safe.

So much on my shoulders now.

Could I bear it?

I didn't have a choice.

We'd cope.

I hoped.

BACK AT THE COLLEGE, the sun was setting, filling the sky with rich colors and fluffy clouds. Hellfire. I wished my life was simple. No murders or abilities or investigations. Just life, Rick, our cat, and our little apartment.

But that was just not meant to be.

This time we tried the dean's office. They'd have the information on record, right?

It was a small, musty room with shelves of binders and awards on the walls. I felt a bit claustrophobic.

"Hi. We're here to ask a few questions about a student," Rick said to the secretary, who looked to be about fourteen and bored as hell. "Can we speak with the dean?"

The secretary rolled her eyes. "He left about three hours ago. But can I leave him a message?" She grabbed a pen and pad of paper.

"It is a bit late, isn't it?" I asked, forcing a chuckle. Of course. He worked normal hours. We were the odd ones, showing up here at this time of day.

"Yes, it is," the secretary said. "But his assistant might still be here. Let me check."

"Thanks," I murmured as she picked up her telephone and made a call. It had a cord hanging from the bottom of the part she put to her ear. Where did it lead to?

"See, she's helping us," Rick said softly. "It's obviously my smile. She likes me."

"Oh, I see," I said, rolling my eyes. "It's all you. I would not be able to get the same results alone because you're just Mr. Hotness."

"Damn straight," Rick said with a smirk.

"Hey," I murmured, keeping my eyes on the secretary. "Where does that cord lead to?"

"You mean the one attached to the receiver?" I nodded. "It is plugged into a port where the outside line feeds into this building." My eyes narrowed. "Right. There are phone lines outside. You've seen the tall poles with cords strung between them? They lead into each building, and each building has a port connected to it. And each phone connects to a port that is connected to that. They're called landlines. Which are quickly becoming obsolete."

"Wow," I said, not even sure what to say. It was amazing, this technology. I wished we'd had these landlines when I was alive the first time.

The secretary hung up her phone and glanced at us. "She's still here. Through that door and all the way to the end. She's on the left. Mrs. Cooper." She pointed out our route, then went back to being bored.

"Let's go," I said, taking Rick's hand in mine and squeezing it.

We went inside and followed the hallway to the end. Pictures of past and present very important people lined the walls, along with what looked like...various awards and things? Hmm.

I glanced at the closed door to Mrs. Cooper's office. A brass sign read "Violet Cooper, Assistant to the Dean." Well, she had an important title. I hoped that meant we'd get answers.

I let go of Rick's hand and knocked on the door. My heart thudded, and was that sweat forming on my forehead?

Was I that nervous?

You bet.

"Come in," a high-pitched voice said loudly.

I glanced at Rick with a shrug. "Here we go."

Rick opened the door and motioned for me to go in first, ever the gentleman. Mrs. Cooper's office was a splash of light and color, with bright blue walls and brightly-lit lamps in strategic places. Lamps now used electricity, and I was still amazed by it. There was a couch with bright-colored throw pillows on it, a set of deep red chairs in front of an ornate desk, and shelves lining the opposite walls. Books, so many of them. I also noticed her degrees and certificates of excellence, and some kind of fancy award prominently displayed at eye level on one of the shelves closest to where I stood.

Mrs. Violet Cooper was slightly overweight, with longish blonde hair and blue eyes framed by glasses. She wore a pink sweater and a black skirt. A heart locket completed the simple look. She wore very little makeup and no other jewelry.

"Mrs. Cooper?" I said, not sure how to begin. Somehow coming in with guns blazing didn't seem like a good plan. But I was tired, and wary, and out of smart entrances.

Mrs. Cooper smiled. "Yes. How may I help you?" She motioned for us to sit, and I slid gratefully into a chair. Rick took the one beside me. I realized—belatedly—that his hair might give her the wrong impression. I loved his black hair, streaked with blue, but it was unusual. I loved him and wasn't ashamed of him...it just made me wonder what she thought of us.

Of course, I was a Grim Reaper turned human with odd abilities, so I had no stones to throw.

Rick cleared his throat. "I'm Rick Ashton, and this is my wife, Leliel. We're—uh—investigating a murder."

"What looks to be a murder," I corrected hastily. "It appeared to be a suicide, but there's...evidence that—evidence of foul play." Wow, look at me, all police-ish. I bet I sounded like a moron. I felt like a moron. But use the jargon, look more professional and competent, right?

Right?

Mrs. Cooper's eyes widened. "Oh my. How is that even possible? And why—oh dear. It's about one of my students, isn't it?"

I ignored the why for the moment. Saying that I saw it in a vision would probably compel her to call the men in white coats. "Possibly, yes. Was there a student here named Samantha who passed away recently?"

A flash of recognition in her eyes, but it disappeared too fast. "I'm not aware of a student with that name that passed away."

Rick nudged me gently in the side, then followed it with a pointed look. What? I had no idea what he was trying to say.

"There was a suicide. Fred Chandler. We heard that he was Samantha's boyfriend. And it seems a bit...odd, don't you think? Two people die and they were once a couple?"

Mrs. Cooper looked at us blankly. "I know nothing about that." Her hands, which were sitting folded on the desk, tightened almost imperceptibly.

Oh. She was lying.

I glanced at Rick. Pointedly.

"We're just trying to find out who killed Fred Chandler," Rick said, trying not to look intimidating but failing. He was walking intimidation. When I first met him, I was sure he was going to kill me for screwing his life up. I had been wrong about that, but Mrs. Cooper didn't know that. "We want to see justice served. We'd appreciate your cooperation."

Mrs. Cooper's eyes narrowed. "Are you with the police?"

I wanted to say we were, because why not? She wasn't being truthful with us. But that could be checked and we could end up in trouble. So... "No, we're not. We're just"—two crazy people— "concerned citizens."

She removed her glasses, giving us an imperious look. "If you aren't the police, then I am not obligated to tell you anything, am I?"

Hellfire.

"Um, no." Rick raked a hand through his hair. "But we'd—"

Mrs. Cooper stood. "I have no information to give—"

"But the student?" I asked, not caring that I was interrupting. I knew a dismissal when I saw one. This was our only chance to find out about Samantha. "Can you at least confirm whether or not she attended here?"

Please.

With a huff, Mrs. Cooper sat down. Put her glasses back on. Typed furiously on her keyboard. "No, she did not attend here." She pointed to the doorway. "I'm sure you can see yourselves out."

We left.

Once outside the miserable place, I let out a scream of frustration. "She was lying through her teeth the entire time."

"That's what I was trying to tell you. I could tell she was being dishonest," Rick said. "Samantha went to school here, and I'd bet money that she was one you saw in your vision."

"Oh, yeah," I said, kicking a rock across the parking lot. "The real question is, how are we going to prove any of this?"

Rick pulled me into his arms, nuzzling my cheek. Sometimes he reminded me of Love. "It's a cover-up. And it's up to us to figure out exactly what they don't want us to know."

"We'll figure it out," I said. "The ones responsible will pay. And things will go back to their natural order."

"I'VE BEEN THINKING," Rick said, startling me.

We were back at home, and I was sitting on the couch, thinking. Thinking so hard that I was giving myself a headache.

"About what? The murder?" I asked. I took a sip of soda. Maybe a jolt of caffeine would bring me back to life.

"Well, Samantha's death would probably be online."

"On that Web place?" I asked. "You've said that it has everything, so why not try to look?"

"Exactly." Rick left the room, then came back carrying his laptop computer. I never really understood the idea of computers. Supposedly, they could do almost anything.

I watched as Rick set it up on the coffee table and pressed a button. The screen came to life.

Rick clicked on a symbol—an "E" surrounded by a golden halo—and a screen popped up.

"Okay, here we are." He typed "www.google.com" into a box up top, then pressed the "enter" key. "This is called a search engine. You can search literally anything." Another screen popped up with the word "Google" in several colors. There was a box underneath it.

"Okay…we don't know her last name, but we know the school." He typed "Samantha Amsburg Law School" in the box.

I held my breath.

A list appeared on the screen.

"Okay, here's something." Rick clicked on a sentence that said "Amsburg Law School Fire, One Fatality." That looked promising.

"What is it?" I asked, my heart pounding.

Another screen popped up.

"'You must have a subscription to the *Amsburg Daily* to read this article,'" Rick read. He moved the screen down, murmuring, "How much does a subscription cost?"

I saw it before he did. "Fifty dollars per year. Is that a lot?"

Rick frowned. "It's not a huge amount, but it is a lot to me. That comes to around four dollars and some change per month." He rubbed his chin. "We really don't have a lot of extra money to spend on this."

We'd talked about money before, and I knew that we weren't rich. That was okay. I didn't *need* fancy clothes or china, or for Rick to have a fancy car. But this was important.

I turned to Rick. "I know, but this could give us a lead. I think it's worth considering."

"This money could pay a bill, Leliel." Rick looked gutted. "I'm sorry. I'd love to give you everything you want, but I can't. I don't make enough for stuff like this."

Now I felt horrible. He probably thought I was thinking he was a terrible husband or something. I put my hand on his wrist. "It's okay. I just...I guess this case is consuming me. I'm sorry. I don't mean to make you feel bad."

Rick took a breath and let it out. "I do feel bad, like I can't provide for you. And that...honestly? It sucks. But I know you don't mean it that way, so...let's just table this, okay?"

I couldn't let it go. "I've heard of these things called credit cards. Do you have one?"

"Yes," Rick said slowly. "I have one. For emergencies only."

I gave him a hopeful smile. "Isn't this an emergency?"

Rick sighed. He took both of my hands in his. "Credit cards are basically money on loan. We'd have to pay it back the following month. If we don't have it...big problems."

"But they're plastic," I said. "I've seen them in pictures and on the television. How can they be a loan when it's a plastic card?"

"It's a representation of the loan," Rick explained. He squeezed my hands. "It basically says that I have a loan with a company and I promise to pay it back."

I thought about it. "So it's a…plastic loan card?"

Rick smiled. "Yeah, that's it."

"Can we try to do this?" I asked. "I'll sell some things. I'm not sure what yet, but I'll try to pay your plastic loan back…"

Rick chuckled. "You are amazing. Don't worry about it. I think I can pay it back if I shuffle some things around."

He was going to do it? Did I hear that right? "We can? I mean, we really can?"

"Yes," Rick said, reaching into his jeans pocket and pulling out his wallet. It held money. And apparently his plastic loan card. He took it out and held it aloft. "Can I trust that you won't run up a bill we can't pay? This is serious stuff."

"I'll never touch it again. I promise." And I meant it. "I don't care about anything else. Just this."

He handed me the card. "No one can have these numbers. If they do, they can use our plastic loan card to take out loans and make us pay the bill. It's seriously not cool."

My heart lurched. "But if they take out the plastic loan with our card, shouldn't they have to pay it back?"

"In a perfect world, yes. But this isn't a perfect world, and there are bad people out there who do this sort of thing so they don't have to pay."

"That's stealing," I said.

"Yes. Anyway, let me show you how to do this."

Rick explained that I had to type in several different numbers in order for it to work.

My head was spinning. Yeah, I wasn't going to do this again. Too damn complicated, and risky, when people tried to steal using your card.

We finally got to read the article.

Apparently, there'd been a fire at Amsburg Law School in the middle of the night. There was one fatality. The police were investigating. At least at the time of the printing, which was a few months ago.

Rick and I looked at each other.

"The time frame fits," I murmured.

"So, maybe the one fatality was Samantha?" Rick asked, rubbing his chin.

"But in my vision, people were laughing. She was hanging somewhere, and—"

"Could she have been murdered, too?" Rick's eyes lit up with excitement. "Could explain why no one will talk to us. It's obviously not something people want anyone to know."

"That's crazy," I said. "Why on earth would someone kill a young law student?"

THAT NIGHT, I had a dream. About a girl. Red, red hair, green eyes. Short. A smirk on her face that said she'd won whatever there was to win.

Flames.

Inhuman screaming again.

Burns. The pungent smell of smoke.

I bolted upright.

Love meowed at me from her place at the foot of the bed. She carefully padded over and sat next to me, curled into a little ball of fur and purred.

"Rick?" I said, gently shaking my husband. I was surprised he hadn't—

He bolted upright with a scream.

"Leliel?" His eyes were distant, seeing something else or somewhere else.

I touched his wrist. "Rick, I'm here. I'm right here."

His eyes cleared, and he looked at me. "I felt it. Every flame, every burn. I freaking felt it all."

"Was it a girl?" I asked, yawning. Having visions and dreams was exhausting.

"Red hair—"

"Green eyes—"

"Shit-eating grin," Rick finished.

I nodded. "That's what I saw, too. So there's another?"

"I don't know," Rick said, laying his hand on Love's head. "But it was so real. It was as if I was experiencing it, too."

"Yeah." I picked at my sheets. "I don't think I can sleep after that."

"So, you're having dreams now, too?" Rick asked.

I sighed. "Yeah. It's like the universe is really pounding me to get this solved."

Rick arched a brow. "Coffee and cookies?"

Coffee and cookies was our go-to when we wanted to think, or we were bored, or if we wanted to just relax and drown ourselves in comfort food. Tonight, all three applied. Well, I didn't think we were bored, but if we couldn't get to sleep, we would be.

Love followed us into the kitchen. The lights were too bright.

Three o'clock in the morning.

Hellfire.

"Who was she?" I asked, taking a sip of my coffee a few minutes later. Rick had helpfully placed a plate of double chocolate chocolate-chip cookies on the table, knowing that they were my favorite. I snagged one and chewed thoughtfully.

Rick grabbed one and dipped it in his coffee. I gave him a confused look. "What?" He took a bite. "Isgood," he mumbled around a mouthful of chocolate-y goodness.

What the hell? I dipped the remaining half of my cookie into my coffee, eyeing it warily. Took a bite. "Very good," I murmured once I was done chewing. "I guess I need to be more open-minded."

"Uh-huh," Rick said with a smile. "So...she was probably a fellow student."

"If Mrs. Blank Face was lying," I said, dipping a second cookie in my coffee.

"Huh?"

"Mrs. Cooper, because she has quite the poker face. Isn't that what it's called?" I asked. Rick nodded. "I could tell, naturally, because I'm cool like that, but it was tough to see. Blink and you miss it."

"But I'm sure she was being dishonest, so between those two things, we're probably right." Rick took a sip of his coffee. "So now what?"

"What about the first two suicides? Mary and…what was the other girl's name again?"

Rick dipped another cookie into his coffee. "Summer."

"Right. So what if they are connected? Hey, could they be students, too?"

Rick rubbed his eyes. He looked exhausted. "Sure. We should run this by David. See what he can dig up."

I sighed. "I just wish we could find something out, not bumble around like morons. Who keep getting either thrown out of places or stonewalled."

"We're terrible at this investigation thing, aren't we?" Rick said, rolling his eyes. "Might need to consider switching careers."

Ye Gods. Careers? He was kidding...no, he didn't look like it.

"I have to work and stuff?" I asked. "I'm kind of...old. Ill-prepared."

"I'm doing okay at the bike shop, but we're not...I mean..." He stopped and took a sip of coffee. He didn't look at me. "Well...you know we're not…some help would be...uh...a good idea."

He was right. I knew he was right. But... "I have no skills except reaping souls. And that's not an option anymore." I hugged myself, feeling utterly unprepared for the realities of human life. I was one of them now. A housewife, because I couldn't be anything else. And we needed money. Sure. "My mother taught me how to cook before I died. I'm not really good with all this new technology. But if I get used to it, maybe I can...cook. Somewhere."

It was tough for me to wrap my head around. But I needed to prove that I could do this, not just to myself but to Rick. I would be more independent. I would try to find a job. It would be okay.

Rick nodded. He'd gone really pale. "I'm not trying to be unkind, Leliel. I just think it would help. It would give you something to do with your time. Not that you don't spend your time wisely—I don't mean that—" He put his head in his hands. "I'm really screwing this up, aren't I?"

I touched his hand. "No, I understand. People work. They don't sit around and dream up murders and conspiracies."

Rick dropped his hands and gave me a hard look. "That's not what I meant. I just think you could use another outlet. Another purpose. I can't imagine how you must feel, being human again and having your sole purpose taken away from you. The world is way different than it was centuries ago." He took both my hands in his. "I'll help you. We could look at the want ads and see if there's anything you could do. Or we could look at the college's programs. But I won't pressure you."

I nodded. "That sounds fair. And you're right. It's a strange thing to be on the human side of things. Very strange."

"You'll be okay," Rick said softly. "After all, you have me."

I mock-smacked him. "Of course. So modest, aren't we?"

"Me? Oh yeah. Totally," Rick murmured, his eyes drifting closed.

We fell asleep at the table.

A HIGH-PITCHED meowing woke me up.

Five-thirty in the morning.

Love was hungry.

I wanted to go back to sleep, but once I was awake, it was tough to sleep again. No weird dreams, thankfully.

I stood and staggered over to where we kept Love's food. She wove in and out of my legs, nuzzling me, purring away.

"I got you," I whispered. I didn't want to wake Rick up. He'd have to get up for work soon. "Just...chill."

I put her food together and set her bowl down. She ate like I hadn't fed her in weeks.

My cellular phone rang, startling me. I grabbed it from the coffee table, but I didn't recognize the number. "Hello?"

"Leliel, this is David Landis. There was another suicide. I wanted to talk to you about it."

I swallowed hard. "Okay, lay it on me."

"All right," the detective said. "Another one via self-immolation. And there was a Tarot card left at the scene."

I sucked in a breath. "Okay."

"The deceased was nineteen and she attended Amsburg Law School."

Could it be the same girl as in my dream? The one with the shit-eating grin?

"So did Fred Chandler and Samantha," I said. "There's a connection there."

"Why don't you come to the station? I have some things that I need to take care of here, or I would come by. Is that okay?" David asked.

I tensed. I didn't drive, but there was no way I was going to admit that. There was nothing wrong with that, of course, but it just made me feel more alien. Less normal. I let out a breath. How would I get there? "That's fine. Just let me get some food in me and I'll be there."

"Great. See you in a bit," the detective said.

We said our goodbyes, and I was left holding my cellular telephone, wondering what was going on. Another suicide! It was number four.

I ran back into the kitchen and shook Rick awake.

He opened his eyes and yawned. "Wha...what's—"

"There's been another suicide. David just called me!"

"Slow down," Rick said, rubbing his eyes. "What exactly happened?"

So I told him. And decided that I would find a way to get there myself.

"Son of a bitch," Rick said once I was finished. "It could be that girl in your dream."

"I bet she is," I said.

"I have a bad feeling about this one, Leliel. A very bad feeling."

Chapter 4

AFTER RICK WENT to work and I had a light breakfast of oatmeal, I jumped into action.

I had to find the police station, but where was it? How would I get there?

I'd watched Rick use the Web, but could I remember how he did it?

I grabbed Rick's laptop computer and set it up in the kitchen. Love looked at me weirdly, and I shrugged. "Supposedly you can find anything on here."

I turned on the laptop. I watched as it went through its startup thing and waited longer until that stopped. That part I remembered.

There were so many little pictures on the screen. Each one did something, Rick had said.

"Which one is the Web?" I asked Love and the room at large. "Hellfire! Why didn't I pay closer attention? I am such a dope."

Okay, fine. I started clicking on each picture randomly. One was a writing program. One was for pictures. One made a weird black box on the left side of the screen. My eyes narrowed. That one looked scary.

I continued being a dope until I hit upon a blue E with a golden halo. Something about it looked familiar.

And ta-da, I had the Web! But Rick had called it the "internet." Was that the same thing? No time to worry about that.

But now what?

I could not remember what the hell to do next.

Love padded up to me and I picked her up and put her on my lap. "Do *you* know what to do next?"

She meowed as if to say, *who, me, Mommy?*

Right. She was a hellcat, not a computer expert.

I stared at the screen.

Something niggled at me. An…address bar?

"Could that be it?"

Love meowed, licking my fingers. Her breath stank of canned tuna. We gave it to her once in a great while as a treat. But it made her breath stink so badly… I made a mental note to get rid of all tuna cat food.

Rick had used something called the Google.

So I typed that in, and was rewarded with a plain page with a single bar in the center. Yes, that looked familiar.

I sighed. I didn't even know what police station it was. But there couldn't be that many, right?

"Okay," I murmured, and Love batted my arm with her tail like a whip. "Sassy thing." I typed in the words "Amsburg Police" and clicked on the search button.

Ta da, I had…wait for it…the Amsburg Police Department.

I squinted, trying to read the small print. I felt like an old woman. Well, I guess I *was* an old woman. Three hundred years old wasn't young.

I looked around for the address and found it at the bottom of the page. But I had no idea where it was. I had no car.

I'd never read a map.

But I recalled hearing someone on a television show talking about taking a cab…I remembered cabs. But surely they weren't pulled by horses now.

Would this internet tell me where to find a cab?

I went back to the Google page and typed in "Amsburg cabs."

And got another listing.

I grabbed my cellular telephone.

Wow, this felt strange. Everything was so new. Cellular telephones. Cabs. Internet. Laptops.

Jeans and tee shirts.

Indoor plumbing.

Air-conditioning.

I shook my head to clear it. I had to stay on task, or I would lose my nerve.

Because this was freaking scary. Taking a cab, going to the police station, talking to David officially...

But I needed to do this. For Fred. For this new victim. For the first two.

I was sure they were connected, but how?

I dialed the number—three times, because my fingers were trembling—and took a deep breath.

"Suburban Cabs," barked a man's voice.

"H-hello?" I said. "I-I'm looking for a-a cab."

"We are a cab company," the man said as if he were talking to a child. "We service all of Amsburg and parts of North Amsburg. Where're you looking to go?"

My mind went blank. *Meow.* Saved by the hellcat! "Amsburg Police Department. 1287 Normandy Street."

"That is within our service area. Where're we picking you up?"

"Uh..." What was our address? Damn, I'd never needed to know these things before!

"Ma'am?"

"Uh, yeah. My address is 487 Brian Street, no, *Bradley Street*, apartment 5C." I squeezed my eyes shut, willing myself to relax, for my heart to stop crazily pounding in my chest.

"Okay, we'll be by in about ten minutes. Two dollars to get into the cab, four-fifty for the first mile, five dollars a mile after." *Click.*

I stood there, staring at my cellular telephone. I had just ordered a cab. To take me to the police station. What the hell.

I paced.

I paced so much that I about damn near made a track in our carpet. My mind raced. What if this cab was a hoax? What if I got lost? What if I didn't have enough money?

I started looking for it. Should have done that sooner. What did the man say? Two dollars…four-fifty…five dollars…how many miles away was the police station?

Damn, I had no idea, and no time to check the Google thing.

I wondered if Rick's plastic loan card was here. But I'd promised never to use it, and I was going to keep my promise. Besides, I wasn't even sure if they'd take a plastic loan card as payment.

After tearing our bedroom apart, I found two bills in Rick's dresser. They looked like twenties, which Rick had explained were equivalent to twenty one-dollar bills, five five-dollar bills, and two tens. Was that enough? I hoped so.

A loud honk.

Was that my cab?

Cautiously, I opened the curtain to my front window. Sitting in front of my apartment building was a gray, nondescript vehicle. The words "Suburban Cabs" were written in blue on the passenger side door, along with a telephone number. Plumes of fumes wafted out from the back.

This was my cab? There weren't any horses. People drove *cars* everywhere.

Oh, boy.

Another honk.

Wow, he was really impatient.

I ran out of our bedroom like His Highness himself was after me, stopping only to give Love a kiss goodbye.

"Wish me luck, baby," I said as I walked out, locking the door behind me.

Meow.

Was it my imagination, or did she sound a bit upset that I was leaving?

By the time I got to the cab, I was breathing heavily. Hey, ex-Grim Reapers didn't really get much exercise.

I opened the passenger side door—

The man inside looked dirty, with greasy hair. He wore a torn tee shirt and pants. "Get into the back, miss."

"Oh." I felt my face flush as I closed the door and opened the back. Well, no one had ever told me *how* to do this, including the guy who answered the telephone. I slid into the seat. Cigarette smoke assaulted my senses, and I coughed.

"Where to?" the man barked.

"Uh," I said, my mind scrambling to remember the address of the police station. "1287 Norman Street. No, it's Normandy Street."

"You sure?"

I nodded. "I'm sure."

"Alrighty then." The tires squealed as he pulled out into traffic and I was violently slammed backward into my seat.

Ouch.

Once I got settled, I watched in awe as numbers appeared on this monitor thing next to the steering wheel. I was pretty sure that was my fee. I glanced down at the money I was clutching in my fist with a death grip (ha, get it? *Death grip!*). Would that be enough? And I hadn't thought about getting home.

The cab driver grunted. "So, you new around here?"

"Yes, I am."

"Never taken a cab before?"

I tensed. Was this a trick question? Would he try to scam me because I was a good target, not knowing anything about taking a cab? "Uh—"

He chuckled, stopping me cold. "It seemed that way, anyway. Don't worry. I'm not going to mug or kill you."

I laughed weakly. Weren't those the ones to worry about, the ones that *tell* you they wouldn't hurt you?

"So, hey, what're you doing at the police station? Being interviewed or something?"

I was not going to tell him about my investigation. I said the first thing that popped into my head. "I'm applying for a job."

He eyed me in the rearview mirror. "Good luck."

"Thank you," I said.

We spent the rest of the ride in silence. Which was fine, because I wasn't very good at chit chat.

Finally, the cab pulled up in front of a tall building. It was very plain and imposing, with at least three floors. Didn't make me feel any better. In fact, I felt as if I were headed to my own execution.

Why had I decided to do this again?

Right. Justice. Natural order.

And David needed me.

The cab driver turned to me expectantly, his hand outstretched. "That will be twenty dollars, ma'am."

I glanced down at the twenties I was carrying. I plucked one out of my hand and handed it to the driver.

The driver cleared his throat. "Aren't we missing something?"

My heart lurched. "I'm sorry…was that not enough? I'm pretty sure I gave you twenty—"

"A tip is customary, ma'am."

Oh, crap! I decided to tell the truth. "I am so sorry. I was in a hurry, and nervous, and I only brought enough for my ride here and back. I promise I will bring enough next time, in a hurry or not." I felt my face flush. Way to go, Leliel.

The driver surprised me by throwing his head back and laughing. When he could speak again, he said, "That's all right, but be sure to bring one next time. Some drivers get horrible if you deny them their tips."

I nodded. "Yes, sir. I promise."

"What's your name?"

I wondered if this was a ploy of some kind—

"I am just curious, is all. No harm intended."

"Leliel," I said. "What's yours?"

"Leliel," the driver said, tripping over the syllables. "That's different. Where are you from? I'm Tom."

I'm from the Underworld. "Here and there. Tom is a nice name."

Tom smiled. "Good luck to you, Leliel. Hope to see you again."

"With a tip," I said with a laugh.

I got out of the cab, my legs feeling like jelly.

We waved each other good bye, and his cab disappeared around a corner.

What a nice guy, I thought. I was lucky to get a nice one. Mental note: when taking a cab, bring a flippin' tip.

And now I was about to do something else I'd never done before.

Walk into a police station and talk to a detective about a murder.

Chapter 5

I WALKED INTO chaos.

People were everywhere, running here and there, talking, arguing, thrusting sheets of papers at each other.

Who would be the most receptive person to talk to?

"Hey, you over there! Are you the new detective?" A man wearing a nice suit approached me, looking frazzled. "You're two hours late! What—"

"Excuse me. I'm not the new detective, sir," I said apologetically. "But maybe you can help me with something."

"You're not the new detective? *Where* is the new detective? She was supposed to help me with this."

I shrugged helplessly. "I don't know anything about that. I am looking for Detective David Landis."

"This have anything to do with the suicides? Are you a witness?"

"I am not," I said. "He called me in."

Another frazzled man dressed in a suit flew past us.

"If you're not a witness, how would you have information about it?"

"I just...do. I'm...psychic." My vision shifted, and everything looked black and white. Except for this man's body. It was edged in a red glow. What did that mean? I blinked, and another set of eyes was looking at me. I got the impression that they were feminine.

And then my vision snapped back to normal.

"We do not believe in psychics—"

"Please. It's a matter of life and death," I said. I'd heard people on the television say that sort of thing, and it worked for them.

He sighed. "I'm sorry, but I can't tell you anything about an ongoing investigation."

I blinked. Everything remained the same. But to my *other* senses, it sounded almost like a woman's voice speaking below his.

"Okay, well…I have reason to believe that the self-immolation 'suicides'"—I made air quotes—"were actually murders."

"Look, I'm working with Landis on this, and I am doing some pretty heavy investigating here. Are you suggesting I'm not doing my job properly?"

Whoa, someone was on edge. "No, sir. I just wanted to investigate the situation, just like you."

His eyes widened. "You're not a detective. What makes you think you can do a better job than people who have done this for *years*?"

I shook my head. Someone was getting his panties in a twist. "I just want to help. Detective Landis wanted me to meet him here."

"I think you need to leave," the man snapped. "Landis knows better than to bring a civilian in on an ongoing investigation."

"I-I—"

"Get the hell out of here!"

I couldn't leave, not after what I had to go through to get here, but he was pretty much kicking me out. "Yes, sir." I smiled weakly, but he'd already headed in the opposite direction, screaming about his MIA detective and how she needed to be fired immediately. And the "idiot psychic" screwing with his investigation.

Nice guy.

I figured he was a candidate for a heart attack.

I wasn't about to irritate or offend anyone else. I'd have to call David and explain what happened.

Hey, maybe I'd get to see Tom again.

I was so intent on finding my way out that I crashed into something that was hard. And smelled of men's cologne.

Blushing, I looked up and saw David. He wore a police uniform and his badge on his hip.

He was smiling. Grinning, actually.

"Hi, Leliel. Don't listen to John. He's not very personable."

This flummoxed me. What the hell did "personable" mean? "Oh…okay."

"Come into my office. Let's talk."

DAVID'S "OFFICE" was more like a cubicle in a dark corner. It was quiet, though, and I was grateful for that.

His desk was neat and tidy, and he had one of those wide computer monitor thingies. Stacks of papers sat on the other side of the desk, plus a couple of folders. Unmarked. I checked.

He gestured for me to sit down on the chair opposite him, and I slid into it, my stomach clenching with anxiety. It was weird being here.

What had I seen around John's body? And the second set of eyes? What did it *mean*?

David smiled, shuffling some papers around on his desk. "There was talk that the deceased was severely depressed. There was a suicide note…"

I leaned forward, pulling a notepad out of my purse along with a pen. "Who was she? What did she look like?"

David consulted a piece of paper inside one of the folders. "Red hair, green eyes, from the description. Her name is—was—Shelby Price."

I made a note. "And the Tarot card?"

"Judgment?" David's brow furrowed. "Judgment?" David's brow furrowed. "I have no idea what that means. Or if it is even relevant." He shrugged. "So…what are your thoughts?"

I took a breath, then released it. "They all involved a Tarot card. Could it be a serial killer?"

David nodded. "That's a possibility we are tossing around. Also, that this could be a copycat suicide. That happens sometimes. One person does it, and someone else gets up the courage. But for now, let's just focus on this one here, okay?"

I took a breath and let it out. "I would like to mention one thing. Have you considered the possibility of the first two suicides being classmates of Fred's? Or even this Shelby being one, too?"

David leaned forward, his eyes focused on me like two lasers. "We have actually confirmed that. All four were students of the Law School."

My heart lurched. "What could this mean?"

"We haven't been able to figure out theories yet. Although you did say you thought the murderer was female? Why would a female law student want to kill her classmates?"

"Too much competition?" I tossed out. "Maybe she caught them copying her work? But that's a really dumb reason to commit murder."

"Yeah. Especially if we catch her and she goes to prison. Could you imagine that? But then again, people find all kinds of reasons to kill."

I nodded. "Good point. What about the suicide note?"

David dug into the same file, then produced a piece of paper. "This is a copy." He handed it to me, and a sense of foreboding gripped me and held me tight.

The note was written in small, cramped writing. "'I cannot take the pain anymore. Please forgive me. Luv, Shel.'" Again, it felt canned.

"I'm positive that someone forced them to write these notes. And, quite possibly, kill themselves." I set the paper down, meeting David's gaze squarely.

"You...? How?"

"I have dreams—"

The room tilted up.

A flash.

Fire. Smoke. Ashes.

Red hair.

Screaming; two women's voices intertwining.

A flash of a white glow.

The Tarot card.

Judgment. Someone judging—

"Leliel? Do you need help?"

David's voice came from a long tunnel. The edges of reality pulled in, containing me within them.

I screamed.

"LELIEL? LELIEL?"

I blinked awake. Everything was blurry.

A man's head hovered above me.

David?

"Leliel?"

"I..." I licked my dry lips. "I...where am I?"

"You're in the ER, honey," a woman's voice said. "You collapsed. This gentleman here called us."

I blinked again. "David?"

"Leliel? Hey, I'm sorry if I overstepped. I didn't know what to do."

And...neither did I. Why'd I lose consciousness?

"It's okay," I said. "I'm..." What did Rick say to Professor Everson? "I'm...I have epilepsy. This happens sometimes..."

"Can I call someone? Your husband?" David asked. "It's no trouble."

I waved my hand, and it turned into three hands. Ugh. "Yeah. Um, where's my purse?"

"It's here," the woman said. She was wearing the blue uniform thing that nurses wore, so she was clearly a nurse. Witness my great powers of deduction!

"My cellular telephone is in there. Give it to David, please."

The nurse nodded, rummaged in my purse carefully, retrieved my cellular telephone, and gave it to David. Following her action made my vision blur and my head ache.

David called Rick. "I'm at the hospital with your wife. She asked me to call you. She had an...epileptic...Okay, great. We will see you in a few." He hit the "end" button and handed the cellular telephone back to me.

I put it back in my purse, thinking about whether or not to mention the Web article. Hell, why not? He seemed open to what I had to say.

"There's something else," I said.

"Oh?" David said. "Do tell."

I met his eyes. "Rick and I were investigating the death of Samantha, another law student. We saw on the Web an article posted a few months ago about a fire and a fatality at the Law School. Our theory is that she was murdered, too."

"That's a bit out there," David said gently. "How do you know for sure?"

"Because I saw it in a dream," I admitted. *Please don't freak out.*

"That puts a whole new spin on things," David said. "As I recall, it was a big thing. All the news stations were covering it, the community freaked—but wait a second. It was a fatality, not a suicide."

"I dreamed this. She was murdered. Someone hung her up somewhere on the school grounds and set her on fire. People were laughing. It was horrible."

"You have to understand my position," David said. "Dreams are not evidence." He held up his hand when I started to protest. "I believe you. But unfortunately, I can't take this to the chief. There's no proof."

"But no one will talk to us about it, so we can't find any proof." I picked at a loose thread in my bedsheets. "But we know Fred's classmates know something. It was obvious that it was being covered up."

David shook his head. "Everyone wanted it buried and forgotten. Samantha was a law student, young, and very popular. It freaked a lot of people out."

"Who did it?" I asked.

"We ruled it a fatality, not murder."

"What happened? Was there a lack of evidence?" I asked.

David nodded. "Exactly. The crime scene was completely clean."

Rick flew into my cubicle, sweating heavily, panting, his eyes wild with terror.

"Leliel, are you okay?" He sat down next to me. "What happened?"

"I had an epileptic episode," I said. "I'm fine. David was kind enough to take me here to get checked out."

Rick glanced at David. "Thank you for bringing her here. You may have saved her life."

I touched Rick's hands. "There's something going on. With the, uh, epilepsy."

Luckily, Rick caught my hint. "I see. Is it worse?"

"Somewhat," I replied, my gaze flicking to David, who was just sitting there. "David, could you do me a favor? Get me some water, please?"

David jumped from his seat. "Of course. I'll be back."

After he was gone and out of earshot, I told Rick everything.

"So you passed out in the police station after having another vision?"

I nodded, the room tilting slightly. "Yeah. And I saw something else. A flash of glowing white."

"A flash?" Rick asked. "What the hell?"

"There's someone else," I said. "Someone else who doesn't want us to know what he or she is doing."

"The murderer," Rick murmured. "Holy crap."

"And," I said, catching his gaze, "there were two women, Rick. The victim and the murderer."

Chapter 6

"A WOMAN IS THE murderer?" Rick asked, his eyes wide. "Are you sure?"

"I'm positive." I heard footsteps nearby, and David poked his head in between the curtains. "Hi, David. Come on in."

"Thanks." He let himself in and held out a large cup with ice water in it. "I was able to get this from one of the nurses."

I took the cup and sipped. And sipped. And...sipped. Dang, my body must have been a desert. "Thank you. I feel better now." I quickly told Rick about what David and I had discussed. Then, "What do you think?"

"I bet they are connected," Rick said.

"But why leave a Tarot card?" David asked. "I mean, most people don't really know about or use them. What's the message?"

"The bigger question is," Rick said, "why leave them at all?"

David said, "Maybe he or she is trying to send us a message." He glanced at me. "Tell me about Tarot cards."

He had a good point. "Well, way back, they were simple playing cards. At some point, they became a way of divining the future. So, in reference to the investigation, we could look at this in two ways." My heart raced. Maybe we'd figure this out yet. "One, they can reveal what lies hidden from us. The Tarot cards have a position called 'ill-dignified,' or reversed. If a card is ill-dignified, it is usually a negative meaning. I wonder if the reversed position would make more sense. And second, and more importantly, this card is telling us the future. As in, more judgments to come."

"I've been giving this some thought," David said, leaning forward and catching my gaze. He looked so focused and thoughtful. "And I have to ask the question: how can anyone burn themselves to death? There are far less painful ways to die. Pills. Slit wrists. I know myself. If I were in their place, burning myself to death wouldn't be my first choice."

"Exactly. I'm positive that they didn't *have* a choice. It was taken from them," I said. "I'm telling you, someone else made them do it. They'd never choose that way to die. They're rich and have influential parents. They'd want to go out quietly and without a lot of fuss."

David made a few notes. "This is an interesting theory."

"It's not theory. It's fact," I said.

"What if this is a serial killer?" Rick said. "So, he or she is saying there's more to come. When will it be enough? Six? Fourteen?" He glanced at me, and I knew what he was thinking. Neither one of us could bear another one, let alone fourteen. She had to be stopped, and soon. "We're having a slight problem with people connected to the victims. They will not budge on giving us information."

"This is a very difficult time for them," David said. "It's like putting salt on a wound. I'd be surprised if they were forthcoming. Keep at it. Someone will fold. Especially if there are more." He checked his watch. "I'd better get back to work. Here's my card." He dug in his pocket, took out a small card with writing on it, and held it out to Rick. "Give me a call. We can compare notes and toss theories around."

I smiled. "Great. Thank you for everything."

"Take care, both of you." And he left, his footsteps whispering away from us.

"What is that small card he gave you?" I asked.

Rick held it out to me so I could read it. "It's his contact information. Conveniently on a card you can tuck in your pocket or purse. It's called a business card."

I smiled. "How totally cool."

"Getting back to the case…what's the reversed meaning for Judgment?" Rick asked, his eyes distant.

I thought about it. "Um...being close to a transformation and feeling blocked. Also, feeling spiritually empty. A call to action, a call to arms. But for the wrong reasons."

Rick shrugged. "So, the murderer feels this way? And wants to start a war?"

"No, not exactly. She feels this 'war' will make her feel better. That it will lead to transformation. But it won't work."

"I wish we knew what position the card was in when it was found," Rick mused.

A nurse bustled in. "How are you feeling, Leliel?" She wore a pink outfit and her hair in pigtails.

"She's been drinking a ton of water," Rick said, gesturing to my nearly empty cup.

"I feel much better," I confirmed. I just wanted out.

"I think we can safely release you," the nurse said, her ponytails a-bobbin.' Mesmerizing. "I'll check with the attending. Be back in a bit." And she bustled herself right out of there.

"So, what's next?" Rick asked, twining my fingers with his.

"Hopefully some rest, because I'm tired." Who knew that visions and murders could be so taxing?

She with the bobbing ponytails rejoined us fifteen minutes later and after filling out several forms, I was free.

BACK AT HOME, I tried to relax. Rick talked me into watching another episode of *Survivor,* so I sucked it up and tried to get interested in alliances and fights about food.

"We should watch *Bones*," I grumbled. "I love watching how they solve murders by examining bones of the deceased. And Brennan is so smart."

Rick was staring at me. "That's interesting. I didn't realize you were into those kinds of shows."

"Just trying to learn new things," I said. "And maybe Brennan's knack for solving cases will rub off on me."

"Cool."

I nodded. "I was thinking about watching *General Hospital*. I saw a—what's it called when this thing interrupts a show?"

"Commercial."

"Right. I saw a commercial. And it looked really entertaining. They were showing something about a mob war. Imagine that."

Rick put his arm around me and pulled me close. "Soap operas could be kind of fun to watch, I suppose. Especially after watching murder and gory stuff."

"Yeah. I wouldn't want to get depressed."

My cellular telephone rang, and I picked it up off the coffee table. I didn't recognize the number, but I didn't want to miss any important telephone calls. Rick encouraged me to "screen" my calls, whatever that was, but I didn't want to miss *anything*. "Hello?"

"Hello? Is this Leliel?" a girl's voice asked. She pronounced my name as "Lee-leel." But in her defense, my name was pretty different.

"This is her," I said, glancing at Rick. He arched a brow in question, but I didn't have any answers yet.

"This is Mandy from Professor Everson's class. I need to talk to you. As soon as possible."

I glanced at the clock. "Is this about Fred Chandler?"

"Yes, and Shelby Price."

My heart lurched. "What about them?" I tried to keep my voice steady.

"Can we meet somewhere?"

"Yes, absolutely. How about in an hour at that diner on Ford Street?" I hoped I'd gotten the street name correct. I wasn't really sure.

"Gerald Street," Rick said.

"Oh, it's on Gerald Street," I said. "One hour."

"Perfect. See you there."

After saying goodbye, I turned to Rick. "We might be in luck. Mandy from Fred's class wants to talk to us."

"That's awesome! Score one for Team Ashton!" Rick held out his hand, palm out.

I looked at it, then at him. "What's that about again?" Hellfire. The world had changed *so much* in three hundred years.

"It's a high five." Rick took my hand in his and touched our palms together. "It's like saying 'way to go' except cooler. Try it." He let go of my hand, and I raised it. He raised his. I brought mine to his and tapped it. "Okay, better, but hit my hand harder. Try again."

"I don't want to hurt you," I said.

"You're not going to hurt me. Come on, high-five me." He held up his hand again.

And I hit it *really* hard. He grimaced and grabbed his wrist. He looked at me, smiling. But it was wobbly at the edges. "Nice job. Maybe you could hit me a bit lighter next time, huh?"

IN NO TIME, we were on our way to the diner.

"Do you think she's got legitimate information?" Rick asked.

"Maybe. I mean, don't people come forward like this? I saw it once on *Bones*."

"Yes, but I have to wonder what her motives are. The whole class, including Professor Everson, was so cagey when we were there. What changed her mind?"

That was a really good question.

"Well, we'll have to see what she says," I said. "And how did she know about Shelby? Only the police know. And us."

"That relative on the force?" Rick asked. He eased into a parking spot in the back and turned off the car. He unlocked the doors and got out. I did the same.

We headed toward the entrance. It was a simple place, small and homey, which was why we liked it. Friendly waitstaff, homestyle cooking, and nice patrons. We'd had several conversations with the regulars, and it felt like being with family.

When we entered, our favorite waitress, Lucy, grinned at us. "Hello, lovebirds! How's it going?"

"Good," I murmured. I still felt shy around her. She was so...animated. And enthusiastic. And loud. I liked her, but she made me nervous for some reason.

"Great. Hanging in there," Rick said with a smile. "We're here to—"

"Yes, there's a young lady here to see you." Lucy sidled up to Rick and pitched her voice low. "What's this all about? She looks a bit rough." She glanced at a black-haired woman wearing all black, including black lipstick and black nail polish.

"She's from the college, actually. We're looking to maybe have Leliel go to school," Rick replied smoothly. Wow, he really was a quick thinker. "She's going to give us the inside scoop."

Lucy beamed. "Well, that's just amazing. You'd do well in school, dear."

I found I couldn't look her in the eye. After saying "thanks," we made our way over to her corner table. We had to dodge several kids running around, and a guy whose legs were so long he had to put them in the aisle. And of course, waitresses milling around taking and delivering orders.

The food smelled divine.

One thing struck me immediately. I didn't remember seeing her in class. Crap, who was I kidding? I'd definitely remember her.

As we approached, Mandy looked up at us, her eyes distant.

And then it happened again.

Things around her went monochrome, her eyes became two sets of eyes, and a red glow surrounded her body.

Hellfire. What did that mean?

"Mandy?" I said, extending my hand for her to shake. "I'm Leliel, and this is Rick, my husband."

Mandy wrinkled her nose. "Have a seat." She did not extend her hand to shake or acknowledge mine. She leaned forward as we sat opposite her.

Her breath reeked of cigarette smoke.

"So, I called because I know something that may help," she said.

"Now, you guys weren't too keen on telling us anything. Why the change?" Rick asked, playing with the salt and pepper shakers.

Mandy pushed her long hair behind her ears. "Well, we would like to help. We still don't believe Fred and Shelby were murdered, but…" She looked to Rick and then to me. "Maybe what I have to say will be useful. Maybe not. But I thought I'd try."

I nodded. "Sounds logical. So what information is this?"

"Well…it's private. I could get into trouble just for meeting you." She folded her arms across her chest.

I had a funny feeling she wanted something in exchange for the information. "We don't have a lot of money. I am hoping you would do this from the goodness of your heart."

"I suppose that will work."

"So, lay it on us," Rick said.

Lucy chose that exact moment to come over and ask for our orders.

"Farmer's omelet with hash browns and rye bread," Mandy said. "And coffee. Black."

That wasn't a surprise.

Lucy made a note, then looked at me. "And for you, Leliel?"

I glanced at Rick. We hadn't discussed getting food. I decided to err on the side of caution. We were already fifty dollars in the hole. No need to add any more. "Just a coffee. Cream and sugar, please."

"And you, Rick?"

Rick tapped the table with his fingernails. "An order of hotcakes. Two plates. And a coffee for me. Cream only."

I arched a brow at him.

"We'll share," he said, taking my hand in his.

"Okay, I'll put this in and bring your drinks," Lucy said, then went to the next table. One of the men sitting there gave a loud belly laugh.

Rick and I both looked at Mandy expectantly. Mandy grabbed a paper napkin from the holder to her side. Napkins confused me because my family had used rags. And reused them. Napkins got thrown away after one use. How weird was that?

Mandy twisted the napkin around three fingers. "It's really sad. They were both really depressed. Like, ready to off themselves depressed."

My heart lurched. Fred's mother had mentioned that. And David had mentioned that Shelby Price had been depressed, too. I glanced at Rick, who gave me an almost imperceptible shrug.

"Okay." Rick set down the salt shaker he was holding. "We know that Fred was. But Shelby, too?" Oh, he was playing dumb. Maybe she'd reveal more.

"Oh, yes. They work us to the bone in school," Mandy said, all serious. "I mean, you basically have no life and nothing to do but work. It's criminal."

Rick snorted. "Well, that is the point of college. To work hard and learn things."

"Yeah, well, I haven't slept in two days. Too much homework," Mandy snapped. "Anyway, they went to this new shrink who promised immediate results."

"A new kind of therapy?" Rick asked, his eyes narrowed.

Lucy came back with the coffees. "Your order will be ready shortly," she said. "So, how's the school talk coming along?" She glanced at me. "Hear anything you like?"

Rick smiled. "It's going wonderfully. Leliel is considering law school. Right, honey?"

I smiled wanly. "I am. It sounds…invigorating." I took a sip of my coffee, wincing at how hot it was.

"That's so cool," Lucy said. She glanced to her left. "I'll be back."

"What on *earth* did you tell her?" Mandy asked.

"It was our cover story. She didn't know we were talking about mur—" I stopped as Lucy passed our table. "We had to tell her something."

"That was kind of smart, I guess," Mandy said softly, tearing her napkin into tiny pieces. She sighed and put it down. "So anyway, the shrink."

"Yes," Rick agreed, watching her closely.

"He, um, had access to a new experimental medication." Mandy took a sip of her coffee. "And there were some nasty side effects."

"Nasty side effects? Death being one?" Rick asked.

Mandy nodded. "Yep. The drug supposedly could cause some people to have suicidal thoughts and you know, um, attempts."

I set my mug down. "So you're saying that this is why Fred and Shelby died?"

"I'm saying it's possible. Not for sure." She wouldn't look me in the eye.

Our food came. I mulled that over while I ate. Rick seemed to be thinking, too, and Mandy scarfed her food down as if she hadn't eaten in months.

"How did you come to this knowledge?" Rick asked, breaking the silence.

Mandy lifted her head and met Rick's gaze. "Fred and Shelby actually told me."

"I don't recall seeing you in class," I said.

Mandy tensed. "Uh, yeah. I was absent. I got your number from someone else." Her voice was shrill. She picked at her hash browns.

Something was really wrong with this situation. I couldn't put my finger on it.

"Well, we appreciate you telling us." Rick took a sip of his coffee, then set it down. "Can we call you if we have any additional questions?"

Mandy froze with her fork halfway to her mouth. Her eyes darted around, not focusing on anything in particular. "No, I'd prefer you didn't. There's nothing else to say." She rummaged around in her big leather purse and produced a ten-dollar bill. "Here, this should cover mine. I gotta go."

And before we could even say thanks, she hustled out of there, her head down.

Rick and I looked at each other.

"That was too strange," I said. "I think she was lying."

We finished eating in silence. This was just too weird.

When we were done, we paid for our meal and headed out, saying goodbye to Lucy.

Rick took my hand in his as we headed to the car. The parking lot was starting to fill up, and I was glad to be leaving. Humans made me anxious sometimes. Even though technically I was one of them now. Go figure.

"I felt her decision to be dishonest." Rick unlocked the car and opened the passenger side for me. Always the gentleman. "But what part was she lying about?"

I got into the car and Rick did the same. "I'm pretty sure all of it is a lie. But let's run it by David, see what he says."

Rick started the car and pulled out of the parking lot. "I agree. It might shed some light on something."

"Or muddy the waters," I pointed out. Then I remembered my hallucination. "I've seen a weird thing twice now. Once at the police station and once just now."

"Tell me about it." Rick glanced at me, then returned his attention to the road.

"It's like I can see and hear other things besides the people I'm talking to. Mandy and the police guy both sounded like two people were talking, and their bodies were edged in this red glow, and—"

"It's the Underworld." Rick stopped at a red light, and then he turned to me. "Your abilities aren't gone, Leliel. They've changed. I bet you're seeing spirits or something."

"The dead?" I asked.

Horns honking. Rick hit the thing that made the car move forward.

"I don't know. It just seems like a logical progression."

"But what does it *mean*?" I knew I sounded like a five-year-old, but I was starting to get freaked out. Crazy things were afoot.

"I don't know," Rick said softly.

"That was pointless," I said with a sigh.

"Not pointless. We learned about the possibility of the suicides being related to drugs," Rick said. "Assuming that part wasn't a lie." He made a sharp turn to the left.

"Hey, don't give me a flippin' heart attack," I grumbled. "Would like to live long enough to enjoy being human." What I didn't say was, *and my last life ever.* I decided he could extrapolate the rest.

"I don't want to kill you," Rick said, glancing at me quickly, then focused back on the road. "I want to loooooove you."

Heart. Melting. "Aww. So sweet."

Rick drummed his fingers on the steering wheel. "That's me. Mr. Sweet. Hey, maybe David has something for us."

And you know what? He came through in a big freaking way.

Chapter 7

"SO, I DID SOME digging," David said.

We were seated in a different diner around the block from the station, coffee and muffins ready for consumption. I got two, because why not. Rick sipped his black coffee but didn't dip his muffin into it. Must only work for cookies.

"Lay it on us," I said.

David's eyes danced with excitement. "I looked into the background of each victim. Found something interesting."

"And that would be...?" Rick asked.

"They were all friends. Connected." He grinned. "And now for the big thing. They were into witchcraft and Tarot."

"Really?" Rick asked. "That is interesting, considering that the killer is leaving Tarot cards at the scenes."

"I know, right?" David said. "Apparently, they held séances and went to the cemetery more than was healthy, according to some people who were close to them. Samantha had an unhealthy fixation on the 'dark arts.'"

My eyes about bugged out of my skull. "How did you find this out? This is a gold mine. Nice job."

David arched a brow. "Just some good old-fashioned detective work."

"We have some information, too," I said, breaking my muffin into equal pieces. "We got a telephone call from one of Fred's classmates. She says Fred and Shelby were on an experimental drug for depression. And she thinks their suicides were due to a side effect."

David's eyes widened. "That's...not what I expected to hear."

Rick and I exchanged a look.

"We're not sure if she was telling the truth," I admitted.

"What? I'm not sure I follow," David said, taking a sip of coffee.

"I think it's a bit suspicious." I took a bite of my muffin. Damn, I had no idea blueberry muffins were *this good*.

"So, let me get this straight." David pulled out a notepad and pen and began taking notes. "You went to where to meet with Mandy?"

"A diner," Rick said around a mouthful of muffin.

"And this student told you that two of the suicides were due to an experimental drug for depression?" He looked up; Rick and I both nodded.

"Evidently they both were seeing this shr—I mean, psychiatrist and he got access to an experimental drug," I said.

"Okay," David said with a nod. "And then what?"

"She refuses to let us call her and she acts shifty," Rick put in.

David made more notes. "And you believe she was lying."

"That's exactly it." More muffin.

"What if she's telling the truth and she was just nervous?" David asked. "Some people aren't good in social situations. Maybe that's all it was."

"But we have no proof either way," I pointed out, picking up the remaining half of the muffin. "And that's a problem."

David nodded. "It is."

"Tell him the rest." Rick put his arm around me.

"I don't think…"

"It might be valuable information," Rick said, glancing at me.

"It's a bit weird." I took a sip of my coffee and carefully set it down, meeting David's eyes. "I'm going to get all woo-woo on you. I hope that's okay."

David grinned. "Woo-woo works." He picked up his cookie, opened his mouth, but must have thought better of it because he set it down.

"I saw *two* females in one of my visions. One was suicide number four—"

"Shelby," David supplied.

"Shelby. The other I believe was the murderer."

"Did you see a face or anything we can use to identify her?" David had gone very still, not even touching his coffee.

"I didn't, unfortunately. But her energy was feminine. I know it." Rick squeezed my hand.

"I believe you, Leliel," David said. "But I'm not sure the rest of the world will. We need more."

"SOMETHING IS bothering me," I said.

Rick and I were at the grocery store. We were out of several things. This case had completely overtaken our lives.

I always marveled at the modern grocery store. Groceries on shelves and shopping carts and canned fruits and vegetables and raw, processed meat. Although I tried not to think of that too often, because it kind of grossed me out.

Rick was studying the label on a chicken soup can. "I'm sorry?"

"I said, something is bothering me," I said patiently. I grabbed a can of green beans and tossed it into our cart. I also added some pineapple chunks.

"And what is that?" He grabbed a can of baked beans, grinning sheepishly. "Beans are good for you."

"They make you *really* gassy, but sure, we'll go with that." I added another can of pineapple chunks.

"What if what Mandy said was true? That they were both on this drug."

"Well…" Rick picked up a package of whole-wheat pasta, shook his head, then set it back down. "Okay, well, there's one way to find out."

My heart gave an uncomfortable lurch. He looked way too squirrely. "Oh, no."

"Yes. It's actually a *great* idea—"

"Will it get us thrown out of another place? Because I really can't take any more rejection." We moved forward a few paces. Wow, this was taking a while, but I loved spending time with Rick. As a Reaper, I really hadn't needed to eat. Not unless I wanted to. I did, but not often. Mostly pineapple.

Maybe I should have been born in Hawaii.

Rick bit his lip. He was so cute when he did that. "Maybe. But it's worth the trouble, I swear."

The uncomfortable feeling became full-blown alarm. "I do not want to get arrested!"

Some people were staring at us. Lovely.

"We won't be." He wouldn't look at me. "Well, probably not."

I sighed. "Just tell me."

We walked down another aisle. I poked him in the ribs. "Hey. What's your great idea?"

He grabbed a box of beer and set it in our cart. "I'm going to need this, okay?" He met my eyes. "Let's pay Ms. Chandler another visit. She would probably know what Fred was on. And this Shelby's mother, too."

"Ms. Chandler threatened to have us arrested."

"I don't believe it. We're not hurting anyone by investigating this," Rick said. "Besides, it would make her feel better knowing we were trying to figure out how her son died."

I grabbed a two liter of soda. Sprite, my favorite. The best thing *ever* about living three hundred years into the future. Or something like that. "She doesn't believe it was suicide. But I guess we could try. Worst case, we end up in matching jail cells. That'd be fun."

"Loads."

Silence descended as we continued shopping. Rick was lost in thought, I figured, and I was trying to figure out how we could avoid being arrested.

But Rick had a point. Either way, Ms. Chandler should have been happy that we were doing this. Then again, many people didn't like other people sticking their noses into their business. Or opening terrible wounds.

Maybe she knew deep down that Fred hadn't killed himself. And maybe she was just too afraid to face it.

Denial was a powerful thing.

We got into the checkout lane. Another awesome invention! There were two people ahead of us, one with a baby in one of those baby carriers. They were cool and all, but I had to wonder how the poor baby felt, being carried around in that thing. Did he or she feel claustrophobic? Or was it fun? Or—

Awww. I hadn't thought about kids at all.

"Help me load these, please," Rick said, bringing me back to earth. I helped him load the groceries onto the belt thingie and then went to the bag area to collect our bags.

I glanced at Rick, who was watching the cashier. "I think you might be right."

Rick arched a brow. "Oh? Well, I think *you* might be right. I'm not really a fan of jail."

"We can try Shelby's parents, though," I suggested. "Maybe they will be more receptive."

"Sure."

"That will be thirty dollars and sixty-two cents," the cashier—a young boy—said.

Rick went into his wallet and pulled out his plastic loan card. He slid it through a strange machine.

"It's thinking," he said. Several messages popped up, but I couldn't read them from where I stood.

I leaned closer to Rick and spoke softly. "We already have a plastic loan for fifty dollars. You said we couldn't afford it—"

"I'm waiting for my paycheck. They are running late again." He didn't look at me; he just stared at the machine.

Oh. He was embarrassed.

"Put in your PIN," the cashier said.

Rick pressed a few buttons, and a sheet of paper came out of another machine.

"How should we approach her?" Rick asked. Changing the subject, I see. Good call. "I don't think what we're doing is working."

"Here you go, sir," the kid said, and handed Rick the sheet of paper.

I finished putting the groceries into the cart and we left the store.

"So, um, what did you mean about your paycheck being late?" I asked Rick once we were out of earshot of the other shoppers.

Rick shrugged. "Well…sometimes they run late. It's never been over a week. We can pay that off immediately with the money from my paycheck."

"But *how*? Don't we have other bills?" I caught sight of Rick's car and steered us that way.

"Of course we do," Rick said, sounding tense. Was I upsetting him?

"Well, how are we going to pay them if we're in the hole by eighty dollars? Is eighty dollars a lot?" I asked, confused. I remembered the value of money from my own time but had no way to figure out what it would be now.

"It's not a whole lot." Rick stopped in front of the car, and I stopped, too. "But it's enough. I appreciate your concern—"

"It's partly my fault. I forced you to get that subscription. But this—this is *food*. We shouldn't be getting plastic loans for it. It seems really wrong."

A flash of something went through his face, but then disappeared. "I'm not sure how to tell you this, but, uh—I wasn't completely honest with you about our finances. We're in the hole. Considerably."

My heart dropped to my feet, rolled around on the cement, then kicked me in the butt for good measure. "What? How? *Why*?"

Rick sighed, his shoulders slumping. "I wanted you to think I was a good provider. And…just before we met, things were kind of getting out of control."

"Because of the late paychecks?" I asked. Hellfire. I didn't know what to do. I'd never had to think about money. My parents had done that because I wasn't old enough to be on my own yet.

"Partly. And, well…I'm terrible at budgeting my money. I tend to, uh, have very little savings."

My eyes narrowed. "Budgeting? What does that mean?"

Rick ran his hand across his face. "Making sure you have enough money every month to pay your bills."

My throat constricted. "So…you're saying we're…are we…" My mouth had gone dry. I couldn't even say it. And damn it, I wasn't about to have a breakdown in this parking lot. It would be okay, right?

Right?

Rick sighed again, fiddling with his keys. "We're late on rent. But I promise you, it's okay. I had a talk with our landlord and he's allowing me to pay late without throwing us out."

My jaw dropped. We could have been *thrown out*. As in, homeless.

Now I felt like puking.

It was worse than I'd thought.

"Damn it," I snapped. "How many times have you been late?"

Rick averted his gaze again. "Uh…several."

I barely heard him. "We have to *do* something. I do not want to be homeless, Rick! The world is scary enough—"

Rick took hold of my arm and pulled me close. "I promise you, we won't be homeless. It's still fixable."

I withdrew, not feeling very romantic. "How?"

"We'll figure something out, okay? I'll try to get a raise, or maybe I could work a second job, or—"

"I could work." I rubbed my temples. It all made sense now. He needed money, and he thought maybe I could work.

Rick fiddled with the keys again. "I want to be able to provide for us, but—"

"It may be necessary. Okay, got it. Let's table this before I have a breakdown, okay? Awesome," I said.

"Leliel?" He touched my shoulder, and I pulled away.

"What if you don't pay your plastic loan back? Hypothetically?"

Rick unlocked the car and opened the trunk. "Bad things happen."

"Like being forced to burn yourself to death?" I asked, sliding a few bags into the trunk.

Rick's eyes went wide. "No, not at all! Why would you think that?"

I shivered, and not from being cold. "Well, what would cause someone to do that to someone else? What if Fred and Shelby took out huge plastic loans and couldn't pay them?"

Rick put his bags in the truck and closed it. He took my hands in his, drawing me close. "Look, I know the world is crazy, but trust me. If it was murder, it was not over a credit card. There had to be something bigger going on."

"But what?"

"Hopefully we will find that out." Rick opened the passenger door for me. I got in, and he closed it.

He got into the driver's seat, putting his key into the thing that started the car.

"I don't know," I said. "People are funny. It doesn't matter where they are from—here or the Underworld. Greed is greed, and revenge is revenge, and people can be cruel. It had to be something horrible. If I'd loaned someone some money and they never paid it back, I'd be mad."

The car started, and Rick pulled out of the parking lot. "Not nearly mad enough to set someone on fire. You know what that feels like. No way."

"Not me, no. But what if I'm someone else and I feel I was grievously wronged? Maybe."

"I'm sorry but that's too crazy, even for us humans. And who says it's payback? Remember, Samantha was into the dark arts. Maybe it was a spell or something."

"A spell gone wrong?"

Rick stopped at a red light. "No. Maybe a spell gone right."

THE NEXT DAY, we formulated a plan.

We were sitting in the kitchen with Love, finishing my first penne rigate dinner.

"We'll see Ms. Chandler, make mention of the medication angle. See what she says. If she seems irritated, we'll abort the mission. And then we'll go see Shelby's parents," Rick said.

"*Any* sign of anyone wanting to arrest us, we abort, you mean." I picked at the tail end of my penne. I was pretty full, but damn, it had been really good.

"Yeah." He fed Love a mostly clean noodle. "What if she refuses to talk to us?"

"Then we respect her wishes," I said. "Now, let me call David."

"And I will wash the dishes." Rick came to where I was sitting. "I'm sorry about all the money issues. I'm sorry I kept it from you. I'm *really* sorry that it's stressing you out." He took my hands in his. "I'll see about getting an account with a higher interest rate, so what money we do have in the bank grows more. And maybe I'll see someone about budgeting—"

I nodded. "And maybe ask for a raise?"

"I've been there a long time. They might give me one," Rick replied. "The thing is, I never had to worry about someone else, you know? But now I have you and Love to take care of, and I would never forgive myself if we were homeless because of my crappy money managing skills."

"That's good. And maybe you can teach me stuff so I can help." I kissed him on the forehead. "I'm sorry I freaked out, especially in public."

"No, you were right to freak out. But now we're on the right track. I appreciate you so much, you have no idea." Rick kissed me, soft and gentle.

I responded with a deep, hungry kiss that showed him just how much *I* appreciated *him*. "It's all right. I'm happy you appreciate me."

"So much," Rick said, his voice husky. When he talked like this, my toes curled and my nerves did a happy dance.

"Okay, well, I need to call David. We can explore your *appreciation* after I'm done."

He kissed me again. "Okay. I'll be waiting."

I called David, and he agreed to meet us here tomorrow afternoon.

"Awesome!" Rick said when I gave him the good news. "Now, about that appreciation?"

My vision went white, and I had the impression of a small, claustrophobic space. A young man. And an inner struggle. Depression? Or something more sinister?

"Leliel?" Rick's voice jolted me to the here and now.

I opened my eyes. "I'm okay. I had another vision."

Rick's eyes widened. "What did you see?"

I rubbed my eyes, trying to will the scene away from me. But it was locked up behind my eyelids. "A small space. A young man. And he was struggling for some reason…"

"Oh. That doesn't sound good," Rick murmured. "Do you think it's happening now?"

"No. It's done. He's gone," I whispered. A flash of something else from the corner of my mind's eye. A Tarot card.

I couldn't quite make it out. It was a Major Arcana card, a low-numbered one. I tried to see it from several different perspectives, then gasped when it became clearer. "The Hierophant."

"What does that mean?"

I slid to the floor. Love nuzzled my hand. "The Hierophant. She's teaching us a lesson."

Chapter 8

SHELBY'S PARENTS were a no go. They were out of town. David said he'd keep us posted on the situation.

But then he came through for us again, telling us exactly where the most recent murder had taken place. The victim's name was Mark Allison.

So, we went there immediately, not caring how late it was.

The pungent smell of smoke hung in the air. There wasn't much left of the garage but some charred siding and part of the roof. A big portion of the house next to the garage was charred and destroyed. The fire must have spread, then.

There were police officers everywhere.

"Excuse me," Rick said to the nearest police officer, well away from the scene of the fire.

He was slightly overweight and balding. And he seemed to be perpetually scowling. Way to pick a receptive one. "What are you doing here? This is a crime scene, and—"

Rick looked taken aback. I jumped in. "Sir, we were hoping to talk to the mother of the deceased for a few minutes. We won't disturb anything—"

"Are you with the press or are you medical people? I don't think you are. You're just going to get in the way and upset the mother."

"We won't," I said, my voice quivering. I hated that people just loved to dismiss us. "We won't be long, I promise."

"See that you aren't. And watch where you're walking. The Crime Scene Unit's already been here, but you just never know. Stay to the walls and don't touch anything," the officer said. "Go on." He made a dismissive gesture toward the garage.

"Yes, thank you, sir," Rick said, taking my hand.

A woman with blonde hair and striking blue eyes stood near the ashes and cried. The garage bore the smell of smoke, with a hint of that oily, musty smell that garages get after a while. One side was completely burnt.

That was clearly the small space I'd seen in my vision.

The mother of the deceased turned as we approached. Tears made her cheeks wet.

My heart ripped open when I saw that, which told me that I needed to find the killer and fast. How many more mothers would lose their children? How many more people would die before their time?

"Excuse me, ma'am," I said.

Mark's mother slowly raised her head and looked at us. "Who are you? Are you more police?"

I wished I could lie, but I refused to. "No, ma'am. We are simply concerned citizens looking into these...suicides." I had almost said "murders." I didn't want to scare her.

"We aren't with the police," Rick added. "But we were hoping to talk to you about your son."

Mark's mother covered her face. "I don't want to talk about this. My husband's away on business and I have no idea how I'll tell him."

"Okay," I said, glancing at Rick. "We are so sorry for your loss and understand how difficult this must be. But can you at least tell us whether or not your son was taking medication for depression?"

She uncovered her face, revealing wide eyes. "Ab-absolutely not! Mark was not depressed! He had everything to live for!"

Okay, maybe my question was a bit heavy-handed. "I'm sorry. The others were rumored to have been on medication, that's all."

"Shouldn't the police be doing this?"

"We're helping. Unofficially," I said. I hoped word didn't get back to David. We didn't want to cause him any trouble.

"What is your name, ma'am?" Rick asked.

"I'm Katherine Allison," Mark's mother said, extending her hand to us.

"I'm Leliel Ashton and this is my husband, Rick," I said as we all shook hands.

"Leliel…that's an unusual name," Mrs. Allison said.

"Well, she's a very unusual woman," Rick said with a grin. Then he sobered. "So, you're saying that there is no chance that Mark was depressed or on medication for depression?"

"That is correct."

"We have reason to believe that your son was murdered, Mrs. Allison," I said.

"What? I d-don't believe that." I could tell she didn't want to believe that, but it seemed that a part of her needed to know for sure.

I nodded. "It's possible."

Mrs. Allison sighed, her eyes sliding to the ashes. "So, what do you need exactly?"

"Who were Mark's enemies?" Rick asked.

Mrs. Allison's eyes narrowed. "Well, there were a few. But the biggest one I think was this group of students."

"Why were they enemies?" I asked.

Mrs. Allison came a bit closer and lowered her voice. "They were rivals. Those students always beat him in class. No matter how hard he tried—and he tried *very* hard—he couldn't get better grades than them."

My eyes widened. "There was a group that was rumored to have been into the occult. Maybe it was a spell."

Mrs. Allison gave me an exasperated look. "That stuff isn't even real."

"Well, I'm not going to debate that with you. I'm just saying, it was rumored." I glanced at Rick. He was looking kind of pale. "Honey, are you feeling all right?"

Rick shook his head. "Not really. But keep going."

"Maybe we should take her number and go home," I said. My guts twisted painfully. What was wrong with my husband?

He shook his head. "No, I'll be fine."

"Would you like a glass of water?" Mrs. Allison asked. "I'd be happy to get one for you."

Rick's face lit up just a bit. "If it's not too much trouble."

"None at all. I'll be right back." Ms. Allison left us, her heels tap-tap-tapping on the concrete. Lucky for us, the kitchen didn't appear to be damaged by the fire.

Once she was gone, I took Rick's hand in mine. "What's wrong?"

He shook his head. "I'm beginning to feel..." His eyes rolled back, and my heart lurched. Then his eyes went back to normal. "Um...I feel something very wrong in here, Leliel."

"Well, this is the scene of a possible murder," I said. "With a very considerate mother of the deceased." Which was quite unexpected.

"No, that's not it. It's like—" He put his hand up, as if to show me something, then dropped it. He looked around, his body shivering. His eyes came back to mine. "It's like I'm feeling a psychic imprint of what happened."

Okay, now I was spooked, and that *never* happened. "What do you mean?"

"I can feel what the murderer was feeling—"

"Was it a female?" I asked.

Rick glanced toward the house, where Mrs. Allison was coming toward us, carrying two glasses of water. "I'm not sure."

"Hellfire. I was hoping to find that out for sure."

"I can't explain," Rick said, shaking his head. "She's almost here."

"Okay, later," I said. I turned and flashed Mrs. Allison a smile. "Hi. Welcome back." Inside, my guts were a seething knot of anxiety. Rick had a new superpower? He was going to have to explain this later.

"Hello. Here you go," Mrs. Allison said, handing Rick one of the glasses of water. She offered me the other one. "I thought you might want one, too."

I took it. She was almost *too* considerate. "Thank you. Very thoughtful." I didn't take a sip yet. I watched Rick. He took several sips. And then several more.

"Better?" Mrs. Allison asked, smiling weakly.

"Yes, thank you," Rick said. "I was feeling kind of nauseous. Maybe I need to eat or something. Anyway…" He glanced at me. "We were discussing the rival students in your son's class…?"

"Uh, yes. Their rivalry was legendary! Everyone knew about it. And some of the women in the group…they are ruthless. More than you can even imagine."

"Well, ruthless is ruthless no matter how you slice it," I said. "What makes them super-ruthless?" This was interesting. But I didn't really understand how it tied into her son's murder.

Mrs. Allison lowered her voice again. As if the ghost of her son would hear her. "It was rumored that they *slept* with certain professors to get good grades. Or…" She shook her head. "It's so crazy. I feel stupid even saying it."

"Nothing's stupid when we're talking possible murder," Rick said, taking another sip of water. He did look better.

"The professors didn't do it of their free will." Mrs. Allison rolled her eyes. "Someone said they were under a love compulsion spell. But that's just crazy, right?"

My eyes widened. "That's entirely possible. If you believe, of course," I added hastily. "If you don't believe…then I guess they are not very ethical professors, are they?"

Mrs. Allison looked paler. "And you believe this"—she gestured to where the ashes and charred bones had been found—"this was a murder."

"Have you heard about the other four suicides?" I asked. "One was a college student named Fred Chandler, and the other was a woman named Shelby—"

"Shelby Price?" Mrs. Allison covered her mouth with her hand.

"Yes," Rick said, glancing at me. "Did you know her?"

"Of course I knew her! She and Mark were engaged once. She was part of Mark's circle of friends."

"SO, LET ME GET THIS straight. Shelby was part of Mark's group of friends," I said. We were in Mrs. Allison's house, surrounded by pictures of Mark—high school graduation, track buddies, birthday parties, his college dorm...you name it, it was there. I could almost piece together his life using those pictures.

And Shelby...she was prominent in quite a few, even though they weren't engaged anymore.

Mrs. Allison's home was small and homey, with gray couches and pastel afghans thrown over them. Flower vases sat everywhere, giving the living room color and fragrance. There was a large fireplace on one side, and this is where Mrs. Allison sat with us.

We were drinking a special kind of tea. Because this stuff calmed anxiety.

And boy, was I anxious.

I felt like we were on the cusp of breaking the case.

Mrs. Allison nodded, taking a sip of her tea. "That is correct."

"Shelby and Mark were engaged for how long?" Rick was taking notes.

"For about a year and a half."

"And do you know why they split up?" I asked, glancing at Rick.

"They had a fight. He never said why," Mrs. Allison replied. Something told me that that was a lie. But I didn't want to push.

Rick jotted that down. "And what about the rival group? What were they competing for?"

"The best grades and the favor of the dean," Mrs. Allison said. She leaned forward, steepling her hands. "See, there's a system in that school. Honor. Every time you get a good grade, or do something extraordinary, you win favor with the dean. It is rumored that the dean will help you in unmeasurable ways. He will induct you into his special society and that will give you lots of power, too."

"What kind of power?" Rick asked, pen poised.

Mrs. Allison tensed. "Power. You know, influence. Prestige. Friends in high places. Things like that."

"And the dean can do all of that? Sounds impossible," I said, mulling it over.

Mrs. Allison nodded. "I doubted it, too, at first. But then I heard about last year's graduates who had been inducted into the society. They are making a ton of money. Their names are always in the news. One of them set up a fund for needy children and I swear, everyone knew his name."

It sounded like these things were important to her. And the students.

"Some even end up working with the dean's most trusted friends. Or the dean himself. He's one of those hotshot lawyers."

Rick looked over his notes. "Changing subjects for a minute. Maybe Mark was about to blow this thing wide open and they didn't like it."

"But why are all the murders the same?" I asked. "You'd think they'd vary them more so it didn't look like a serial killer."

"True." Mrs. Allison took another sip of her tea.

"There was a Tarot card found here, too. The Hierophant?" I said. "That card usually means a religious figure or a teacher." I paused. "Or a lesson."

"A lesson," Mrs. Allison murmured. "Of course! They're in college. They're learning lessons every day!" She stood and began pacing.

So much for calming the nerves.

"So, you're saying this points to what, exactly? The school? A clue?" Rick asked.

"No." Mrs. Allison stopped pacing, running a hand through her hair. "The perpetrator is giving you a clue. This whole thing started at the college. And maybe it will end there, too."

A shiver went up my spine, as if the ghosts were touching me. Trying to get my attention.

And then it happened.

A flash.

More flames surrounding a person. Inhuman screams.

Screaming—feminine-pitched, male-pitched. Two distinct voices.

A compulsion—

My eyes widened. "I'm seeing something. If this was Mark…he was forced to do what he did. He didn't want to die, Mrs. Allison."

Chapter 9

"ALL RIGHT, that's enough," Ms. Allison snapped, her voice hard. "How can you say such things? How can you coerce me to give you information about my son's passing? He wasn't coerced. He was depressed about his breakup with Shelby, of course!"

Rick glanced at me sidelong. What the hell was going on? It was as if we were talking to a completely different person.

"Calm down, ma'am," Rick said, making a soothing motion with his hands. "We didn't coerce you. And if you say he was depressed, then we believe you. Right, Leliel?"

"Absolutely." I nodded. "Clearly this was a big misunderstanding. Maybe we should get going now, huh? Surely you need some rest—"

"I do not need rest," Mrs. Allison said through gritted teeth. "I'm going to call the police and have you arrested." She jumped from her seat and went to her telephone. I glanced at Rick again, trying to tell him that we needed to get out of here ASAP, and to keep her talking.

She picked up the telephone.

"Wait, don't do that," Rick said, coming toward her slowly. Carefully. As if she were a wild animal. "We didn't mean to upset you. We just want justice."

"Justice would be you two behind bars!" She dialed the telephone, her finger jabbing the buttons.

And then I saw it. Black and white. Two faces. Two sets of eyes. A red glow around her body.

Something weird was going on.

Three people. Three dual faces. Three dual sets of eyes. Three glowing in red. Three times the world turned monochrome.

I grabbed Rick's hand. "She's one of them," I whispered. "I don't think she's herself right now. We need to get out of here–"

"Run for it?" Rick asked, one eyebrow cocked.

Could we get out of here in time? Or would the police catch up to us?

"On three. To the front door. You ready?" Rick whispered, his eyes flicking toward Mrs. Allison, who was now talking to someone. 911, from the sound of it.

"One," Rick said, glancing at the door. "Two…three!"

Holding hands, we ran to the front door, opened it, and ran outside, slamming the door behind us. By unspoken agreement, we headed to the car, Rick getting into the driver's side. I got into the passenger side. Without putting on his seatbelt, Rick started the car and floored it, squealing the tires.

And we were on the road.

Once I could breathe again, I put my seatbelt on.

"She had two…sets…of eyes," I said, panting.

"Like the others?" Rick looked in the rearview mirror, presumably for police cars. "I'm not sure if we're out of the woods yet. It didn't sound like they could do anything, but still…what the hell happened?"

"She flipped out." I glanced out the window, looking for the police, too. "Something must have upset her. But, she gave us some great information."

"If it's really true," Rick said. "What if she lied?"

"I actually feel like she's telling the truth," I said. "And it's creepy about the secret society. Something bothers me about that."

"How so?" Rick asked.

"I don't know. It's like…I feel like there's some dark purpose to it besides influence and prestige. They were rumored to be into the occult."

Rick nodded. "Maybe we need to research magic?" He made a turn to the right, down a side street. "We need to figure out what's going on with the weirdness. I think that might be the key to figuring this out." Rick stopped at a red light and glanced at me. "Could it have anything to do with your Reaper abilities?"

"Which are gone?" I said. I let out a huff of air. "Yeah, I suppose. It's just that there's nowhere to look for that information. I don't know any former Reapers."

Rick nodded as he made a turn to the left. "You *could* theoretically still have something besides the visions. It's not impossible."

I smiled weakly. "Nothing's impossible." And then it hit me. "I need to talk to His Highness!"

"The king of the Underworld?" Rick asked, his eyes narrowed. "I thought you didn't really like him."

"I don't. But he'd be able to tell me what's going on. Except…I have no way into the Underworld." I banged my head against the headrest. "I've never heard of a human—besides you, but you had me— going to the Underworld. It just doesn't happen."

"Hmm," Rick murmured.

We sat in silence the rest of the way home. I was on fire. I wanted to *do* something, not sit around and talk all day.

Our trip to Mrs. Allison's had almost gotten us arrested. Again. And for what? Sure, we got information, but who knew if it was even true? And why had she turned on us?

Need you, Your Highness. Would be great if you could give me a way to talk to you without going to the Underworld.

I could hear music, something Rick called "heavy metal" in the background. Instruments screaming, the lead singer screaming, a heavy drumbeat I actually liked, a bit…

I thought about it. I had visions, which wasn't normal. I was seeing things, and that wasn't normal, either. Could it have something to do with the fact that I used to be a Grim Reaper?

But my Reaper powers were gone…weren't they?

I thought back to my time in the Underworld…and found that the memories were hazy, almost as if they were a dream. What did the Underworld look like? I didn't remember.

I must have made some sort of sound because Rick turned the music off and glanced at me. We were stopped at a red light again with lots of cars around us.

I felt a bit claustrophobic. The world felt like it was contracting, that things were getting too close and I would be crushed—

And then I saw it again. A driver with a red glow. Just ahead.

"Leliel? Is something wrong?" Rick asked, taking my hand in his. "You look like you've seen a ghost."

As I watched the driver, he turned around fully—almost impossibly—and I saw two sets of eyes, two noses, and two mouths.

And he smiled.

I SCREAMED.

"Leliel, talk to me," Rick said. He pulled out of traffic and onto a side street. There was a church on the corner, and he pulled into the small parking lot. I found that ironic.

I was shaking, I realized. My mouth was dry and my heart felt like it would jump out of my chest at any moment.

Rick squeezed my hand. "Leliel? Something's wrong. I know it."

"Yes, something is very wrong," I said. I took a deep breath, and then another. I willed my heart to stop its frantic beating. Yeah, okay. Like that would change anything. I looked into my husband's eyes. "I saw another one of those strange people. You know, with the red glow and two sets of eyes. The driver ahead of us turned and smiled at me. But he had two faces."

"That sounds terrifying." Rick squeezed my hand again. "I wish we knew what is causing you to see that."

"I've been wondering…" I said, looking down at our joined hands, then looking up at Rick again. It reminded me of our wedding ceremony, and how joined hands represented our joined hearts, souls, and lives. Whatever happened to me affected Rick. He was my partner, my rock.

"Go on."

"Is it possible that my Reaper powers aren't gone, or maybe changed into seeing things for some reason?"

"Maybe they never went away in the first place," Rick said. "Maybe you're seeing how people would look in the Underworld?"

"That's just it. I don't remember the Underworld. Do you?"

Rick's brow furrowed and he got a contemplative look on his face. "You're right. I don't remember anything except being with you. Is it normal for your memory to fade like this?"

"I don't know. I've never spoken with another Reaper before."

Rick let go of my hand. "So...maybe you're seeing what's really there, not what everyone else can see." He pulled out of the parking lot and made a right turn into traffic.

"That sounds very possible," I said, tapping my fingers on my thigh. "But why?"

Rick shrugged. "Maybe His Highness isn't through with you yet."

"I doubt that," I scoffed. "Once you're no longer a Reaper, you're done. I have never heard of His Highness messing in former Reapers' lives after they left his service. It just doesn't happen."

"Neither did us saving each other," Rick countered. "That was unprecedented. Why not this?"

I nodded. "You have a point."

"Of course. Your husband is a genius." He grinned at me.

I mock-smacked him on the arm.

THE NEXT DAY, we brought David up to speed on everything.

We were back in the diner eating scones. We'd decided that we'd go where the scones were, instead of meeting at home.

David grinned at us. "That's some pretty impressive investigative work there. Ever consider being detectives? You'd do amazingly." He took a bite of his scone.

"I don't know," Rick said, his face turning red. "I do better working with my hands."

"What about you, Leliel? You seem very passionate about justice."

If only he knew. "Uh, I don't really think it's for me. Rick and I kind of fell into this. It wasn't like we planned to fight crime together."

David held up his hands in a surrendering gesture. "Okay, okay, I'll leave it alone. Just think about it." He took a sip of coffee. "So, what's next?"

"You tell us," Rick said.

"Well, you need to follow up on your leads. I'd suggest going back to the college and talking to some of the victims' classmates. See what you can dig up there. And see if what

Mrs. Allison said was true or not. Especially since she turned on you like that."

"Could she have had us arrested?" I asked, nibbling on my second scone. Detective work made me hungry.

"Possibly. You were invited in, so I'm not sure if one of my colleagues would even take it seriously. But you never know. I know I wouldn't."

Rick leaned in close. "So, what else have you got?"

"Well, apparently they weren't just into the occult. Several of them are witches," David said. "They are members of a coven. And this has been going on for quite some time."

I'd heard of people being accused of witchcraft and casting "spells" using Tarot cards. I had been a Reaper, and I considered that to be a form of magic, so anything seemed possible to me. "Interesting," I said, taking a sip of my coffee. "I wonder if it's serious, or they just want to 'cast spells and tell the future.'"

"Good question," David murmured.

"Do you know who's in the coven?" Rick asked. "That might help."

"Students from both rival groups." David's brow furrowed. "And rumor has it that they are constantly jockeying for power over each other."

"What do witches do for power?" I mused.

"I need to research covens," David said. "If we find out more, we can connect the dots better."

"Most definitely." Rick took a bite of his chocolate-covered chocolate donut. He wanted something other than a scone today. Maybe a sugar coma.

"And you two follow up on those leads. You may hit on something big." David checked his watch. "I hate to eat and run but work calls." He stood, throwing a few ten-dollar bills on the table. "It's on me today. Good luck with your detective work."

And he left us.

Rick and I looked at each other.

"This is getting crazier and crazier."

"Where should we go first? Both options are kind of scary," Rick said, standing. "What do you think?"

I thought about that for a minute. "The kids might be more receptive"—Rick scoffed at that—"or at least, relatively speaking."

"Let's do it, then."

MINUTES LATER, we were in the car heading to the college. I was not looking forward to seeing any of the students. I figured we'd be thrown out, but hopefully not until after we got some information.

Rick put on that "heavy metal" music again, and I let my mind drift.

What were these students doing, playing in the occult? They did not know about the Underworld, and what horrible things there were.

And there was a rivalry in a coven?

Rick turned onto the road that would take us to the college. "You look like you're deep in thought. Talk to me."

I watched a strip mall go by, complete with people lugging groceries and walking dogs. "How many witches are in a coven?" I asked. "Must do some research."

"Let's not try to get into the classroom like before," Rick said as we turned into the college's parking lot. He glanced over at me. "That way, we can't be tossed out."

"Right." I got out of the car, and Rick did, too. We linked hands and walked toward the law school.

And right away, we hit upon a few of the students. I recognized three of them.

"Hey," I said, waving. "I was wondering if we could talk to you guys again? Just for a minute?"

The tough guy, who was wearing flannel again, glanced at me and grimaced. "Not you again! We have nothing more to tell you."

"That may be true," Rick said, glancing at each student in turn. "We wanted to discuss some new information with you."

One of the girls said, "Okay, *fine*. Then you'll go?"

"You have my word." I held up my palms in a surrendering gesture.

"Okay, what's it this time? A double murder or something?" the tough guy asked with a laugh that wasn't humorous.

"Not exactly." Rick ran a hand through his hair, looking unsure about how to proceed.

"We were told you guys were into the occult and a coven," I blurted. "And apparently there is a rivalry between you."

"Really, Leliel? Couldn't you just, I dunno, *ease* into it?" Rick asked, his eyes wide.

"And," I said, since I was on a roll, "a few of you are sleeping with professors in order to get better grades."

Rick banged his head with his fist several times. Once he was done, he said, "Sorry about her, uh, candor. She's doing her best."

"Hey." I nudged Rick in the ribs. "Might as well go all-in. Why waste time?"

One of the other students, a tall guy with hair in a bun—wait, didn't only women wear buns?—pointedly looked at his watch. "And your time is running out."

The thin girl who used to date Fred gasped. "What the hell? The answer to all of that is no way. We're not witches, and we're not whores."

I held up a finger. "I never said witches."

"Everyone knows that witches form covens," the tough guy scoffed. "Your point?" He leered at me. He actually freaking *leered* at me.

I stepped forward, my hands in fists. "I think there's something up with you all. You're all pretty tight-lipped for being rivals and such. Maybe the police would have an easier time cracking you open like a—"

"Really?" Rick said softly, flicking his gaze to me.

"Scare tactic," I said through clenched teeth.

"Oh, no, the police," another girl said, feigning fear. "Whatever will we do?"

A petite blonde stepped into our little circle. "I'll tell you everything you need to know."

"Jodie, no," the tough guy said. "You can't do that! What about the promise?"

"What is that?" Rick asked, arching a brow.

"Never mind," Tough Guy said quickly. "I don't even know what I'm saying. I've been up for twenty-four hours straight. Big exam."

"She's not talking to you," Fred's former girlfriend snapped, grabbing Jodie by the arm, her fingers digging in. "If you say anything, you will regret it."

Jodie pulled herself away from the other girl's grasp. Her nails had left angry red marks. Jodie looked me in the eyes. "I will tell you everything. Someone needs to know the truth."

"I don't think so," Tough Guy said. His fist came up and made contact with Jodie's jaw, making a sickening *crack*. Her face whipped to the side, and she cried out.

Then she dropped to the ground, her head hitting the pavement hard.

Rick called the police.

Chapter 10

BELIEVE IT OR NOT, Tough Guy wasn't arrested. His lawyer father did some legal tap-dancing and got him off with a warning. And his name was Lance. As in Lancelot.

Jodie had to have her jaw wired shut. And she had a severe concussion. We were told that it could lead to brain damage.

"What the hell?" I asked. "Was hiding the truth so important that he was willing to go to jail and give an innocent girl brain damage?"

"He knew he'd get off," Rick said. We were outside Jodie's hospital room, waiting for her to wake up. She'd been operated on and was now sleeping.

"Question is," I said, taking a sip of coffee, "what's he trying to protect?"

"What are they *all* trying to protect?" Rick rubbed his eyes. "I need to get back to work. I don't know when she'll wake up..."

"I can stay here and wait."

Rick's eyes widened. "Oh, no. You are *not* staying here! You could be hurt!"

"What? I'm in a hospital—"

"He could be anywhere." Rick pointedly looked around us. "He could try to hurt you. Hell, he could attack Jodie again."

"There's a cop out here. Not to state the obvious." Okay, part of me was happy that he cared so much, but I needed to talk to Jodie. I had a feeling she could tell us a lot. Assuming she could talk with her jaw wired shut. Maybe she could write it all down on paper?

"Cops can be distracted. How many cases have you heard of with all-important witnesses dying right under a cop's nose? I know you need to talk to her, but this is risky as hell."

"Everything's risky." I finished off my coffee, resolving to win this argument. Why didn't he understand?

"Leliel." Rick took gentle hold of my shoulders. The love in his eyes made my heart melt. A bit. He was slowly getting me away from my former Ice Queen ways. "I love you and want to protect you. I'd like to believe that that cop will do his job, but you are too important to me to leave this to chance. Please let me drop you off at home."

I glanced at Jodie's door and bit my lip. Who knew when she'd wake up? "I guess."

"Don't sound so excited to come home with me." He kissed me, gently, and then with more passion and fire.

Fire.

I broke away from him.

Amber flames licked at his beautiful body, burning his hair—

He was on fire!

I screamed. "Rick—" My throat had constricted.

"What's up?"

He could not be standing there acting like—

"Lie down on the floor and roll! Do it!"

"What? Is this some kind of—"

"You're going to get burnt! Get on the floor!" I pushed him so hopefully he'd fall, trying to avoid the flames. He didn't. They surrounded him, smoke rising from his body—

But why couldn't I smell it?

The cop came over, his gun cocked. "What's going on? Is there a problem here?"

"He's on—" The flames were just *gone*. And he wasn't burnt anywhere. "I thought I saw something. I'm sorry."

The cop holstered his gun. "It's all right. Better be safe than sorry. You okay?"

"Yes, sir," I said, my voice quivering.

"I'll be right here if anyone needs me." The cop resumed his post at the door.

"Leliel?" Rick asked. "Did you see something?"

I studied the ground. My shoes. "Yeah. Something really scary."

Rick tipped my chin up. "What just happened? You can tell me."

"I thought you were on fire. I saw flames surrounding you, burning you."

"That is scary." Rick took my hand in his. "Let's get out of here. I think we've done enough today."

I nodded and let him guide me out of the hospital.

As we walked toward the car, I wondered how the hell that meant.

Was Rick destined to die by fire?

I WOKE UP screaming, my bedsheets clenched in my fists. Love gave a distressed *meow*.

Rick stirred, opening his eyes slowly. "Leliel?" He sat up, gathering me into his arms. "What's wrong?"

Love padded her way to us and curled up next to me. I reached out and petted her, feeling the vibrations of her purring like a tiny motor against my hand.

"Leliel?"

I took a deep breath. "I think there's been another death. I—I felt it." I glanced at Rick, who was blinking against the sunlight. "Did you feel anything?"

"Maybe…"

I had a truly scary thought. "What if it's Jodie?"

"I doubt that. It's just on your mind. We can check right now." Rick felt around for his cellular telephone, which was on his nightstand. After a few unsuccessful attempts, he finally used the Google thing to get the hospital telephone number and called the nurses' station on Jodie's floor. "Yes, hello. I was calling to check on Jodie Seagul. She was brought in last night." He took my hand in his. "Okay. Well, I'm not. I'm the one who called the police after she was assaulted…I see…crap. Okay, thank you." He set his telephone down after hanging up. "She wouldn't tell me anything. We're not family."

"Call David. He would know if someone called it in," I said.

"Good idea." He dialed the telephone and waited. "Hey, David! It's Rick. Leliel and I were wondering—well, that's the problem. While we were at the college, there was an incident. Oh, you know about it. Of course." I wished I could hear what David was saying. "Anything you can do to help us find out what's going on with Jodie would be awesome. Leliel thinks something might have happened to her. Okay, I'll wait." Rick turned to me. "He says he hasn't heard anything, but that doesn't mean there isn't anything. He's checking with his colleagues to see what they know."

"Okay, great." I stroked Love's back.

Ten minutes passed. The longest ten minutes ever.

"Yep, I'm here. Really? Wow, that was fast. And you don't know—I'm guessing the same guy who assaulted her. Yes. Great, thank you." He put the telephone down and sighed. "Son of a bitch. Jodie was murdered."

I wasn't surprised, but I felt for the poor girl. She'd been trying to help us. If she hadn't, she might still be alive. "Do they know how?"

"Suffocation. The old pillow-in-the-face trick. What a horrible way to go."

I wanted to punch someone. "This is our fault! We've got to do something! Figure this thing out. Figure out what *Lancelot* was hiding."

"What he killed to hide," Rick said grimly.

We got out of bed. Rick went to work, and I was left alone with my thoughts.

What were we going to do? If the students wouldn't talk, and *killed* to make that clear, where the hell were we? Back to square one.

I wondered if we should give Mrs. Chandler another go. It'd be a long shot, maybe impossible now, but anything was better than sitting on our hands and doing nothing.

And there was literally nothing for me to do right now.

So I got out my Tarot cards.

I rarely used them now. They were old, falling apart. I'd had them for at least a century.

Nowadays, I'd heard, they were used to access one's intuition. Sure…that might work.

I shuffled them, and they smelled of old parchment. I could even detect a bit of a burning smell. Which spooked me.

I kept shuffling. Cut the deck three times, as was customary.

Shuffled some more.

To my shock, a card flew out of my hands and landed right in front of Love, who was sniffing around curiously.

I was afraid to look at it.

Bracing myself, I turned it over.

Death.

My heart lurched and my mouth went dry. Supposedly, the Death card did not predict a death. Rather, an ending.

But given the circumstances, and the fact that a flyout card usually signaled a message…I was forced to conclude that it was a message for me.

That whoever was behind all of this was coming after me.

Even if I wasn't a believer, it was pretty scary.

Hand trembling, I set the card aside. Love let out a distressed *meow*. As if even she knew what this meant.

"Okay, we're going to ignore that for a sec, okay, Love?" My voice quivered. And I needed to talk this out, and talk to my cat, because I was seriously creeped out.

Where was the murderer? Was she in the apartment, creeping along with an axe or gun, ready to take me out?

That was utterly ridiculous. Crazy talk. Rick and I were all about safety. Even before the murders. We kept our door locked and used the chain lock, too.

"Okay, I'm going to also ignore the fact that I'm creeped out and continue." Love came over to me and nuzzled my outstretched hand. "You'll protect me, right?"

In answer, she licked my fingers.

"I'm going to shuffle the hell out of these cards," I said. "I want no funny business." So, I shuffled, leaving the Death card out. And shuffled. And freaking shuffled until my hands and wrists hurt.

Cut the deck three times again.

Shuffled again.

Pulled a card.

My hand shook as I turned it over.

And I dropped it.

Love whined.

It was Death.

Chapter 11

"SO, WHAT DID you need to tell me? You look like you've seen a ghost," Rick said. We were eating dinner—well, he was eating dinner. I was moving food around my plate, my stomach a mess of nerves so bad I thought I might throw up.

He'd asked me what was wrong. And I had said I needed to tell him something.

But hellfire, the words felt stuffed in my mouth. With no way to pull them out.

I clamped my mouth shut. The food didn't look like spaghetti and meatballs. It looked like weird shapes with weird paint pasted on.

"Leliel?" Rick reached out and brushed my fingers with his. "Whatever it is, you can tell me."

"Death," I blurted. "I got the Death card. Twice."

Rick swallowed. "What do you mean?"

I explained what happened, ending with, "And I'm sure the murderer is after me now."

Rick scoffed. "I doubt that. You're just freaked out about the case—"

"How do you explain having *two* Death cards show up when there's only one in the deck?"

Rick's fork clattered onto his plate. He was pale. "Maybe you always had two Death cards."

"No." I waved my fork in a slicing motion. "Tarot decks never, ever come with two Death cards."

"Maybe—how many decks do you have?" He speared a piece of broccoli unusually hard. "Maybe a Death card from a different deck got mixed in."

I took a sip of soda. "Just one. And it had a burnt smell."

"Was it in the fire that…you know…"

"Was it in the fire that killed me?" I looked him straight in the eyes. "No. I've had it for at least a century. It never smelled that way before."

"Can I see it?"

I looked down at my food, my appetite gone. "Sure. But just so you know, I'm not seeing things."

"Leliel, I wasn't about to suggest that." Rick's voice was soft. "You thought I was on fire at the hospital…I'm just trying to understand."

"This is different. It was actually there." I nibbled on a slice of bread, but even that didn't taste right. It tasted like…ash. "Rick, something's wrong with this bread."

"Huh?" He finished chewing his spaghetti, then looked at me. "What's wrong with it exactly?"

I handed it to him. "Try this. Tell me what it tastes like."

"Okay," he said with a shrug. He looked confused. He took a bite, chewed it, and swallowed. "It tastes fine."

"Take another bite," I said, my mind racing. Clearly, I *was* losing my mind, because if it tasted normal to him, how could it taste like ashes to me?

I didn't like thinking that I could be mentally ill.

Or maybe so obsessed with this case that my mind was playing tricks on me.

"Still normal," Rick said after swallowing his second bite. "Tell me what's wrong with it. I don't understand."

I reached over and took my bread back. "I'm going to try it again. Then I'll tell you." I took another bite. Ashes. I almost spat it out. "I think I'm losing my mind, Rick. This bread"—I held it up, with four bites taken out of it— "does not taste like bread. It tastes like ashes."

Rick's hand immediately went to mine. "I do not believe that you are losing it. Maybe you're stressed out or something. Or," he said, arching a brow, "could it be true? That the bread actually *does* taste like ashes?"

"But it doesn't. You said it was fine."

"Yes, but maybe something sinister is going on. Someone's messing with you. First the cards, now the bread."

"But how?" I stood and walked over to our balcony door. "This door is locked." I went to the front door. "And this one is locked, too. And we'd know if someone were here." I went back to the kitchen table. Rick took my hand in his again. He did not seem to want to let go of me.

Rick squeezed my hand. My heart lurched. "Not a *person.* Magic."

"I suppose. But how? It's not like we've been hexed by a witch or—"

Rick and I both looked at each other.

"This case involves witches," I said softly.

"And remember, they're into the dark arts," Rick said just as quietly.

It was as if we were building on something.

"What's next?" I asked.

"LET'S TALK TO Lancelot," I said. Rick and I were driving around, tossing theories back and forth. The idea had just popped into my head.

The night had an almost oppressive feel to it, with shadows lurking and clouds obscuring the moon. We had wanted to get out of the apartment after the whole bread-tasting-like ashes thing.

"That's too dangerous. He *killed* Jodie to keep her quiet," Rick said. "Who knows what he'd do to us?"

"But we're smart," I protested. "We can beat him at his own game."

I looked out the window, not looking at anything in particular when—

What?

I blinked. There was a school field. And in it was a portal to the Underworld. It glowed, and I could feel the subtle *don't-come-here* magic all portals had around them to keep humans out.

"Hellfire," I spat.

"What's wrong?" Rick asked as he moved the car to the lane beside us. What was it called again? I didn't remember. Not with my stomach trying to come up my throat.

"Um, I just saw a portal," I said.

Rick glanced at me. "Really? I thought humans—"

"—can't see portals," I finished. "Yeah. But maybe because I have other abilities, I can see them?"

Rick shrugged. "It's weird."

"I didn't know there was one in that field." I turned around, trying to see it again, but we were too far away. "Maybe it's just a fluke."

We sat in silence for twenty minutes and fifteen seconds. Rick played more of that "metal" music, and I got lost in my own thoughts.

Rick frowned as he made a right turn down our street. "Getting back to what we were discussing...let's think of someone else to talk to. Someone less dangerous."

"Everyone is dangerous," I grumbled. "And we aren't the police."

"No, we're not."

Rick pulled into the parking lot of our apartment complex and parked the car. "Do you feel that?"

My eyes narrowed. "Feel what?"

"Sadness." He looked around, but everything was silent and dark. Only the street lights illuminated the space. "I don't know. It seems to be coming from..." His eyes widened. "Our apartment?"

He got out of the car and I followed suit, my heart racing. Was there someone in our apartment? Or near it, waiting to mug us or worse?

What if it was one of the students? Anyone could find anyone else with the right skills—

"Stay behind me," Rick said softly.

He led me to our apartment. Nothing looked out of place outside; no one was lurking in the shadows. We checked. Thoroughly.

"I guess maybe it was just a fluke?" Rick unlocked the door and went in first, turning on the lights. I felt horribly vulnerable out here in the dark with my husband inside. Anyone could attack—

Rick appeared in the doorway. "Nothing weird. I think it's safe."

"Okay." I went inside, and a blast of cold hit me. "Um…is our heater working?"

"I think so." Rick checked the thermostat. "Yeah, it's fine. Seventy degrees."

I shivered. "Feels like about forty."

Rick came to me and put his hand on my forehead. "No fever. Huh."

"I feel fine," I said, heading to our bedroom for a sweater.

And stopped at the doorway.

Ice-cold air wafted out of our bedroom.

There was only one thing that gave off such cold air…

Love growled from the floor. She padded to where I stood, presumably to defend me.

"Rick?" I said, not moving.

"Yes, baby?"

"I found the source of the sadness. I think."

Rick let out a huff of air. "Okay?"

"It's a ghost." I took a deep breath. I'd dealt with ghosts when I was a Reaper. But it was seriously messing with my mind now.

I could no longer assume that I was just human anymore.

I decided to get the party started. “Hello?”

Nothing.

“We can feel you but we can’t see you,” Rick said. “And I know you’re sad about something.”

“Hey…I know you’re there.” I had a thought. “Are you responsible for the Death card and the bad food? Are you trying to tell us something?”

Nothing.

“You went to the trouble to come here. What is it you want to tell me?”

Still nothing.

But…

The lamp on my night table flickered.

I turned to Rick. “I’ve read that ghosts can affect electronic equipment.”

“I think I’ve read that, too,” Rick said. His brow drew down. “But let’s put this into perspective. It *could* be a power surge. It *could* be that our thermostat is malfunctioning and giving us the wrong reading. It could be simply a mundane thing and not a ghost.”

I moved farther into the room, stopping in front of our bed with its colorful, whimsical comforter and pillow shams. “But why the sadness?”

“I don’t know. Maybe it’s not connected to this, but to a death to come?” He scratched his head, looking confused.

I turned to face him. "I hope not."

The light flickered three times.

"Hello?" I said. "We are listening. Say something."

The light flickered three more times.

I had an idea. "If you are here and willing to talk, make the lamp flicker twice."

"Leliel?"

"Just roll with it," I said softly.

Rick nodded.

"If you're here—" The lamp flickered twice. "Oh my gosh…it's real."

Rick took my hand and squeezed it. "Be careful."

"Always." I squared my shoulders and took a deep breath, then released it. "Okay. Are you male or female? Flicker once for male, and twice for female."

Two distinct flickers, as if the ghost wanted it to be very clear.

"Who could she be?" I asked.

Rick smiled. "I have an idea. So, Miss Ghost, were you a student at Amsburg Law School? Once for yes, and twice for no."

My jaw dropped. *Of course.* If this was connected, we'd know by her answer.

One flicker.

The room spun around me. My heart raced so fast—

This ghost was one of the victims. She had to be.

Rick put his hands on my shoulders to steady me. "Okay, so you were a student. Excellent. Are you one of the recent victims? Once for yes, and twice for no."

One flicker.

Then, two more.

I turned to Rick. "Huh? What does that mean?"

Rick's eyes narrowed. "Oh. I bet she's not a recent victim but someone who's been—"

"Jodie," I said. "She's not technically a victim, but she's still connected."

"Leliel, you're brilliant! Keep going."

I smiled. "So, you're Jodie? Once for yes, two for no."

One flicker.

Yay for being smart.

I let out a breath. "Now what?"

"Well, what do we need to know?" Rick said.

"How about the Death cards and the nasty-tasting food? Did you do that? Once for yes—"

Two flickers.

"Huh. She wasn't warning us," I said, wracking my brain for another smart question. "Do you know who is responsible for those things?"

One flicker.

"Crap. How on earth are we going to—"

"Is the murderer responsible?"

"Leliel, what—"

I held up my hand to stop him.

One flicker.

"Is the murderer trying to scare me? Because she sure as hell succeeded—"

One flicker.

"She wants us off the case," I said. "So no one will know what really happened."

"Of course, isn't that always how it works?" Rick said, running a hand through his hair, messing it up.

"Another question," I said, my insides twisting with anxiety. "Are either one of us in imminent danger?"

One flicker.

"Is something bad going to happen to one of us?" I asked, my mouth going dry and my palms sweating.

One flicker.

"Who? Once for—"

One flicker.

Rick and I exchanged a look. "I was going to say you." His eyes glistened with tears. He drew in a breath, then let it out. "Is something bad going to happen to me?"

I grabbed his hand. "No."

One flicker.

"Crap," I said. "Something is telling me that I am next."

Rick squeezed my hand. "No way, that can't be it."

"I was first in your questioning. She answered before you finished asking," I said.

"I refuse to believe that." A muscle twitched in his jaw. "I *hate* this, just for the record. Does the murderer want us dead?"

Nothing.

I noticed that the room wasn't cold anymore. "I think she's gone."

Shattering glass brought my attention to the hallway.

Our wedding picture had fallen off the wall and shattered.

Chapter 12

THE NEXT DAY, there was another suicide. Pamela Carson.

Neither Rick or I had any visions or dreams.

And no more visits from ghosts.

What the hell had happened? Were our powers gone now?

And was this what Jodie was hinting at?

We decided to see Ms. Chandler again because we still needed to know if Fred had been on any medication.

"What're we gonna do about the ghost?" I asked, wishing that I smoked. I needed to do something with my hands.

Rick glanced at me, then refocused on the road. "You mean what she told us?"

"Yeah…that."

"I'm beginning to feel like I'm losing my mind. Did that actually happen?"

"Yeah. Unless you think our thermostat was malfunctioning and we were, I don't know, hallucinating?" I said, rolling my eyes.

For the record? I believed it.

"The picture falling and shattering really freaked me out," Rick said. "And then the whole imminent danger thing, and the bad things happening thing, and also the wanting us dead thing. More than I care to admit." He glanced at me. "And this crazy idea you have about being next. Nope. Not happening."

I shook my head, not wanting him to feel worse. But I knew. "I don't know. Somehow, I don't believe that Jodie made the picture fall. Maybe it was the murderer? Scaring us?"

"Maybe," Rick said.

"If the murderer played with my Tarot deck and made my food taste bad, I'm sure she could knock the picture down. But to what end?"

"Lots of questions and so few freaking answers," Rick said. He parked in the driveway, shut off the car, and turned to me. "Whatever you do, *don't* mention the ghost. She already thinks we're unhinged."

"But aren't we? Just a little?" I held up my thumb and forefinger close together.

Rick chuckled. "I suppose."

We got out of the car and linked hands as we headed for the front porch.

Rick rang the doorbell.

Nothing.

He glanced at me. I nodded.

He rang it again.

The door opened, and a man dressed in a suit stood in the doorway. "Can I help you?" He had some sort of accent.

"We're here to see Ms. Chandler," I said. "I'm Leliel, and this is Rick, my husband."

The man frowned. "I've been advised to tell you that Ms. Chandler is not interested in another meeting."

This wasn't a surprise. But we needed more information. "Please, we just need a few minutes of her time."

"I was told to tell you that Ms. Chandler does not want another meeting," the man repeated with exaggerated patience.

"Please, this is a matter of life and death," I said. Hey, it worked for people on the television.

"No. Please leave."

Rick stepped forward. "Look, my wife here is distraught over these suicides. We are trying to figure out what's going on. Which includes what really happened to Fred. Can we please talk to her? For just a few minutes?"

The man sighed. "All right. I will check with her. Just a moment." And he was gone.

"There's a name for what he is, isn't there? I just can't remember it," I said.

"A butler," Rick supplied. "Right down to the pseudo-English accent."

It wasn't a moment. It was more like ten minutes. Any longer and I would have wondered if they'd forgotten about us.

The butler returned. "Come in. She will see you for ten minutes." He did a funny bow, and we walked inside.

He led us through the foyer and down a dimly lit hallway and into a room off to the side.

It had been cleaned up some, but the room was still in bad shape. The smell of smoke was too strong, and it made me want to flee.

Ms. Chandler was sitting on the sofa. The butler announced us, then left. I caught the smell of pressed flowers.

"Ms. Chandler?" I said, feeling seriously outclassed.

She stood and crossed the room to where we stood. She was wearing a lovely pants suit, complete with diamond stud earrings and a pendant that looked like a ruby. "What do you want?" she asked sharply, looking down her nose at us.

This again?

"Ms. Chandler, we wanted to talk to you about Fred," I said.

"You're just dredging up memories." Ms. Chandler sighed, and her eyes glistened with tears. "I would rather not."

Rick said, "If we are right, don't you want justice for Fred?"

"But you're *wrong*," she said, her shoulders slumping. "But I suppose I can hear you out. Be quick about it."

"Thank you," I said. "I would rather not be in this room. This reminds me too much of…you know."

"We should bear witness," Ms. Chandler said softly. "A bright, loving young man perished. Right here. In my study. All alone."

I was pretty sure that he hadn't been alone, but I kept that to myself.

"So, what did you want to tell me?" Ms. Chandler asked, motioning for us to follow her into her beautiful living room.

It was as if we'd entered a different world. A world where Fred hadn't died.

"We're here to discuss some things," Rick said, sitting down on the other sofa. He gently tugged on my elbow so I'd do the same.

"What is there to discuss?" Ms. Chandler asked. "My son took his own life."

"Yes, but we've learned some new information," I said, glancing at Rick. I was pretty sure she'd shut us down, but we had to try.

"We've recently learned that the two other students who committed suicide were on an experimental drug for depression," I said, watching Ms. Chandler closely. "And we were—"

"No, absolutely not," Ms. Chandler said. "Fred would have *never* been on any medication, much less an experimental drug. That's preposterous."

"Okay, that answers that question." Rick glanced at me, then looked at Ms. Chandler again. "Also, we learned that there is a coven of witches," Rick started. "Apparently the deceased—including Fred—were part of it—"

Ms. Chandler gave a dramatic sniff. "My son would never be part of *those* types of things. Whoever told you that was mistaken. Or was lying."

"Well, okay. But what about the rivalry for the dean's favor? And this secret society thing?" Rick asked, meeting Ms. Chandler's gaze and holding it. Good. Maybe we'd get somewhere.

Her brow furrowed. "I know of no such thing. Freddie wasn't into that."

"Do you think he could have been, but didn't tell you?" I knew I was pushing some, but someone had to ask the question. If her son was involved in these things, he was not the perfect angel that Ms. Chandler proclaimed him to be.

"He told me everything." She folded her arms across her chest and stared down her nose at us again. Way to make us feel small. And poor.

I did not like the vibes she was putting out.

"What about Samantha? Did he mention his relationship with her?"

Something strange happened. The very air grew cold and Ms. Chandler's hands balled into fists. "I do not know what you are talking about."

I glanced at Rick, and he looked pale. I had an idea. "Ms. Chandler, my husband looks pale. He might be dehydrated. Could you be so kind as to get him a glass of water? We'd really appreciate it."

Ms. Chandler's lips pursed. I was sure she would throw us out, but she surprised me by saying, "I'll have the maid fix you some tea." And she left the room.

"Rick?" I asked. "What's going on?"

"I'm sensing something," he said, and he seemed to be in a trance. "There's something on this property. It feels...very emotionally charged. I think it might be a clue to this whole thing."

How amazing! "Okay, can you narrow it down to a room?"

Rick shook his head. "It doesn't work that way. We'd have to walk around and hope the feeling gets stronger."

I mentally counted how many floors there were in this house, plus the sprawling front and back yards. "That's a lot of house and yard to cover. How are we going to do this?"

"Maybe she'd give us a tour?" Rick asked. "If we ask nicely?"

"She's very annoyed with us—"

"If we kiss up to her, maybe she'll do it." Rick smirked. "I can pretend I am in such awe of this place, never seen anything like it."

I thought about it. That was as good an idea as any, and time was a-wastin'. She'd be back any minute. "Unless one of us could cause a distraction…"

"And here she is," Rick said with a smile as Ms. Chandler walked into the room, followed by a maid carrying a tray. It held a teapot, cubes of sugar in a pretty glass holder, small, dainty teacups, and more of those mini cakes.

She must have loved them.

"Rick, Leliel, have a seat. The maid here has tea for you both. And sugar. I wasn't sure how you took it."

Why was she suddenly calling us by our first names?

We sat down on the couch and the maid set the tray on the coffee table.

"Sugar for your tea?" she asked softly.

"None for me," Rick said.

"Very good, sir." She poured him some tea and handed him the teacup carefully. "And for you, ma'am?" she asked me.

"A few cubes, please," I said. This was too weird. I was not used to be served and asked things like this when I could get it for myself.

She did the same and dropped two cubes of sugar into my tea, then stirred it up really well. And finally handed me the teacup.

"Thank you," I murmured, afraid that I'd drop the thing and upset Ms. Chandler even more.

The maid curtsied and fled.

I could relate.

"So, Rick, how are you feeling now? And Leliel, have some petits fours." Ms. Chandler pushed the tray my way, and I felt like I had to eat at least one…

Rick glanced at me as if to say, *What the hell? Why is she being so nice?*

"I feel…better." He looked at her and took a sip of his tea.

Ms. Chandler smiled. "Good, good. Now can we *please* forget about medication, witches and covens and the dean's favor?"

Ah. She wanted to smooth this over, maybe buy our silence.

Which meant she knew something.

We needed to find out what it was.

"You know, I'm feeling much better now." Rick smiled what I called his Prince Charming smile. He was looking less pale than before. "And I was just telling Leliel that I am astounded by this place. You have a palace! Could you possibly give us a tour? It doesn't need to take a long time," he added hastily when Ms. Chandler's eyebrows went up in question.

Ms. Chandler's eyes narrowed. "What is there to see? Many rooms. Acres of lawn in the back and front. It's nothing special."

I jumped in. "Maybe to you, it isn't. But people like us...we live in an apartment. Nine hundred square feet. White walls and beige carpeting and old tile in the bathroom. Trust me, we'd love to see something more lavish. Might be our only chance."

Rick nodded. He took my hand in his and squeezed it. So apparently I was doing okay and not screwing everything up.

Ms. Chandler stood. "I...suppose I could? I'm not used to this sort of thing."

"Just walk around and tell us things," I said, getting into it. I stood, too. "Pretend like we're buying the place or something. Which we aren't."

"Nope, totally not in our budget, regrettably," Rick said as he stood. "Maybe in an alternate universe."

"Well, let's begin, then?" Ms. Chandler bit her lip and her eyes flicked between Rick and me and her maid, who'd just entered the room.

I had a strong feeling she felt stupid.

But...this was a totally reasonable thing to ask, right? Right?

"Sure! After you, ma'am," Rick said oh so enthusiastically. It was almost too fake, and I shot him a warning look.

"This is the sitting room," Ms. Chandler said, making a gesture to encompass the entire room. "It is where I receive guests."

Who received guests? His Highness used to. But no one else I knew.

Talk about hoity-toity. The house reeked of it.

We followed Ms. Chandler out of the "sitting room" (be sure to say that with a sophisticated accent), and into a different hallway than before. It was bright, with a row of pictures down each wall. Brass lamps-on-walls provided said bright light.

"Who—"

"These are generations of Chandlers," Ms. Chandler said. "Many, many, many. My poor Freddie is at the end, there." She pointed. "He won't be able to carry on the family name."

"I'm sorry," I said, because there was nothing else to say.

"Thank you, dear. Come along." She led us into a room that screamed *I have money*. Everything was brass, from the feet on the coffee table to the doorknobs to more lamps-on-walls. I saw a pattern forming.

This room was done in pastels, mostly lavender and pink and cream. The couch was velour and the curtains were lavender, tied back from large windows with brass holders.

Two large windows.

They looked out into the backyard with a deck and an in-ground swimming pool with perfect, crystalline water.

Not a single thing out of place.

The room also bore end tables. Gold edges, naturally. Brass vases held tall flowers—mostly tulips.

Rick glanced at me. He was thinking the same thing, I bet. That this place was too perfect.

"This is my reading room. I have a library off the room there"—she gestured toward a door that didn't look like a door at first glance—"because I have too many books. Displaying them all in here would make the place look cluttered."

"What kind of books, ma'am?" Rick asked.

"I can't bring you in there, Rick. Maybe another day. The staff needs to deep clean it. I have mostly the classics, as well as some current things. Do you like to read, by chance?"

"If I had the time, I would," Rick said with a shrug. "I was never very good at it."

"It's never too late to learn." Ms. Chandler led us out of the room and into a different hallway. This one was dark.

And then came a procession of rooms, each more perfect and fancier than the last. I was starting to get nauseated.

Maybe poor people were allergic to rich people?

About forty-five minutes in, Ms. Chandler excused herself to use the "facilities."

I turned to Rick. "Anything?"

He shook his head. "Nothing."

"I'm feeling a bit sick," I said softly. "I don't think—"

"You could be feeling the psychic imprint, too. When did it start?"

I thought about it. "Um, I don't know. Twenty minutes ago?"

Rick ran a hand through his hair, his brow furrowing. "So maybe it's close. Maybe I'll start feeling something really soon."

"I hope so," I said.

Ms. Chandler reappeared, a fake smile on her face. Was she ill, too? "Are you ready for more?"

"Yes, we are," Rick said.

"Come on, then."

She led us through a serpentine hallway, showing us the maids' quarters—and yes, she called them that. Onward to the kitchen.

When I stepped inside, I was astounded to see so much stuff—elaborate pots, pans, and gadgets. And the room was *huge*.

Ms. Chandler got in front of me. "The cooks are on break. Come, let's go outside."

She led us outside, past some maids who were dusting in the hallway. She showed us the front yard, which was beautifully manicured with trees and bright flowers everywhere.

In the back there were more beautiful flowers. She must have had a thing for them.

We edged around the pool to a small gazebo. There were a few seats and a table, all polished wood.

"Have a seat. The weather is pleasant," said Ms. Chandler, sitting.

Rick and I sat across from her.

I noticed something. The area was in the far corner of the yard. The flowerbeds did not look like they'd been planted at the same time as the others. They appeared freshly planted. "Ms. Chandler, did something happen to the flowerbeds over there?" I pointed.

Ms. Chandler blinked. "I had an unfortunate incident. The neighbor's dog got in here and dug everything up. I had to have it replanted. It is still unsightly."

"That's too bad," Rick said, tilting his head.

Ms. Chandler didn't look at us. "I am not a dog person, so you can imagine how upset I was."

That made sense. She'd probably freak at the slightest bit of dirt or God forbid, if the dog had an accident in the house.

"We have a cat," Rick offered. "We, uh, took her in. She was feral at one time."

Ms. Chandler made some sort of sound that told us she was listening, but she appeared to be tuning us out.

"It's surprising that a dog can do that much damage," I said evenly.

"Well, she is a mix," Ms. Chandler said, still not looking at us. "Some people do not train their animals very well." She stood. "Well, that's it for the tour." She glanced at both of us. "Now you know every nook and cranny of my property—"

Rick was choking, his eyes wide and his hand on his throat.

But he hadn't eaten or drunk anything besides the tea.

"RICK? ARE YOU okay?" Stupid, I knew it, because he probably couldn't speak—

"I'm…" He coughed a few times, looking pale, his eyes bloodshot. "…all right. Just...need…to…"

"Do you need medical attention?" Ms. Chandler asked. "I can call an ambulance."

Rick shook his head. "No…I can…" He took a deep breath and let it out. "Breathe."

"What happened?" I asked, purely for Ms. Chandler's benefit. I was pretty sure I knew what had happened. He was most likely faking it to get me alone again.

"Allergies, I'm sure…" Rick coughed again. "Can I bother you for some water? I'm so sorry…it would help."

"Of course." Ms. Chandler left, heading back into the house.

I turned to Rick. "You found it, didn't you?"

He nodded and coughed again. "Bingo. It's somewhere near the flowerbeds that were dug up by the dog. If you hadn't pointed them out..."

"So, what's next? We have to see what's in there!" My heart raced. I knew we were close.

"How, Leliel? Ms. Chandler is not going to let us dig it up, especially if there's something she's hiding there."

I bit my lip. He was right. Hellfire and a half. "We'll have to sneak in here and dig it up at night."

"And get arrested for trespassing and who knows what else? No way." Rick coughed again. "If I could get closer, I could maybe see if this psychic imprint stuff can tell us what it is."

"That'd be great," I said. "But what excuse do you have to get closer?"

Rick winked at me. "You'll see."

Ms. Chandler returned with the water herself, plus one for me. "Here you are. Are you feeling any better?"

Rick took the glass and drank it all at once. "Yeah. But I was wondering—"

"Another tour?"

"No, not that! I have a bit of a green thumb, and I wondered if you could plant those differently to make them look more attractive. May I have a closer look?" He made a motion to indicate he wanted to go over there.

Ms. Chandler smiled. "Of course you may, dear."

Rick held out his hands, palm up. "I won't touch anything. I just want to see it, okay?" He began backing toward the flowerbed. I was amazed at how he managed that without tripping or taking a dive into the pool.

"It's not a problem. But I suppose if you have any suggestions…" Ms. Chandler said. He was already halfway there.

"Rick can help," I said. I lowered my voice. "In fact, he's sort of obsessed with flowers. But you didn't hear it from me."

Rick was getting closer. Just another few feet.

Ms. Chandler leaned in toward me. A muscle twitched in her jaw. "Really?"

I nodded. "Totally. It's actually kind of cute."

My little plan to distract her was working. She wasn't even looking at Rick now.

And he was almost there.

"He has some sort of mystical ability with flowers," I said, glancing at him to see his progress. "I'd swear it was magic."

Rick staggered back, holding his stomach. "Something's very wrong here."

Dirt and grass flew as the flowerbed exploded and the smell of ozone filled the air.

Ms. Chandler just stared as Rick crumpled to the ground.

Chapter 13

I KNELT AT MY husband's side, taking his hand in mine. "Rick? Rick, wake up! What's happening?"

He wasn't waking. He wasn't—my heart felt as if it would explode—

"Oh my," Ms. Chandler said. She didn't come near us. "Is he all right, dear?"

I glanced at her. "I don't know."

"Is he breathing?"

I leaned down and tried to feel the warmth of his breath. "Yes."

"Is his heart beating?"

I put two fingers against his neck like I'd seen people on television do. There were beats, but they were faint. "Yes."

"Are his pupils—"

"I'm calling an ambulance," I said, pulling my cellular telephone out of my pocket. After I dialed, I said, "What was that explosion?"

"Nine-one-one, how may I help you?" an operator said.

"Yes, my husband is passed out from an apparent explosion and I don't know what to do," I said, then took a breath. "He's still alive—"

"That's good," the operator said. Then she rattled off some directions, none of which penetrated my brain, then asked me for the address.

What was the freaking address? I glanced at Ms. Chandler, who was looking kind of…blank. Like her face was made of stone. "Ms. Chandler, what's your address here?"

She blinked at me. "Oh. 457 Pinecone Lane."

Weird. I gave the operator the address, and we hung up.

I went back to my regularly scheduled panicking. I put my hand on Rick's shoulder. "Wake up, baby…come on. I'm here."

I felt as if someone were watching me, and looked up. Ms. Chandler was standing over us, her lips in a straight line. "You shouldn't have meddled in things that weren't your business."

"What?" I said, standing. "I don't understand. Wasn't that an…" Oh, no. No, no, no. "You did that on purpose so…what? We'd stop 'meddling?'"

She actually looked down her nose at me. "I cannot confirm anything. But it would serve you right. This doesn't concern you!"

Anger boiled my blood. "People are dying and you don't even *care*?"

"People would not be dying if—I've said too much. When the ambulance gets here, leave and don't come back!" She turned on her heel and strode toward the house, not looking back.

Hellfire. What had just happened?

My husband was unconscious, there'd been an explosion, and it was all my fault. I'd pushed to do this investigation.

And then the police arrived.

MAKE THAT THE police *and* the bomb squad. Apparently they were concerned that there might be another bomb on the premises.

"Can you tell me what exactly happened, Mrs. Ashton?" an older police officer with graying hair and kind eyes asked me, pen poised to take notes on a notepad.

I rubbed my eyes. This was all so surreal. Another police officer was questioning Ms. Chandler, who had had to come back out and talk to them. She was making animated gestures with her hands, her face a mask of anger.

"I can't. I have to go with my husband. He just collapsed," I said. "Can we talk later?"

"Please come down to the station at your earliest convenience to give a statement. Sooner rather than later," the police officer said.

I nodded. "No problem."

The EMT who'd loaded Rick into the ambulance caught my gaze. "We gotta roll."

"Okay." I turned to the police officer, smiling apologetically. "I'm sorry, but I have to go." I got into the ambulance and took Rick's hand in mine.

So many thoughts raced through my mind as the ambulance took Rick and me to the hospital. He had some bruises on his face, and his clothes were dirty. I also noticed a bump on his head.

It was so surreal. I'd never imagined that he'd be the one who wasn't well. I was the one with the lingering Underworld powers. Sure, he could feel these psychic imprints...but somehow, I assumed he'd be fine.

Until he wasn't.

I held his hand with a death grip. "Rick, please wake up. I know you found something. Please come back to me...and Love. We need you. We love you." I kissed his knuckles. I wasn't much for praying, but I did look up to the ceiling of the ambulance, to whoever or whatever was out there. "Please, don't let him die on me. He's all I have besides Love. We're a family, a team. I don't know what I'd do without him. He's my tether to this world." Tears fell down my cheeks, and I didn't even bother wiping them away. I wanted him to wake up. I wanted Love. I wanted…I wanted this to not have happened at all.

Ms. Chandler was in her beautiful, perfect home. I thought it was coldhearted to not even make the trip with us. It had been an explosion on her property that had caused my husband's collapse. *At least try to look like you care, why don't you?*

"Okay, we are here, Mrs. Ashton," the EMT who'd put the tube in Rick's vein earlier said. "We've called ahead to the ER and they are ready for you now."

I nodded numbly, more tears falling down my cheeks. I thought distantly that maybe I *should* wipe them so I didn't look like such a mess, but forget it. I was sure they were used to wives being messy. This was not the time for perfection.

The EMTs unloaded Rick from the ambulance very efficiently. As one, we all walked into the ER.

And…chaos.

A doctor introduced himself as Dr. Hill and quickly began assessing Rick's condition. Dr. Hill was a short young man, and he looked a bit disheveled. But he had caring eyes and an efficient manner. He snapped out orders to waiting nurses. And the nurses rushed to fulfil those orders, whatever they were.

Don't ask me. I didn't know anything about medicine or hospitals.

After what felt like a century, the doctor took me aside. "Mrs. Ashton, I'm sorry to say I don't know why your husband isn't responding. He's showing all signs of brain activity and alertness, which is good. I will need to run an MRI to check for things like a stroke or aneurysm. What was he doing when he collapsed?"

Poking into something he shouldn't have been poking into. Trying to be a hero. Cracking a case. I wiped my cheeks. "Uh, well…we were at someone's house and we were talking."

"That's it? Do you remember anything else? Was he acting differently? Even the slightest thing could be important, so think hard, okay?"

"He choked. He'd had some water and tea," I said. This was pointless. I knew that this had everything to do with the explosion.

"Anything else?"

"We'd been invited in. My husband wanted to see one of the owner's flowerbeds. To help," I added quickly when his brow drew down. "And as he was walking toward it…" I made a gesture toward Rick, still unconscious. "There was an explosion. He passed out. Well, the choking came first. And then he seemed to be okay. And then that." I let out a breath. Hellfire, this stuff was exhausting.

Dr. Hill patted my shoulder. "So, there's the possibly of a concussion. You did well. I will need you to sign some paperwork giving us permission to give your husband an MRI, and then once that's done, we will do the test. I will do everything I can to figure out what's going on."

"Thank you, Doctor," I said softly.

I wondered if a human doctor *could* figure out what was wrong. I had a bad feeling it wasn't a human thing, but a psychic thing. He'd said he'd found something just before the explosion. What was there?

And…would he ever come out of his slumber?

I couldn't lose him. I just couldn't.

A nice, quiet nurse brought the paperwork over. I read everything, especially after having heard on the television about horrible mistakes made because people didn't read their medical paperwork. Everything looked good, so I signed it.

Signing my name was a weird experience, too. In the Underworld, we signed things, but not with pen and ink. Usually we signed contracts in blood. This just didn't feel as final— or as binding—as a blood contract.

But I figured that this was the human version of a blood contract and thus was just as binding.

"Mrs. Ashton?" the nurse asked.

Her voice jolted me to the here and now. "Yes?"

"Do you have any questions?"

Had I been staring off into space, possibly delaying what Rick needed done?

I handed her both the clipboard and pen. "No, I'm fine. I was just…praying."

"We will do everything we can for your husband," the nurse said. "Would you like to go with him? You can't go into the room because it's not safe, but you can watch."

"Sure," I said. It sure beat daydreaming out here, thinking the worst.

Rick was taken into a small room with a huge tube in it. The MRI machine, I was told. It was a huge magnet. No metal could be anywhere in the machine, so we had to remove Rick's wedding band.

They strapped him to a thin table-like surface and slid him into the tube. I felt claustrophobic just watching him. I touched his legs, which protruded from the machine.

"Stay strong. We'll figure this out," I said softly. "Just come back to me."

"We have to leave now," the nurse said gently, leading me out into a hallway and into the adjacent room. There was a window where I could watch Rick.

I clutched his ring so hard my hand turned white.

The test seemed to go on forever. The nurse explained everything to me while a technician operated the machine and watched the results on a screen. It was supposedly very loud in there, with taps and beeps and weird sounds, and I thought about Rick jumping from fright instead of lying still. He was lying still because he was unconscious, and that just started the tears again.

"Okay, we are done," the technician, a young man with a beard, said. "We should have your results in a few hours. Dr. Hill put a rush on it."

My heart lurched and my stomach twisted. "Don't you know what they are?"

The technician shook his head. "I wish I did. We don't read them. We just perform the tests. I'm sorry."

My eyes blurred with more tears. "It's okay. I'm just so worried about him."

"Well, don't worry. We will get to the bottom of it," the technician said.

The nurse took me back to Rick's cubicle—we weren't even given a room yet—and assured me that Dr. Hill would be with me shortly.

My mind drifted. Why hadn't I seen the most recent death? And what were the police doing now?

"Mrs. Ashton?"

I looked up. Dr. Hill stood there. "Do you know something?"

Dr. Hill met my gaze squarely, no flinching. Your husband is a very peculiar case. He has a concussion, but we've found no neurological reason why he's unconscious. So here's what I suggest. Talk to him. Spend time with him. Let him know you are still here, and you are waiting for him to wake up."

"Can he hear me?"

"Absolutely. There is evidence that supports it," Dr. Hill said. "We're keeping him for observation. Tomorrow we will do a second scan in case there was swelling or something that did not let us see the entire brain. Occasionally, swelling will do that. So it's not over yet. I also suggest you get some sleep. You will do no good for him if you are exhausted." We shook hands, and he left, disappearing down a hallway.

He was my only link to my husband. While I was off getting coffee and navel-gazing, Rick was moved to an actual room. That would be nice. Quiet. Less chaotic.

I entered Rick's room, my insides doing a nervous dance. I didn't know why. I was just supposed to talk to him. It was like any other conversation, except it would be one-sided.

I took a deep breath and sat down next to Rick. His breathing was even, and I could clearly see his chest moving up and down with each breath. His eyes were closed, and he seemed to be sleeping. But he couldn't be just sleeping, and that was the part that scared me—the possibility that he'd be sleeping forever.

Taking hold of his hand, I started talking, the words tripping over themselves in an effort to come out. "The doctor said to talk to you, that you'd hear me. So here I am talking. I'm going to investigate and see what is going on with our sixth victim, maybe talk to David. I'm not sure about visiting the next of kin, even if I find out who that is. We haven't had the best of luck. Hopefully when you wake up, you'll be able to tell me exactly what you saw or felt. I feel like this is going to be big. And important. Are you dreaming, Rick? What are you dreaming about? Us maybe having a quiet, yummy dinner at home? That's definitely a good dream. I hope you aren't having a nightmare. You don't need that."

I let out a breath, inhaled, exhaled, and kept going. "It's so hard talking to the relatives. And Ms. Chandler knows something, doesn't she? She must. She was very rude before the ambulance came."

And…I ran out of steam. I wanted him to answer me. Give me his thoughts. Which gave me an idea. "Okay, so you would probably tell me to get some rest and forget about the case for a while. And then I'd tell you no, I want justice served, and things to go back to their natural order again, and there's another suicide and we need to investigate. And then you'd back down, wouldn't you? You'd understand. I *know* you would. Because we're a lot alike, you and me. We're from totally different worlds but we're more alike than you know." I squeezed his hand. "I still can't believe I get to be your wife. It's so unreal. I never married, not even before…" I glanced at the door. At any moment, a nurse or doctor could pop in and hear me. Best not to show them how unique we really were. "Not even before what happened so long ago. I wonder if I knew somehow, on a subconscious level, that I'd find my perfect mate someday. In the oddest of circumstances."

I shifted. How long was I supposed to keep this up? I was getting tired. "But the thing that bothers me the most is...why haven't we seen this suicide?" I kept my voice low. "We saw the rest. And now...it's almost as if I am tapped out, that the visions are done with me." I bit my lip. "I hope not, but what if they are? And your imprint thing...you have a concussion and you can't wake up—" I choked on a sob.

Don't cry, I told myself. *He can hear you.*

I took Rick's hand in mine. "We're-we're going to make it through this. But I need you to wake up."

Chapter 14

THE FIRST THING I did when I woke up was call the hospital for an update on Rick's condition. No change. As much as I wanted to see him, I was pretty certain he'd rather me investigate than sit at his bedside.

Tell that to my broken heart.

I was eating a bowl of oatmeal and blueberries, keeping Love away from my breakfast, when it hit me.

The explosion.

Why did it happen? How did it happen? I needed to investigate. I'd been in shock and worried about Rick, but now was the time to do something.

"Who could tell me about weird explosions?" I asked Love. She gave me a wide-eyed look that said, *hell if I know*. Yeah. She was a cat. "Okay, let's reframe this. Who would do something like this? Was it on purpose? Could it be…" I took another bite, running through possibilities in my mind. "A chemist? No, a chemistry student who knows how to…no. It doesn't *feel* right." I stood and paced. Love followed me with her eyes. "Okay. Okay. Wait. What if this was the work of a witch? A spell of some sort?" My heart thudded and my mind raced again. I'd seen a little Tarot/fortunetelling shop not far from here. I'd been meaning to go in and check it out. Maybe the owner, or an employee, could tell me something. Surely they were psychics, or Tarot readers, or witches. Love meowed, which I took as agreement.

Time to get a ride with Tom.

In ten minutes Tom was waiting for me. I got into the cab and smiled. "Hi. How's it going?"

Tom smiled back. "Same old, same old. Heading for another interview?"

I shook my head. "No interview…just shopping."

"Oh," Tom said as he backed out of our apartment complex driveway and turned onto the main road. "That sounds like fun."

"It should be," I murmured.

We rode in silence while I freaked out about virtually everything—who to talk to once I got there, what the answers would be, Rick not waking up….

"Here we are," Tom said, breaking into my thoughts. "That'll be five dollars."

"Thanks." As he pulled into the parking lot, I dug in my purse for my money.

I gave Tom a smile as I handed him a five-dollar bill, plus two dollars for a tip.

Tom flashed me a grin. "Thank you. Have a wonderful day."

I opened the cab door and got out. "Have a nice day, Tom."

He waved and took off.

Feeling much better about this whole thing, I walked into the psychic shop. Which was actually called "Esoteric Creations." Not a bad name for a place like this.

Chimes clicked as I crossed the threshold. The pleasant smell of incense wafted near me. Crystals, Tarot decks, and assorted other books sat on shelves. Many shelves, I realized as I moved farther into the small room.

There were a few customers here. One was sitting on the floor, poring over books of spells. Another was in an animated conversation with an employee, something about astral projection. And the third was looking through the different crystals, muttering to herself.

There were dowsing rods to one side, and I Ching kits on the other. There were also lovely cloths one could use for Tarot readings. I remembered them from when I was first alive. My gaze fell on a really pretty one. It was the moon and stars on a navy-blue background. I reached out to touch it.

"Like that one?" a female voice asked.

I jumped and dropped my hand. Standing in front of me was a thin, black-haired woman wearing a tank top and a long, flowing skirt. A necklace of crystals hung from her neck and a few pretty bracelets she wore glinted in the light. Her hair was straight and went down to her waist. Her eyes were lavender and piercing.

"Um, yes. It's gorgeous," I said.

"Do you read the Tarot?" Her voice was lilting, with an accent I couldn't place.

"I do. Although I've just started again after a long absence." Three hundred years long.

"Oh, how wonderful! This is just the thing. Understated, but gives a feeling of peace. Can I interest you in a new deck? Or maybe some crystals?"

Talk about laying it on thick. "No, thanks. But I do have a question."

"Ask me anything."

Here goes. "If someone was a witch, could he or she cast a spell that would cause an explosion?"

She blinked at me. I was pretty sure she wasn't expecting that. Oops. "Uh...I, uh..." She glanced at the employee at the counter, then looked at me. "Sure. A witch with a reasonable amount of power could do that. But why would someone want to create an explosion?"

"Back up. Is there any way to tell that after the fact? Like, I don't know, a magical residue or something?"

She backed away a few steps, which confused me. The employee at the counter was on her telephone. "There would be something that someone who is sensitive to such things could…sense. But finding someone…" She shrugged. "I don't know anyone like that."

"Well, that kind of sucks. I'm trying to figure out why someone caused an explosion near my husband. He's in a coma. And I don't think it was by mundane means."

Her mouth made a surprised "oh." "Um, can I recommend a Tarot reading? Perhaps the cards might reveal something like that." Her hand twisted in her hair. "Um…"

"I haven't done a reading yet. But I suppose I could."

"Crystals? They absorb negative energy." She sounded almost desperate now. "Dowsing wands? Good for locating water and…stuff."

"No, thanks."

"Books of magic? Maybe you'll find a spell there?"

"You know, that might not be a bad idea." I moved in the general direction of the books. When I got to one of the shelves, I picked one up at random and started reading.

I flipped through the pages, losing track of time.

"Ahem?" a male voice said, making me jump for the second time. Wait. That was—

"David? What are you doing here?" I put the book back. It didn't have a single thing I could use in it. Figured.

"I should ask you the same question. A young lady called 911 complaining of a woman talking about explosions. I was sent here. So, uh, what's going on?"

I sighed. Damn it, they ratted me out. "You know I'm not looking to explode anything. But I wondered if a witch could cast a spell. And that girl right over there says it's possible. And there could be residue. But only someone who's sensitive could tell."

David nodded, his expression blank. "Well, unfortunately, I have to remove you from the premises. I hate to ruin your experience, but these ladies are scared."

It finally sunk in. "I scared them? But how? I was just asking some questions!"

"Very odd questions, Leliel," David pointed out. "Hey, miss—this is the woman you were talking about?"

"Yes. Sorry," the black-haired woman said. "Sometimes we get mentally unbalanced people. You can never be too careful."

"Okay, let's go," David said, gently taking hold of my wrist.

When we got outside, I remembered that I needed to get to the police station. "Any way I can get a ride to your station? I am supposed to give a statement about the explosion."

"I was going to bring you in anyway. Hop in," David said, shaking his head. We both got into the police car. What a weird thing, to have this metal thing separating me and David.

"I hope things improve from here," I said as David pulled out of the parking lot. "I'd hate to get arrested."

"I'M GOING TO let this go. I'm supposed to take statements and file a ton of paperwork, but I know you and know that you didn't mean to scare those people. But I must caution you," David said as we walked to the entrance of the police station. "Try to be less…overt. I've got no problem with you investigating but getting called on what amounts to a BS call is wasting my time. Understand?"

I hung my head, feeling terrible. "Okay. I'm sorry."

"I know you are. Let's do this."

It was good and bad to walk into the police station again. Good because I'd be helping solve the case—I hoped. Bad because I was afraid they'd find some way to arrest me over what just happened.

"Come into my office," David said, motioning for me to follow him, and I did, like a good little sheep.

My heart raced. What if I said something that inadvertently screwed things up?

Maybe I should have stayed in bed this morning.

Still, I followed David into his cubicle office.

"Have a seat."

I sat. "So…um…how is this done?" I asked, swallowing hard.

"First of all," David said, putting a device on the desk between us, "do you mind if I record this?"

I sort of knew what recording was. "Um, sure."

He pushed a button on the device. He said his name and gave the date. Then he said, "Tell me what happened at Aimee Chandler's home yesterday."

I took a deep breath, then let it out. "Okay. Well, my husband Rick and I went over there to investigate her son's murder." I swallowed hard. This was when he told me I was an idiot, probably. "We didn't feel that his death was a suicide. So we wanted to talk to Ms. Chandler."

"Why didn't you feel it was a suicide?"

"I didn't believe that his suicide note was authentic. And the Tarot card was a weird touch. It was more of a gut feeling, sir."

David's lips pursed. "Go on."

"We were talking and my husband Rick wanted to see the rest of her house. Because we'd never seen anything so huge and beautiful. So, Ms. Chandler gave us a tour."

"So, you went from, 'your son was murdered' to 'let me see the rest of your house?'"

I nodded, meeting his gaze. "Yes. And we caught sight of a flowerbed that was dug up. Rick wanted to see it better, to see if he could help fix it, and he started choking for no apparent reason."

"No allergies?"

"None that we're aware of. After he'd recovered from that, he headed to the part of the flowerbed that had been dug up. And there was an explosion."

"We didn't find any evidence of an explosive there."

My jaw dropped. "But there was an explosion. It happened. I was there."

"Leliel, we're still investigating how and why it happened." He pressed another button on the device. "We aren't being recorded right now. I wanted to tell you, in the midst of our digging, we found some things. Does the name Samantha Rhodes mean anything to you?"

I gasped. "That's Fred Chandler's girlfriend? The one that died that no one will talk about."

"Yeah, that's her. We got curious about her connection to Fred Chandler, so we looked back at the autopsy findings." He paused. "She was pregnant when she died."

My mind raced. Pregnant? "Could it be that Fred didn't want the child…?"

David met my eyes. "Samantha Rhodes committed suicide, Leliel. Self-immolation. Because it was shameful to both families, no one speaks of it anymore."

"Oh," I said. Something wasn't quite right about this. "I can't believe that Samantha, a mother-to-be, would kill herself and her unborn child."

"There were rumors, of course," David said. "But nothing concrete to point to an alleged murder."

"I would bet several plastic loan cards that that was a murder," I said.

The detective's eyebrows went up. "I'm sorry?"

I felt my face flush. "You know…those cards. With money that is loaned to you…" He probably thought I was crazy.

And maybe I was.

"*Oh*. Credit cards?" he asked, his lips quirking as if he were fighting a smile.

"Right. Those. I'm not weird," I said defensively. "I just never used any before." *I'm also living in the wrong century.*

David took a sip of his coffee. "Would you like some coffee? Water?"

I shook my head. "No. I'm fine."

He gave me an assessing look. "You seem nervous." Another sip.

"Well, I *am* in a police station. It's kind of scary."

"Don't worry. As long as you didn't break any laws, you're fine. Now, let's talk Tarot cards. Mind telling me how they work?"

"They used to be playing cards, way way back." I hooked an errant strand of hair behind my ear. "But over time, they became divination tools. For me, it's more like a way to tap into my intuition. Maybe even my subconscious. And I've had some theories for a while. But let's look at this for a minute. Two of Cups and Judgment. The soulmate card and the card of, well, judgment. What does that say to you?" My turn to give him an assessing look of my own.

"Uh…passing judgment on a lover?"

"Bingo. She's judging him and finding him lacking. Thus, the murder. And don't forget, there's that rivalry and the coven. The first two are interesting, too," I continued. "The Fool, for a new journey, maybe even a foolish action. And then the Ten of Swords, a disaster and the 'death card' of the Minor Arcana."

"I do recall that," David said. "The murderer seems to be wanting to send someone a message. Is it us? Is it someone else? We're not sure." He took another sip of coffee. "I'm going to set you loose. If you remember anything else at all, or have more incidents with the Tarot cards, let us know."

"Sure." And then I remembered. In all the chaos, I'd completely forgotten about the Death card. And Ms. Chandler. "There's something else. Ms. Chandler wasn't very nice at the end, telling me to stop 'meddling.' And I got *two* Death cards."

I could see the wheels turning in his head. "Explain that."

"I got two Death cards. There's only one in a Tarot deck. And Death isn't always Death, but I believe getting two must mean death and…" I realized that I was starting to sound like a mental institution escapee. "I think the same person who's doing this killing is after me." Anxiety was a knife to my heart. I needed to get back to Rick, back to Love. Back to normalcy. But I had a bad feeling that normalcy had given up the ghost.

"All because you got two Death cards?"

The way he said it, it made me sound like an idiot. "No, sir. I also have a strong feeling."

"Because you're psychic," David said.

I forced a shaky smile. "Sure."

The detective stood and held out his hand. "Thank you for coming in and sharing your thoughts. We will continue to investigate this."

I shook his hand. "Thank you for hearing me out."

As I left the building, I had to wonder. Did he believe any of it at all? Or did he think I was full of it, not worthy of listening to?

I figured we'd find out soon enough.

"SO, WHAT ARE YOU saying?" I asked David. Rick was still unconscious, so I was in the hospital bathroom, practically whispering. David had called me with information about

Pamela Carson, the most recent death. And I wasn't sure I was hearing correctly.

"They are not ruling it a serial killer yet," David repeated patiently. "Death by self-immolation, just like the others. Pamela was also a law student at the college, and part of the coven."

"So, they are all connected," I said, running my finger over the pristine counter. "Now we just need to figure out why."

"Also?" I said, my heart racing. "I have to wonder about Samantha Rhodes."

An undrawn breath. "So, what's your theory?"

I shrugged, even though he couldn't see me. "I have to wonder…what if she was killed because Fred didn't want the baby?"

"That's pretty extreme," David said. "I mean, she could just have an abortion or give up the child. No need to murder her."

"So…let's say she decided to keep the baby for some reason and he didn't like it. That could maybe cause him to murder her."

"Still extreme. Unless he's a total psychopath."

"His mother is a real piece of work. Maybe it's genetic," I said. Hellfire. I was *so* tired. "Maybe the explosion was meant as a warning to us."

"Really? Could it have been an accident?"

"I doubt it. The things she said to me before the ambulance arrived give me the impression that she didn't like us nosing around."

"It's a thought," David said.

"Great, thanks. And I will try to be useful here," I said.

"I'll let you know if anything comes up. Later," David said.

"Later," I murmured, wondering what on *earth* I could do from a hospital room.

Couldn't go to the police again. They'd *really* think I was a whack job. A whack job who believed in what amounted to conspiracy theories.

Couldn't visit the school. They'd made it clear that I wasn't welcome.

Hellfire.

I sat on the commode and tried to be useful. Somehow, my visions had dried up. I was effectively blind. And that just wasn't going to work.

I went back into the room and got out my Tarot deck. My heart gave a lurch when I touched them, and I was pretty sure this was a big mistake. I'd probably find a third Death card or something.

But I had to try. It was my only option until David provided me with more information. And that could take a while.

With shaking hands, I looked at every single card before shuffling. And there was no second Death card.

Had I imagined the whole thing?

Just for kicks, I went through it a second and third time. Looked in my bag. Nothing. It was just a normal Tarot deck again.

A chill went up my spine. Something strange was going on.

My hands continued to shake as I shuffled the deck and cut it. I put it all together, counted out four cards. Another card flew out.

A message. If one believed in such things.

I almost didn't want to flip it over.

My heart damn near burst out of my chest with the force of its beating.

"Please, don't be weird," I whispered, glancing at Rick. He had to wake up. He just had to.

I flipped it over before I could change my mind.

Three of Cups. A celebration.

Huh?

I pulled another card.

Moon. The occult.

What did these things point to?

Think, Leliel, think….

A celebration. And the occult. Did covens celebrate? I remembered hearing about festivals... or...was it more serious...like a ritual, maybe?

Something inside me loosened. It *felt* right.

But was it true, or was my imagination getting carried away?

Chapter 15

TWENTY-FOUR LONG hours passed.

I was in the hospital cafeteria, looking for some food because I was starving and Rick had given me some money for emergencies.

This was an emergency.

I went down the line, not really seeing the items offered. I kept wondering what the hell a coven ritual would have to do with any of this. And when my husband would wake up.

Someone bumped into me.

I realized that I'd been standing there, still as a statue, staring at the food.

Oops.

I grabbed a plate of some kind of vegetable and noddle thing and moved my butt forward. I also grabbed a few sweet rolls and a soda.

And kept myself moving until I got to the cashier. I paid for my food and found a table in the back corner.

Got a good look at my food. It was…noodles in some kind of brown sauce, along with some vegetables. It looked and smelled interesting.

I decided to call David.

"Hello? David Landis here," David said, a bit breathless.

"David?" I said, picking up my fork. "Do you have a few minutes?"

"Leliel? For you, sure."

I picked at the noodles and vegetables. "I did a Tarot reading. Want to know what I found?"

"Sure," David said.

"It points to a coven ritual. The Three of Cups points to a celebration, and the Moon card points to the occult. Or madness."

"Yeah, how crazy are we for even doing this?" David sighed. "I guess we need to figure out what coven ritual they were doing."

I found some chicken, speared it, and put it in my mouth. It was pretty damn good. "That's where I start to draw blanks."

"I don't know much about covens," David said. "Maybe you can do some research?"

I thought about it. "I remember a woman from my childhood that had been rumored to be a witch. She was a bit creepy, and lived in an old, run-down farmhouse, but she seemed nice enough. But I know nothing else about her."

"That's a shame."

"Yeah." I took another bite. And another.

"Listen, I got another call coming in. Can I call you back later?" David asked.

"Sure. I'll see what I can come up with in the meantime."

We said our goodbyes, and I was left with my very different but yummy meal.

After I'd eaten every bite, I headed back to Rick's room, making a mental note to ask him, once he woke up, what it was. I also wondered if I could make it for dinner sometime.

Doctors and nurses walked past me, talking animatedly. One nurse pushed a man in a gurney past me and around the corner.

A woman with a child hanging onto her hand and looking scared also passed me. I wondered who they were visiting. The father, maybe? Or a grandparent?

At last, I got to Rick's room.

My cellular telephone rang. I pulled it out of my pocket, hit the "accept call" button, and said, "Hello?"

"Leliel?" David said.

"David," I said. "That was fast."

"Yeah, it is me. Look, something weird just happened. One of the CSIs found a Tarot card at the scene of Pamela Carson's suicide/murder. Maybe you can tell us what it means?"

Score! "I knew it. Which card?"

"I'm looking at a picture, obviously. The card is pretty bloody." Rustling papers. "Yeah, it's hard to tell. There's a person in a seated position and there are golden cups."

My heart lurched. "How many?" I tried to think of what card that was, but I was out of practice. "I'll need to look at my deck. I'm kind of rusty."

"Okay."

I walked into Rick's room, and he appeared to be sleeping soundly. I walked over to his bedside and took his hand in mine. "Please, wake up," I whispered.

"Leliel?"

I almost dropped the cellular telephone. I also dropped Rick's hand. "Hmm?"

"Everything all right?"

I mentally shook myself and tried to focus on the here and now. "Yeah. It's just…Rick. It looks like he's sleeping." My throat constricted, and I busied myself with rummaging around in my purse for my Tarot deck. Again.

David said, "I'm sorry. Here I am bugging you when you have bigger things to worry about."

"It's fine. I need something to distract me. And the case is important to me. And Rick." I set the telephone down and put it on speakerphone. Thank goodness I remembered how to do that. Then I picked up the deck and began going through the cards. "How many cups?"

An indrawn breath over the phone line. "I don't know…the blood—well, what we believe unofficially to be blood—is obscuring most of it. I want to say…seven or eight? Or maybe six..."

I kept going through the cards, my heart racing. This could be it, the thing that broke the case. "The seated man sounds familiar, but I can't remember which cups card he's on." I made two piles: one for the cards I'd looked at, and one for the ones I hadn't.

"Okay, I'll wait."

It took me a while to go through them. I was almost to the end when I came to the Nine of Cups. I picked it up, my hand trembling. "I think this is it. The Nine of Cups. The wish fulfillment card."

"So, I have to wonder if this will stop," the detective said. "If the murderer got what he wanted, is he done?"

Something deep inside me said *no*.

"There's more to be done," I said softly. "I know it. And," I added, feeling as if I were throwing myself to the wolves, "I still believe it's a woman. Don't ask me how. It's…complicated."

"Leliel," David said warningly. "What aren't you telling me? Did you witness this or something?"

"No. Nothing like that. Just call it a feeling."

"I can't do anything with that," David said. "Get me some proof, then we can revisit this idea of yours."

"Okay, fine. Do you think it will be ruled a serial killer now?" I asked.

"I believe we will. Unless others believe it's a copycat. Then we're back to chasing our tails."

"They can't possibly do that," I said. "The Tarot cards tie it together. I'm sure of it."

"Listen, I've got to go," David said. "I'll relay this the police chief and if he has questions, can he call you?"

"Sure." I put my cards back together and started putting them into the bag when one fell onto the floor. I bent down to pick it up. The picture was face down, and I felt a shiver work its way up my spine. "A card fell onto the floor, Detective. Whenever a card falls out of the deck for any reason, it's considered a message from the Tarot—"

"What do you mean, a message?" he asked.

"It's supposedly the Tarot doing it. To tell us something," I explained oh so patiently. I snatched the card quickly before I could chicken out and laid it on the table, taking a breath.

The Page of Wands.

"Okay, young person, fiery personality, could be literal fire."

"I believe you, Leliel," David said with a sigh. "I can't believe I'm even saying this. I'm just not sure how the others will react to this."

"The police have used psychics before. At least on television," I said.

"So, this page, could it be a woman?" the detective asked. He sounded legitimately curious. Did he really believe in it now?

"A young woman or man. Possibly even a child. Could even be Samantha's unborn child."

"That muddies the waters a bit," he said. "Theories?"

"There's something about the fire," I mused. "Fire ties the deaths together, too. And now this card, a wands card, which is about fire. Literal or figurative."

"I agree," David said. "Sounds logical."

"Thanks, sir," I said, "for believing in me."

I WAS HOME briefly to check on Love when my cellular telephone rang. I jumped, my heart racing. Love nuzzled my legs.

I pushed the "accept call" button. "Hello?"

"Hi, is this Leliel?" a guy asked. He sounded young.

"Yes, this is her. Who's this?" I sat down.

"This is Eugene, a classmate of Fred's," the guy said. He cleared his throat. "Um, can we meet?"

I blinked. What were the chances of hearing from *two* of Fred's classmates? I forced myself to pay attention. "We can, sure. When and where?"

"I want to help," Eugene said. "I can't say anything about the actual—thing—"

"Why not? What do you know?" I asked, my mouth going dry. What could he tell me?

"I-I-I can't. I'm under a compulsion spell. I can't physically do it. But I c-can maybe help with oth-other things."

I thought of the explosion. "Do you know anything about casting spells?"

"Y-yes," Eugene replied, his voice quivering. "I am a witch."

"Then you *can* help," I said. Finally, a freaking break!

We made arrangements to meet at the diner in an hour. I had just enough time to call David and give him the news. He couldn't meet us, but I promised I'd give him a call when we were done.

"I should start picking you up every day," Tom said with a grin as I got into his cab. "You could be a regular customer."

"Do I get a discount? Like those, um, flier things?"

"Frequent flier miles?" Tom laughed, pulling out of the driveaway. "Yes, frequent cab miles. That'll catch on. So where are we heading today?"

I gave him the address.

"So, how are you doing today?" Tom said, glancing at me in the rearview mirror.

"I'm doing all right. My husband hasn't woken up yet."

Tom sighed. "I am so sorry. I will say a prayer for you." He made a turn to the right. "And they don't know why he's unconscious?"

"Thanks for the prayer," I said. "They don't really know. We're just waiting."

"That's too bad," Tom said. "I hope they figure something out soon."

"Me too."

I wanted to take my mind off of things, so I decided to figure out how much money I had. My emergency fund was rapidly depleting. Although I loved talking to Tom, I realized taking a cab wasn't very cost effective. Was that what Rick was talking about? The budgeting thing? If I blew all our money on cab fare, I wouldn't have any left for food. And I had no idea how to get more. Or where Rick's plastic loan card was. But I had promised him that I'd never use it again.

"Here we are, milady," Tom said, breaking into my thoughts. We were already here.

I glanced at the meter and counted out the correct amount of money plus a generous tip. Because he deserved it. "Here you go." I handed him the money.

Tom glanced at the money and shook his head. "This is a huge tip. You should save it." He took the cab fare, plus a few extra dollars, and gave me the rest. Was he a mind reader?

"Okay, thanks. I just—"

"Not to worry. Enjoy your day."

I got out and waved him goodbye, then went into the diner.

Lucy wasn't there, so I could duck in without worrying about anyone asking tough questions. That was a good thing. I really wasn't in the mood for it.

A black-haired young man wearing a sweatshirt and jeans waved at me. How did he know who I was? Was *everyone* reading my mind today?

I smiled and went to where he was sitting—in the back, right near the bathroom.

"Eugene?" I asked, sitting down. He nodded, his eyes dancing in the light.

"And you must be Leliel." And he pronounced it correctly! Nice.

We shook hands. I found myself unable to form words. My mouth had gone dry, and it felt like cotton had been shoved in there. My tongue felt wrong.

"What's happening is a compulsion," Eugene said conversationally. "No one can know that we're working together. After our business is concluded, you will not be able to speak my name or remember me. You will remember the details of this conversation and any other conversation, however, in case you want to take whatever we find to the police. I won't interfere with that."

I swallowed, and the cottonmouth feeling dissipated. "I'm not feeling very comfortable with this, especially right after meeting you."

Eugene shrugged. "Well, that's the price you pay for my help. Take it or leave it."

This was not good, but I needed his help. At least I'd be able to go to the police if we found anything. I sighed and tried not to panic. "How long?"

"Indefinitely."

I really didn't like this. My stomach knotted with anxiety that was really hard to tamp down. "So, I won't remember you or your name, and that's it? No other effects?"

"Right," Eugene said.

I nodded. "Fine. If this is what you require from me."

A waitress came up to our table and took our orders. I ordered an ice water, and Eugene ordered just about everything on the menu that was breakfast food, plus a coffee and a soda. Talk about hungry and thirsty. And breakfast during the day? That was odd.

I hoped he didn't expect me to pay.

"I'll share some with you," Eugene said. "Since you are saving money and stuff."

My eyes narrowed. "Is it that obvious?"

"To me, yeah." He smiled. "Don't worry, I'm good with it. I just want to help. I-uh…don't like what's happening and I want to stop it."

"What part do you play in all of this?" I asked.

"I'm p-part of th-the…" Eugene said. He sighed, and his mouth moved, but nothing came out at first. "…part of the…thing. B-but I don't d-do what they are d-doing."

I took that to mean that he was part of the coven but wasn't one of the perpetrators. I could work with that.

"Okay, cool. Here's what I need. My husband was put into a coma from an explosion on someone's property. I want to know if it was magic based. I was told by someone that there would be a residue."

Eugene nodded. "Yes. Typically. But I am wondering if there might not be, so whoever did this can hide it. I mean, you could press charges."

The waitress returned with our drinks, then went to another table.

I took a sip of my water, mulling that over. "What if there's no residue? Is there any other way to determine if it's magic? Or are we screwed?"

Eugene put sugar into his coffee and stirred it. "I have a few tricks up my sleeve," he said, looking at me. "No need to worry. Where did this happen? Is it private property?"

I swallowed hard. "Um…yes. Is that a problem?" Please, please, let this work out. I needed to know.

Eugene took a sip of his coffee. "I have a trick for that, too."

Our food came, and Eugene generously offered me some hash browns, some of his scrambled eggs, and toast.

"So, s-something was d-done. I'm sure you know that-that much," Eugene said. "And it wasn't c-cool. I was against it from-from day one. But I was-was overruled."

"By your coven?" I asked. Interesting how the stutter had come back.

Eugene nodded. "Yes."

I took a bit of hash browns and chewed them, trying to figure out how we could use Eugene's abilities. "I'm wondering if we could go to the property—at night, so we wouldn't be seen, I hope—and see where the explosion happened. And then hopefully figure out the how and why."

Eugene smiled. "That could work. I have an invisibility spell, but it only works for one person. So maybe I could go there and poke around. Sound good?"

I nodded and took a sip of my water. "I'd like to be there. But yes, it sounds good."

"Sure. What can you tell me about the property?"

"It's huge. She's rich. And it's beautiful inside, with—"

Eugene held up his hand. "Just the outside."

I took a bite of toast. "Okay. There's an in-ground pool and a gazebo. There's a flowerbed on one edge. Part of it was dug up, according to the owner. A dog supposedly did that. But it doesn't look dug up now. New flowers were planted there."

"How much was dug up?"

"Not a lot. But my husband can sense psychic imprints, and he believed that something was there."

"So you're saying that the spell would be in that area?" Eugene took a bite of his scrambled eggs. "And are the police involved?"

I hoped that wasn't a problem. He was my only way to figure this out. "Yes. My husband and I are neighbors of one of the police officers. He brought us in unofficially." I took another sip of water. I realized that I didn't really like water, and saving money sucked. I had no idea how to fix this.

"Leliel?" Eugene's voice brought me back.

I shook my head. "Sorry. I spaced out for a second. What was your question?"

"You believe the spell is in the area that was dug up by the 'dog'?" Air quotes.

"Yes."

"Okay, then. I think this is possible. I can track the spell and hopefully find out who did this." He smiled and moved a few hash browns around his plate. "When do you want this to go down?"

I smiled. "Tonight."

"Tonight, it is," Eugene said.

"SO…WHERE ARE we headed this time?" Tom asked.

I was *not* going to tell him the truth. "I'm meeting a few friends for dinner. Should be fun." Fun if your definition included an invisible witch, trespassing, and a spell that might or might not exist.

"Cool. It's good to have friends."

"Yeah," I murmured. *Let's hear it for invisible friends.*

"How is your husband?"

"I was just at the hospital," I replied. "His condition is unchanged."

"So sorry," Tom murmured.

I didn't tell David about going back to Ms. Chandler's property. I was afraid he'd have to arrest Eugene and me. I would tell him after. Assuming we found anything out.

My stomach was a mess of butterflies, and I was pretty sure I was going to throw up. What had possessed me to do this? Oh, right. I needed to know what happened to Rick. That was too important.

As Tom turned down Pinecone Lane, I said, "Why don't you stop here? It's a nice night. I can walk."

Tom pulled over to the side and gave me a quizzical look. "Why? I'm supposed to drop you off—"

"I need exercise," I said. It was the first thing that came into my mind. "I've been gaining weight, and every bit helps."

Tom put the money into a cloth pouch. "All right, then." He looked like he was about to say something but must have thought better of it. "Have a nice evening, Leliel."

"I'll see you around," I said, and began the short trek to Ms. Chandler's house. I kept a lookout for Eugene's car, but didn't see anything yet. I watched as Tom passed me and made a turn at the corner, then disappeared from view.

A cool wind gusted past, and I shivered.

As I got closer to Ms. Chandler's house, I let out a breath I hadn't realized I was holding. It was dark, with clouds covering the moon. I could hardly make out the house.

It looked so terribly evil, standing tall, with no hint of the life inside. I wondered if everyone was sleeping. It looked so imposing, so wrong…

A *honk* made me jump. I spun toward the noise. Eugene! In an old beat-up car of some sort. I wasn't familiar with all the different kinds yet.

He poked his head out the window. "Want to wait in here and plan?"

"Sure." I went around to the passenger side and opened the door. It creaked and got stuck. "Um…"

"Just give it a little shake," Eugene said with a laugh. "It's really, really old."

I did as instructed, and the door started moving again. I got in, sat down, and closed the door. The inside of the car smelled of old fast food, body odor, and cigarette smoke. "So, um, how are you?"

Eugene pulled over to the side, just a few houses away from Ms. Chandler's. He turned off the engine and turned to me. "I'm doing all right, I guess. I haven't told anyone about this, but I swear, our High Priestess has some type of sensing because she was asking some really weird questions." He shrugged. "I made something up. But she's getting close."

"Who is your High Priestess? If you can tell me, that is." I looked out the window, going for casual. This might be good information for the case.

Eugene said, "That's pretty safe. Michelle Dumas. She took over when Pamela…you know…"

I looked at him. His face was impassive, but his fingers were tapping on his jeans. "Can you tell me how Pamela got to be High Priestess? Is there an election, or…?"

I hoped he'd tell me something useful.

Eugene shook his head. "No. But…huh. I don't remember."

"Was your memory tampered with?" This was getting weirder and weirder.

"I don't think so." He shrugged. "I don't go to meetings much. I'm more of a loner."

I tucked an errant strand of hair behind my ear, watching as two cars flew down the street opposite us. Once I was sure we wouldn't get hit, I asked, "Do you want to make that plan?"

Eugene smiled. "Yep. So here's the deal." He leaned in closer to me, and I smelled onions and alcohol on his breath. Great. Hopefully he wasn't too intoxicated to do a good job. So much was riding on this. "I have a spell to make myself invisible, as I mentioned. There's only one catch. It's not very long-lasting. So I need exact directions on where this thing is so I'm not running around and getting my ass arrested."

"Of course. I wouldn't want that."

"Right. And just FYI…if I go down, so do you."

I swallowed hard. I was pretty sure David wouldn't look the other way this time. I'd already cashed in my freebie. "I figured as much."

A dog barked.

Another dog answered.

I pictured Ms. Chandler's backyard in my mind and hoped I remembered it correctly. "There's a pool and a gazebo. The place we're looking for is past all of that and in a corner.

There's a flowerbed. The explosion went off near the part of the flowerbed that's replanted." Something occurred to me. "How are you going to prove this? You could walk in there, pretend to look for the explosion and a spell, and come back and tell me anything. I want to be able to trust that what you say is the truth."

Eugene smiled. "I anticipated that. I'm going to cast a truth spell on myself so I can't lie." His eyes narrowed. "And maybe on you, too, just so you know it's working."

"You could still pretend," I countered.

"At this point, you will have to trust me, okay?" He held his hands out, palm up. "There's not much else I can do."

"You did say you wanted to help," I said. "But we already think we've been lied to. You have to understand. We don't want to end up chasing the wrong theory or the wrong person."

Eugene dropped his hands and let out a breath. "Why is this so important to you? Besides the whole justice being served thing? *Everyone* wants that." He rolled his eyes. Just in case I didn't catch the sarcasm.

"Well…these deaths are not in the natural order of things. They're all *wrong*. I have to fix it."

Eugene smiled. "Fair enough. Now I'm going to cast the truth spell. It shouldn't last too long. Just long enough for us to do this."

"Will it hurt?" I asked, biting my lip.

Eugene chuckled. "No! You may feel a slight tingle. That's it." He lifted his hands and his eyes went distant. "Ready?"

"As ready as I can be," I said, shivering again.

Another car blew past us.

And then I was feeling kind of tingly, but sort of relaxed, too. Like floating on a cloud.

"Leliel?" A snap.

My eyes flew open. "Hmm?"

Eugene's face emerged from nothingness. "I may have made that too strong. Um, how do you really feel about me?"

I heard him. I felt my mouth and tongue make the sounds, but I swear, I didn't have any control over what came out. "I'm still trying to decide if I can trust you. You seem cool and I needed a witch and you fit the bill."

"Excellent." I blinked at him, still feeling dopey. "The truth about you. I like you. You're pretty. And I wanted to help your investigation. And get revenge on the ones who did the bad stuff. But I'm not allowed to tell you certain things and I stutter because I am fighting against the compulsion that was laid on me by Michelle." He let out a breath. "*Now* do you trust me?"

I nodded. It was as good as it could get. "Yeah. I do."

"Okay, I'll get closer to the house, then." He opened the door and looked at me. "I'll go on foot so no one notices the car."

My heart lurched. What if we got caught? What if Ms. Chandler had us arrested? And if so, we could be in so much trouble.

"You should stay here. Just in case," Eugene said, breaking into my thoughts.

Good thing he did. I was about to have a panic attack.

"But I could help you if you get lost."

"Leliel, you're not going to even *see* me. And I have limited time. It has to be fast. And a fast getaway. Wait three minutes, then turn the car back on." He held out his keys. "That way, I can jump in and we can go."

I bit my lip, my gut clenching with unease. The truth spell! I did not want to tell—

"Leliel?" He shook the keys in front of my face.

"Um." Wow, I was a *brilliant* conversationalist. "I—uh—I don't know how to drive."

Eugene's eyebrows shot up. "Really? That's kind of strange." He gasped. "Sorry. Truth spell."

"It's all right. Actually, it's not. It's very judgmental of you," I said. Crap! We were going to have an argument, and we needed to get the information and get out. Stupid, stupid, stupid.

"I'm a judgmental kind of guy," Eugene countered.

"Look—" Through sheer force of will, I focused on Ms. Chandler's house. "Let's just get this going. We can argue later."

"I'd love to argue now." Another gasp. "Wow, this spell is *crazy*. Okay, let's...um...get to work. I'll turn the car on. Just watch for anything weird. You're kind of useless." He cleared his throat. "I mean—"

This was a disaster. I let out a huff of air. "I know. I know. Truth spell. Go. Before I decide to—to do something." Way to go. I was still dopey, too. Useless indeed.

Eugene nodded. "Right." He got out of the car and headed into the darkness that was the street and headed to Ms. Chandler's house.

I worried. What if he got lost, or couldn't find where the explosion was?

Was I really useless?

Crap.

I was going to talk myself into a nervous breakdown.

Okay, I decided to stop thinking.

Yeah, right.

Sleep?

No. I needed to be focused in case anything went wrong.

Follow him in?

Bad idea. Bad, bad, bad idea.

A quiet voice in my mind kept telling me to go. That he *needed* me. That I couldn't be useless.

That decided, I got out of the car.

Another car blew past me, making me jump. Maybe this was a bad idea.

I crept along to the curb. And wondered again—

The snap of a twig.

My heart raced and my fingers trembled.

Keep. Going.

I plunged into the darkness, hoping I wouldn't be seen.

The rustle of leaves.

I made it to the gate. I could make out the vaguest shape of a person. Eugene was creeping around, but he was doing it very randomly. Had he forgotten my instructions? Or were they unclear?

"Eugene!" I whispered. "Farthest corner. Flowerbed. Replanted section. Go!"

The shape stopped. "Leliel? Get out of here! Now!"

"Yeah, but—"

"Just go! Someone will hear us!"

I felt another odd tingling, then the oddest compulsion to go back. Right now. Nothing else. He knew what he was doing.

Don't be useless.

With a sigh, I headed back toward the car.

And waited for a million years. Or so it seemed.

Eugene reappeared at the car door, keys in his hand. "I've got your information," he said.

THE NEXT DAY, David and I were at the police station. I was giving him a rundown of what happened.

My friend, whose name I couldn't remember, had been furious at me for jeopardizing the mission. He'd been just about to do whatever it was he had to do when I'd showed up. In the end, he'd lost his invisibility after I'd left and was convinced we were going to get caught.

We hadn't. Luck had been on our side.

"So, he says that the spell was not for an explosion," I said, taking a sip of coffee. "The explosion was just a bonus. The spell was supposed to render one of us unconscious. Whoever was closer. And keep that person unconscious until the spell was broken. Which he says he can't do." My shoulders slumped. "And apparently, Ms. Chandler was behind it, but she didn't actually perform the spell."

"Let's assume I believe in spells and invisibility," David said, steepling his hands. "Let's also speak of this in hypotheticals. Just in case."

I nodded. "Right. So, um, he hypothetically found out that the only person who could break it is a powerful witch. More powerful than he is. He wasn't happy with that."

David leaned forward. "How precisely did your friend discover all of this?"

I swallowed hard. The words were out before I could stop them. "Because he went to Ms. Chandler's backyard and checked it out."

David arched a brow.

"Hypothetically." Hellfire! The truth spell! "Um, I'm sort of under a truth spell right now. I can't lie."

David's lips quirked up. "Really? Now that is interesting."

"I wasn't sure my friend would be truthful, so he cast a spell on us both. He said it wouldn't last long." I looked down at my hands, feeling incredibly stupid now. "I guess it hasn't gone away yet."

"I see," David said. "So your friend hypothetically trespassed onto private property to determine things about this alleged spell to render someone unconscious."

Crap. We were going to get arrested. "Yes."

David cocked his head to one side. "So, what was the point of the spell?"

"They wanted to take one of us out of the equation," I said. "And the other one would be wrapped up in figuring out what happened. Distraction and misdirection."

"But they didn't think of me," David pointed out. "I'm still working the case."

"Yes, you are."

"We finally got hold of Shelby Price's parents. They said something very interesting."

I leaned forward, my heart racing. "Tell me."

"Professor Everson is apparently a witch, too. And she's doing some very nasty things. Like, for instance, black magic. Devil worship."

"That's why I felt so wrong near her and in the building. Want to bet me they do their rituals there?"

"I would love to get a gander at it. But we need a search warrant. And unless there's something in plain sight, that's not going to happen."

That was disappointing. "Well, at least we got confirmation that it's bigger than we thought?"

"Yes. Let's run through this crazy thing again, shall we?" He went to a small whiteboard tucked in a corner, then picked up a dry-erase marker and wrote as he spoke. "The first two deaths, Mary and Summer, had Tarot cards. The Fool and The Ten of Swords." He kept writing, his handwriting getting progressively worse. "Number three, Fred Chandler. Two of Cups."

"Number four, Shelby Price. Engaged to suicide number five. Judgment."

David wrote that down. Then, "Number five. Mark Allison. Hiero—what's it called again?"

"Hierophant," I said.

He nodded. "Samantha was pregnant when she died." He wrote her name off to the side.

"Possibly the first?" I put in.

"Possibly. Your visions showed what again?"

"She wasn't alone, people were laughing, and I still believe the murderer is female."

"Right." David nodded and added that information. "Fred and Samantha were together prior to her death."

"Number six, Pamela Carson, suicide by self-immolation. Tarot card was The Nine of Cups."

"And then we have the spell," I said. "Putting my husband in a coma." Which made me want to cry every time I thought of it. I took a deep breath and let it out.

"You okay?" David set the marker down and faced me. "How is Rick?"

I hugged myself. "No change. But we need to focus on the case. I'll go crazy if I dwell on it."

"Fair enough." David picked up the marker and started writing again. "Tarot cards. Go."

I visualized each card as I spoke. "The Fool, beginning of a journey or the unknown. Ten of Swords, an ending, the 'death card' of the Minor Arcana. Two of Cups, soulmate card. Judgment, or possibly feeling on the verge of a transformation. Hierophant, teacher or religious figure—"

"Would the devil count? Pointing to Professor Everson's um, extracurricular activities?"

I thought about it. "If it was reversed, yeah."

He put a question mark by the notation. "To be determined. Next."

"Nine of Cups, wish fulfillment card. Which should point to an end, but I am getting the feeling that she's not done. That there's more to come."

"Could it mean that she's gotten her wish? Maybe this was all revenge, or something."

"Yeah. I heard the word 'vengeance' in one of the visions," I said. "Vengeance, revenge, almost the same thing."

"Revenge for what, I wonder?"

"The classmates all being killed could have been revenge," I pointed out. "But why?"

"The rivalry?" David murmured. He wrote more stuff on the board. "Anything else?"

"Flyouts: Death and Death, possible death or ending. And a beginning. Three of Cups, coven ritual or celebration. Moon, occult. Page of Wands, immature, fire, maybe Samantha's baby."

David put down the marker and backed away, studying the board. "What the hell does this mean? What does *any* of this mean?"

"Serial killer who hates the students?" I guessed.

"Copycats," David countered.

"And don't forget the ghost," I blurted.

David faced me again, his eyes narrowed. "What do you mean?"

Crap. I hadn't meant to tell him. That was my own problem. "Uh…truth spell strikes again. Yeah. Rick and I got a visit from Jodie's ghost."

David blinked. "So, did this ghost do anything? Move stuff around, or make noise?" He added a notation about Jodie's murder. "Lancelot killed her to keep her quiet."

"About what?"

"I don't know yet. So, what exactly happened?" David asked.

"She was just there. We asked her questions, asking her to flicker the lamp to answer. She said that the murderer was causing—" I paused. I hadn't told David about the weird stuff, either. David was looking at me expectantly. "I—uh—was tasting ashes instead of bread." I swallowed hard, remembering how crazy it felt. And sounded. "She said we were in imminent danger and that something bad was going to happen to me and Rick. And then our wedding picture fell off the wall and shattered. I took it to mean that we were in trouble. But I don't think Jodie did that."

"This gets weirder and weirder," David murmured. He turned back to the board and wrote: *Ghost. Maybe Jodie? Murderer causing weird crap.*

"It's not a maybe. She said that's who she was," I said.

David erased the question mark. "Who would make you taste ashes? And why?"

"It was a warning. I'm convinced that I am next."

RICK WAS STILL in a coma.

It had been almost painful to leave his side, but I knew he'd want me to find the killer instead of sitting by his bedside crying.

The first task was to "be present" while the father of the sixth victim, Pamela Carson, was informed of Pamela's death. Those were David's words, not mine.

Once we got there and were walking toward the house, David said, "Let me do most of the talking, okay?"

"Okay, but I could really help," I said. Gasping, I covered my mouth with my hand.

"Truth spell?" David's lips quirked up like he was trying to hide a smile.

I nodded, feeling stupid.

The yard was mostly unkept, with weeds overgrowing in what might have been the flowerbed. There was a wooden railing on one side of the steps, but I was pretty sure there was supposed to be another one on the opposite side. The grass was long and brown. The windows looked dingy. And the house itself was tiny. The shutters were loose and the wooden door looked like it had been painted over several times.

There was a porch swing frame that was missing a swing. Some hoses and nails were scattered around. The roof was missing shingles, too.

The place gave me the shivers.

The detective stopped just before the porch and glanced up at the address. Then checked a notepad. He shrugged and rang the doorbell.

"Some place," I said.

"I thought maybe I got the address wrong," David said. "But this appears to be the place."

A dog barked. There was a banging sound inside.

David knocked on the door. "Bryce Carson?"

More barking. More banging.

Finally, the door opened. An emaciated man with white hair standing straight up in all directions stared at nothing. He wore a dirty pair of jeans and a stained undershirt. His arms looked like twigs, and there were several bruises on them, along with scabbed-over wounds. "Huh?" His eyes were unfocused, almost rolling back into his head.

"Are you Bryce Carson?" David asked.

The man did not look at either of us. "Yeah."

"I'm Detective David Landis with the police." He flashed his badge. "This lady with me is my associate. We couldn't locate your wife—"

"She took off after our divorce," Bryce said flatly. "Haven't heard from her since."

"I'm sorry to hear that," David said. "We've come to inform you—"

"Yeah? What about?"

"Sir, we have some potentially troubling news. May we come in?" David asked.

"No."

David let out a huff of air. "Okay, we can do this here. I'm sorry to inform you of this, but—"

"Yeah?"

I was pretty sure he wasn't quite right in the head. He didn't appear to be understanding any of this—

"It's Pam, isn't it?" he asked, his expression softening and his gaze focusing on the detective.

David shifted on his feet. "Yes. We found her—it appears that she took her own life, sir."

Bryce Carson nodded. "Yeah. I knew she would someday. She's always been very melancholy and dark. Used to write this horrible bleak poetry when she was a teenager. I never understood it." He ran a hand through his hair, which just made the mess worse.

"I'm sorry for your loss, sir. However, we had some questions to ask."

Bryce's eyes widened. "You don't think—she killed herself. You said so yourself."

"True." David's eyes went to me. "But we have reason to believe that it wasn't a suicide."

"But you just said—"

"What he's saying," I cut in, "is that we think it's possible that someone else killed her and just made it look like a suicide."

"Why would anyone…" Bryce looked so confused, so stunned that my heart went out to him.

"We're not sure, sir. Did she have any enemies?" David grabbed a pen and the notepad from his pocket.

"Enemies?" Bryce scratched his head. "I dunno. Everyone has enemies, right?"

"Sure," David said. "But do you know of anyone specifically?"

"Well, now that you mention it…" Bryce let out a loud belch. "Well, there was that group she used to go on and on about. The one that always got better grades. Said she was going to get them good. Mentioned an attraction…what did she say?" He scratched his head again. "My memory is not what it once was." He glanced at me. And then the detective. "I'm sorry. It had to do with magic, though. I had a good laugh over that one! Magic!"

David glanced at me. "You said there was talk of some improper behavior that was caused by a so-called spell?"

I nodded. "Yeah. We can discuss it later. It's kind of—it's not something a father would want to hear about his daughter."

Bryce waved a hand. He did not seem upset at all about Pamela's death. Which was just weird. Maybe he was in shock. "Ah, say anything. Ain't gonna bother me. I'm not even her real dad."

Everything kind of stopped.

"Oh," I said. "What exactly are you to her, then?"

"I'm her stepfather. But I divorced her mother a long time ago, so I guess I wouldn't be anything?" He chuckled weakly. His hands rooted around in his pockets until he got hold of a pack of cigarettes. "Do you mind if I light up? Nerves are bad today." Without waiting for a response, he pulled a cigarette out, put the pack back into his pocket, and lit up, the tip of the cigarette turning amber. He took a long drag on the cigarette, then blew out the smoke. Thankfully away from us. "Only really horrible thing? The kid. I would have liked to meet the kid."

"What kid?" David asked, and my heart beat double time.

"Pam was pregnant. That's the real loss."

"WELL, I HATE TO say 'I told you so,' but I told you so," I told David. We were back at the police station again.

David sat at his desk; I sat opposite him. He looked ready for a stiff drink. "Okay, okay, no need to hammer on it." He sighed. "*Pregnant?* That's unbelievable." He added the information to the board.

"Actually, it's believable," I said. "I'm sure that's happened before."

"I suppose we could look into her medical records and verify that," Detective Landis said. "And then figure out who'd want her—and her baby—dead."

I held up my hand. Why, I didn't know. I wasn't in school. "If we can also verify where she went to school, that would help. Apparently, that stuff I mentioned earlier was rampant."

The detective took notes. "What was the inappropriate behavior?"

"Students sleeping with professors so the students could gain 'favor.'" I made air quotes. "And the love spell thing, too. Meaning it wasn't of their own free will."

The detective shook his head. "This is *insane*."

"I'm almost positive that Pamela went to school with the others," I went on. "She was the High Priestess of the coven.

Assuming she did…and there was indeed a rivalry…although I can't imagine why she'd get pregnant, because that would be inconvenient when going to school. It could have been an accident." I turned that over in my mind. "Or, maybe…what if she was *trying* to get pregnant? For some arcane reason? Like, I dunno, pregnancy makes witches more powerful."

"You may be on to something," David said. "I'll make some calls, see about the school angle. Since you're into this woo-woo stuff, maybe you could find out about pregnancy and how it affects magical powers." He rolled his eyes. "I can't believe I'm actually saying this. Holy crap. My mother would roll over in her grave if she knew what I was saying."

I arched a brow. "She thought witchcraft is evil?"

"She was old-school Catholic," the detective said. "Oh, also, we talked to Ms. Chandler. She denied everything. And neither one of her next-door neighbors has a dog. Very peculiar."

"Absolutely. Hey, I had another thought."

"Lay it on me," David said.

"Well…let's say that this whole love-spell-compulsion thing is true. It follows that maybe the murderer compelled the victims to commit suicide, right? If you recall, I've been getting that feeling all along."

David rubbed his chin. "I suppose we can roll with that idea. Some proof would be nice, though. Because without proof, it's just a theory." He let out a breath. "Keep in touch."

"I'll let you know what I find out," I said.

We both stood and shook hands.

"Good work. Maybe we'll crack this case yet," David said.

"Thanks. And it's not maybe. We will."

After I left the police station, I ran through everything we knew so far.

What a tangle. I wasn't sure if we could untangle it before the murderer struck again.

Chapter 16

"RICK, PLEASE WAKE up. I need you," I said, wiping tears from my eyes. Dr. Hill had told me that the longer he was unconscious, the less chance of him waking up. And that scared me, worse than anything I'd ever experienced. Losing him…would kill me. I was sure of it.

He continued to breathe, to sleep, but he did not move.

"Okay, Leliel, you gotta be strong," I told myself. "He'll wake up and everything will be okay. It has to be."

I took his hand in mine, kissing his knuckles. He was so cold.

I'd checked in on Love this morning. She was fine, but I could sense something off about her. It was as if she knew that Rick was here, unconscious. I'd thought about bringing her here but decided against it. I would probably be thrown out.

I hadn't heard from anyone at all today. When I'd left for the hospital, the weather had turned chilly, reminding me of the Underworld. I didn't want to think about the Underworld, but I couldn't stop thinking about it. And trying to remember more.

My thoughts moved to the Tarot cards. I got my deck out of my purse and laid them out: The Fool. Ten of Swords. Two of Cups. Judgment. Death. Hierophant. Three of Cups. Moon. Nine of Cups. Page of Wands.

What was she trying to say to us?

We were embarking on a new journey. No kidding.

An ending.

The murderer was passing judgment on Fred…

The Tarot wanted me to know about the murder attempt…

It might end in the school…

There was a ritual in the coven for something…

The murderer got her wish…or something…

And there were two children: Pamela's and Samantha's unborn babies…

I just couldn't figure it out.

A flash.

I was sitting in a chair, my muscles protesting, and I was writing in a journal, my fingers clenched on the pen. Someone was talking to me, making me do it…everything inside me was rebelling. I was nauseous, and dizzy, and I couldn't stop myself from doing what *she* wanted me to do.

Someone threw alcohol onto my body. I felt cold, and the smell was so strong…

My thumb—without my conscious thought—flicked a lighter.

And then I was on fire.

I SAT IN RICK'S hospital room, curled up in a ball in a chair. What had I seen? Was it a vision, or some kind of daytime nightmare?

How could I possibly set *myself* on fire?

And that was when another puzzle piece slid into place.

I'd been right. The murderer had compelled the victims to set themselves on fire.

But what about Pamela? Had she been compelled to burn herself to death?

And she'd been carrying a child.

I had another thought.

Uncurling, I remembered that I'd brought Rick's laptop computer with me today.

To do research.

If I could find out how pregnancy related to a witch's power, maybe we could figure out if the reason why both Pamela and Samantha were pregnant was related to the coven.

I watched Rick, watched the rise and fall of his chest, as I turned on the computer. I hoped I would remember how to use it.

There was something called a search engine…

Rick's hand twitched.

My heart lurched. "Rick? Are you there? Do it again?"

I watched him, my heart racing. Was he waking up?

What if he didn't?

I wasn't sure I could bear it.

Rick's hand didn't move.

Maybe I'd imagined it.

I turned back to the computer, typing the word "Google."

That did not work.

How did that go again?

Address, it had to be an address.

Right…www…something.

I typed in the address and watched Google appear like magic. Technology was cool. I wished we had this stuff when I was alive the first time.

Next, I typed *witch getting pregnant.*

There were thousands of entries in the list that popped up.

Okay, let's see…Wiccan Rituals, Fertility Spells, Pregnancy Spells…nothing seemed to be remotely what I was searching for.

I went through page after page of seemingly random stuff. I felt disheartened by the whole thing, feeling that maybe I was wrong and the pregnancies had nothing to do with the murders.

But deep down, I knew I was right.

I kept looking.

And looking.

Finally, on page twenty, I found *the effect of pregnancy on a witch's powers* in some kind of a thing I didn't recognize. It had a list of sentences and what looked like names. Interesting. I clicked on the link.

Someone was asking that very question.

And got answers!

WiccanWoman: The fact that you are creating a life inside you amplifies your innate abilities.

GoddessGirl: Oh, yes. When I was pregnant, my spells were almost *too* powerful. I had to alter the ingredients and the chants so I didn't mistakenly level the whole city.

Don'tFearTheReaper: It will be HUGE and amazing.

I immediately called David. "I've got some more information for you."

"Hello, Leliel," the detective said. "What do you have?"

"I found something on the World Wide Web," I said. "Someone asked if a pregnancy can affect a witch's powers. And several people said yes. And quite a lot, too." I thought of something. "So, what if Pamela and Samantha were rivals for power? Or," I added, "what if the babies would be evil?"

"This is all very interesting, Leliel," David said gently. "But I need more than just stuff on the internet. Something concrete. I'm sorry. They're great ideas—"

"But you need proof," I finished, my heart sinking to my feet. Damn. I was pretty sure I was on the right track. But how could I prove it?

"Right. But keep me in the loop."

"Okay, I will endeavor to do better, Detective," I said, glancing at Rick. I knew he could help me, but who knew when he'd wake up? And he *would* wake up.

I wouldn't accept anything else.

THE NEXT DAY was Halloween, the human holiday with kids in costumes going door-to-door asking for treats. It is also when the veil between the living and the dead is thinner. And, spirits always tried to leave the Underworld. Returning them was always tough—I'd get bribes, or threats, or tearful pleadings. I *hated* that, but it was all part of the job description.

A shiver worked its way up my spine, and it wasn't from the cold. Something big was going to happen tonight. I could feel it.

I was at home, researching stuff on Rick's laptop computer.

The place was so lonely without him. I could still smell his cologne. I sent a prayer to whoever would listen to please help Rick come back to me and Love.

Love sat on the table, tail swishing and ears perked.

"Why don't we look for covens? That might give us a clue." I typed "witch covens in Amsburg" into Google. I bit my lip. It was a long shot—

I found something.

It was a website for the Dark Moon Coven, based in our hometown. And even better, there was a list of members.

Samantha's name was on there as a past High Priestess and deceased.

And Pamela's name was on there, too. As the *current* High Priestess. They apparently hadn't updated the list to reflect the new High Priestess, Michelle something-or-other. So my friend had been telling the truth. I couldn't remember his name.

Who'd want to murder Pamela? Fred? But someone had killed him.

It didn't make sense.

I shook my head, then pulled my cellular telephone out of my pocket and dialed the cab company. I booked my pick up and went to the living room to wait. They were starting to get to know me, so I didn't need to even give them my address anymore.

Who would want to kill Samantha, the previous High Priestess, and her successor, Pamela? Something niggled at me. Something big. It was a stirring in my gut. A feeling. Something.

A loud *honk* outside jolted me from my thoughts. I went outside, said hello to Tom, and got into the cab.

I was running out of money.

And I had no idea how to get more.

"Back to the hospital, huh?" Tom asked as he pulled out into traffic.

"Yep."

"Your husband still unconscious, then?"

"Yeah. And they're saying the longer he's like that…" I couldn't even bring myself to finish.

"Oh, man. What a horrible thing. I'm so sorry," Tom said. "I will say another prayer for you two."

"Thank you," I said, even though I doubted the human deity would help us. I appreciated the thought, though.

The ride passed in silence after that. I wasn't feeling up to conversation. I felt hollowed out; empty. I wanted to go back to the apartment, get into bed, and not come out for a while.

Tom pulled up in front of the hospital. "Do you have any plans for Halloween?"

I shook my head. "No. Just being with my husband."

"That's perfectly okay," Tom said gently. "I don't have any plans, either. No kids in my neighborhood. I'm diabetic, so candy is too tempting. Might just watch a horror movie or something."

I counted out Tom's fare plus a small tip. "Tonight's a good night for that." I held out the money, and he took it from me.

He grinned at me. "Try to have a nice night, Leliel. You deserve it."

"Thanks, you too." I got out of the cab and gave him a wave. "See you soon."

He saluted me, then left.

I went inside, breathing in the scent of antiseptic, flowers, and death. Nurses passed by me, frantic to save someone; a doctor smiled at me.

I just wanted my husband back.

It felt as if I were walking in a nightmare. My eyelids drooped. I could hardly see where I was going, but instinctively knew the way.

When I came to his room, I opened the door.

Rick was gone.

I gasped.

Chapter 17

"WHAT DO YOU mean, he's been released?" I asked the head nurse. I was at the nurses' station, trying to puzzle out what had happened.

And was getting exactly nowhere.

"Dr. Hill signed off on it," the head nurse, a tall, thin woman, told me.

"But he's in a *coma,*" I protested. "Unless he woke up, but no one told me that."

The head nurse shook her head, sending her short brown curls flying around her face. "No, it says here that he remains the same but stable." She flipped through a binder that I had learned was his chart. "Someone came to get him. We assumed—"

"Assumed what exactly?" I asked, my heart racing, my blood heating, my hands sweating. If he was lost…or taken somewhere else by mistake…I would commit murder. No question. He didn't need to be anywhere but with me. I had very little money left to get myself someplace else—

The head nurse averted her gaze. Her words were quiet, almost mumbled. "We assumed it was a relative, taking him to another facility."

What?! "Why didn't anyone call me to confirm that? Do you just let patients go with anyone who walks in?" I leaned forward, and I swear I saw red. "You need to fix this. Get on the telephone and find him. *Now.*"

The head nurse nodded. "I will find him, Mrs. Ashton."

"Great."

I went to the lobby area and sat down. Naturally, I couldn't freaking *think* with the chokehold panic had on me. I felt as if I were suffocating—

My cellular telephone chose that moment to start ringing. Rick had put some kind of rock song on it, and my heart constricted. "Hello?"

"Leliel." A woman's voice. It sounded vaguely familiar.

"Who is this?" I asked, my hand clenching on the receiver.

"I am someone who will become very important to you very soon."

Huh? "I don't know you, so probably not." I glanced at the head nurse, who was busy making telephone calls.

"I know where Rick is," the woman said in a singsong voice.

My breath caught.

The entire world stopped.

"Leliel?"

I took a deep breath. "Tell me!"

"Meet me at Amsburg Law School tonight at eight o'clock. Come alone."

Click.

I nearly dropped the telephone.

I had to get to the college.

How?

David could give me a ride.

I dialed his number, my finger shaking. I tried to take deep breaths as the telephone rang. And kept ringing. Hellfire! Where was he?

This couldn't wait.

Rick could be in danger right now.

The cab. I'd just have to have Tom drop me off somewhere close. I'd have to use the last of my money, and hope it was enough. I was supposed to come alone.

That decided, I called and booked my pickup.

Was Rick okay? Was he dead?

What if she'd killed him?

Who was she?

I frantically searched my purse for money. And found…ten dollars. Was it enough?

It had to be enough.

I spun around to face the head nurse, who was watching me with concern. "Mrs. Ash—"

"I've got to go," I said. "You have my cellular telephone number. Call me once you know something." I ran to the elevators, my hands shaking and my heart pounding. Was this a trap? Of course it was a trap, but there was nothing I could do. I had to get to Rick.

This meeting could be the thing that solves the case. I'd finally get answers. I needed to calm down so I could think clearly.

I had my Reaper cloak with me. It was familiar, and soothing, and looked badass. I put it on, leaving the hood hanging in the back. I didn't want to scare the nurses. Then again, it was almost Halloween, and maybe I'd just blend in with the kids.

Who was the woman who'd called? What would I do once I got there?

As I entered the elevator, a short man with blond hair stepped forward and pushed the button for the fifth floor.

I tried to breathe deeply. Tried to relax. But who was I kidding?

My husband could be dead.

Would I die with him, by fire, just like in my vision?

AS I APPROACHED the law school, my cellular telephone rang again. "Hello?"

"I see you made it," the woman said.

"Where is my husband?" I asked. "Please. I'll do anything!"

"You sure will," she said with a chuckle. "Come to Building A, room one hundred thirty. I'll be waiting."

Click.

Okay. I took a breath.

What if he was dead?

No, I had to be positive. He was alive. He had to be.

After what felt like eons, I made it into the law school.

I headed for Building A, taking deep breaths. I could do this.

A man was headed for me. Was he involved with this? Did he have instructions for me?

What was going on?

I braced myself for an assault, paying close attention to my surroundings.

Footsteps behind me.

Hands on my shoulders.

I hadn't heard the footsteps. My hearing was human normal. I tried to pry the hands off—

A pinprick, then the gaping maw of darkness.

I WOKE UP IN white.

It was a small room. White blankets hung from the walls, concealing any windows. The chair I was sitting on was painted white.

And apparently someone had changed my clothes. I was now wearing a white tunic and white slacks. White socks. White shoes. No Reaper cloak.

Hellfire.

I looked up. The ceiling was white, too. Even the ropes that bound me were white.

What the hell?

Who had done this?

And... could I somehow free myself?

Something crackled above me. It sounded like one of those things that people listen to...what was it called? A radio!

"Leliel," a woman's voice said. It sounded like the one who had called me, but I couldn't tell for sure.

"Who are you? Why am I tied to a chair in a white room?"

She chuckled. "All will be revealed in due time."

"That's not an acceptable answer!" Rage and fear burned my veins. "Where is Rick? I need to see him!"

"You will."

"I want to see him *now*," I said through clenched teeth.

"You do *not* make demands of me. Now, sit tight and enjoy your stay."

"Release me!" I struggled against my restraints, feeling nauseous and anxious all at once.

She had Rick, and who knew what she was doing to him? He was defenseless!

I had to see him—

A television screen in the front of the room came to life. The image was of—hellfire!—Rick. In a bed. He looked like he was sleeping, but I couldn't tell. He could be dead.

He could be freaking dead.

"Hey!" I cried. "Where is he?"

"He is safe," the woman said. "Now, you need to calm down and pay very close attention. We are going to play a game. You do as I say, and he lives. Disobey me, and he dies. Do you understand?"

My eyes filled with tears. What was she going to—oh, no. Oh, no. The vision!

I was going to die.

"Leliel, do you—"

"Yes," I snapped.

"There's someone else," the woman said. The view on the television screen widened.

David lay on a second bed, looking like he, too, was sleeping peacefully.

Hellfire.

"He will also die if you disobey me. I understand he's become a trusted friend. You wouldn't want to be the cause of his death, would you?"

I closed my eyes. She was right. I couldn't let him die, either.

"Leliel? When I ask you a question, you are to answer me. Or there will be consequences." Her voice was as hard as steel.

I opened my eyes. "Fine. No, I don't want to be the reason he dies. Assuming he and Rick are still alive." I don't know what got into me. The thought just burst forth.

"They both live. Currently. Here are their heart rates." The screen changed to something

I recalled seeing in the hospital. A green line jumped up and down with their heartbeats. Two lines jumping. Two sets of beats.

I let out a breath. "Okay."

"I will be there momentarily. I am bringing a friend," the woman said.

I wasn't sure how long it was before I heard the sound of a key opening the door. Then two women stepped in.

One was a police officer I hadn't met yet. She had long, brown hair tucked into a bun and brown eyes.

The murderer *couldn't* be her. She was a cop.

But...

It was back. Black and white. The two sets of eyes. The two voices. The red glow.

What did that mean? I had to freaking figure it out. It was too important—

Footsteps brought me out of my haze. The other woman was short, with black hair and blue eyes. Her black dress hung to the floor. She wore a necklace with an oddly shaped symbol hanging from it.

The woman stopped in front of me with a grin that said she was *quite* satisfied with things. "Hello, Reaper Girl."

What? I'd never seen her before, but she seemed to know me. "Don't 'Reaper Girl' me. I am no longer a Reaper," I snapped, pulling at my restraints. I just got sore wrists and ankles for my trouble, but it felt like I was doing something instead of things being done *to* me. I glared at her, letting my anger fill my gaze. "Who are you, and what are you doing? And how do you know who I am?"

She smiled, and her eyes mesmerized me. I blinked and looked away. "My name is Mercy, and I am a witch."

"I am Officer Carlos," the female police officer said. "You have been brought here for a very specific purpose."

"I figured that," I said, yawning. "Skip to the part where I save my husband and friend."

"But it'll be so much fun," Officer Carlos said.

"I highly doubt that," I said. "So, what am I going to have *so much fun* doing, Officer? By the way, you suck as a cop."

Officer Carlos's eyes widened. "I am *not* a bad cop. I'm not—"

Mercy waved her finger in Officer Carlos's face. "Don't you *dare*, Juanita."

I looked from Officer Carlos to Mercy. "What's going on? Might as well let me in. It's not like I can actually *do* anything. Yet."

"So, let's get this party started, shall we?" Mercy said.

I struggled against my restraints. "I am getting out of here, and when I do—"

"You're not going anywhere," Mercy snapped.

Officer Carlos looked at me, and I felt the weight of her gaze. "You can't see it, but there's a very powerful ritual circle on the floor here. I need you to finish what I started."

What? She was a cop. She shouldn't be into this stuff.

Then again, professors and students from the law school were into the dark arts. It was possible.

I looked down at the floor and saw what looked like a dagger, a few vials of liquid, and some herbs, maybe? The room was dim. "What do you need to finish?"

"I'll get there." She circled me, never taking her gaze off mine. I blinked several times. "I want you to know that I did all of this so I could live again. Me and my child." Her hand went to her abdomen, but I didn't see what humans called a "baby bump." I was pretty sure Officer Carlos wasn't pregnant.

Or was she?

"How are you the murderer? You're a cop, and you're on the side of good. Unless you're a dirty cop," I said.

Officer Carlos chuckled. "Wow, you must really be a genius."

"Yeah, but the Tarot ratted you out," I said. "It kept giving us messages and readings. I knew it had to do with a coven, and a ritual."

Officer Carlos frowned. "I did not account for that. But you're here and we're here, so we will continue with the plan."

"And that would be?" I asked, my mouth going dry.

I had to think of something, and fast.

Rick's and David's lives could depend on it.

Mercy spread her heads. "Tonight's ritual. The one where I raise Samantha from the dead and she takes over the coven as High Priestess."

Chapter 18

I STARED AT THEM, dumbfounded. "Raise the dead?"

"I'm a necromancer," Mercy said. "But I need something to power my spell. A sacrifice. That's where you come in. And your Reaper powers will transfer to me, too."

"I don't have any Reaper powers." My stomach twisted. What was she talking about? Were they both crazy?

But then again, I *had* felt Jodie's ghost. Psychics could sense ghosts, so that didn't mean anything.

"You mean you don't know?" Mercy asked, giving me a dumbfounded look of her own. "Your powers are dormant. That's why you had visions. That's also why I had to take them away."

"What? I don't understand," I said. How was that even possible?

"It was a powerful spell to suppress your abilities." Mercy glanced at Officer Carlos. "Took a lot of work, but it was very effective. You were getting close to figuring it out. And we couldn't have that."

"Yeah, right. Besides, I'm fully human. And I like it that way."

Mercy came closer. "But wouldn't you like to reap souls again? Have power? Control over the living and the dead?"

It was tempting, but I'd been lonely and heartless then. I shook my head. "No. I rather like being human and married to a wonderful man. I may even go to college someday." I smiled. "I'm fine the way I am. Really."

"You are too *human* for me." Mercy wrinkled her nose. "Well, soon it won't matter because you'll be dead."

That scared me. I didn't have Reaper powers, and I was fully human, which meant that I could actually die…

As could Rick and David.

But wait. I'd also seen a portal to the Underworld.

Could it be possible?

I didn't know.

My hands clenched into fists. I couldn't die. Not when I was happy, Rick was happy with me, and we had our own little family with Love. And maybe babies someday.

My vision blurred as tears filled my eyes.

I realized that I wanted that. All of it.

I had to fight.

"If it wasn't for that ghost girl, giving you hints…I couldn't control her," Officer Carlos said.

Score one for Team Ashton! I smiled. "Good. Just think, if Lancelot hadn't *murdered* her, you'd be in jail right now."

"I'm not going to jail. Not because some ghost decides to grow a conscience!"

"Well, maybe she took exception to being controlled. I know I would."

"If that's the case, you are going to *hate* this part." Officer Carlos flashed Mercy a smile. "Mercy?"

"So, I have a surprise for you," Mercy said, watching me closely. She pulled a notebook and a fountain pen out of a bag I hadn't noticed she was carrying. She showed them both to me with a flourish, like that Vanna White chick on Wheel of Luck. Except she felt unspeakably evil to my senses.

"What's that for?" I asked. As soon as the words left my mouth, I knew.

Hellfire and a half.

I freaking *knew*.

"No," I said, my throat constricting. "I won't do it!"

"I will force you to do anything I want," Officer Carlos snapped. "Once Mercy lays a compulsion for obedience on you, you'll do anything we ask."

"What's in it for you?" I asked Mercy. "Seems like the good officer here has everything to gain from your hard work." Distract, distract, distract.

"Well, it's very simple," Mercy replied. "We rule the coven together. As High Priestesses."

Something didn't add up. "But Samantha won't want to share power. She got herself knocked up to ensure that." I wanted to antagonize her. Get her thinking. Maybe turn them against each other.

"She will. We have a deal."

"Enough small talk." Officer Carlos, who'd been watching our conversation with interest, clapped her hands to get our attention. That was pointless, as I was already a captive audience. "Mercy, lay the compulsion."

My heart raced. I couldn't let this happen. "Now that I know your game, it'll be harder to compel me."

"It doesn't work like that." Mercy came closer. "This won't hurt you at all. It'll be like going to sleep. Except not."

"Don't fight it," Officer Carlos said. "It hurts more if you do."

I remembered His Highness's compulsion on us Reapers to do our job, and what awful pain I went through with Rick. But I'd rather bear the pain than succumb. Whatever it took to fight.

Because once I stopped fighting, it was game over.

My vision blurred and shadows surrounded us both.

"You will do as Officer Carlos says," Mercy murmured. "You won't be able to fight it. You will be the perfect slave, Leliel. The perfect end to the perfect circle."

Her words reverberated through my mind, echoing and fading, slowing and speeding up. I could feel them in my body like insects burrowing. They were digging into my skin and becoming a part of me.

A tingling feeling spread through my body and...

I felt...wrong.

There was no Leliel. There was only Officer Carlos and her wishes; Mercy and compliance.

I was theirs now.

Officer Carlos came to me, lifted my chin, and smiled with two faces. There was something important about that—

Mercy held up the notebook again. "This is your journal, Leliel. You will write in it what I tell you to write."

"No," I said. My voice was raspy, as if I hadn't spoken in decades.

"We'll see about that," Officer Carlos said with a smile. Again, I got the impression of *two* mouths smiling. I remembered that I needed to figure out why, but it seemed so distant now. So...unimportant. "Since you're a Reaper, Mercy and I decided to give you the VIP treatment. I am going to leave you for a bit so you can think about how you want to spend the last hours of your life." She walked away, Mercy following, and I heard the door close.

What followed was horrific.

There was absolutely no sound. I felt as if I were underwater.

White surrounded me; cocooned me. But I felt anything but safe.

Sometimes I thought I heard voices and footsteps, but I was imagining things.

No one was there.

No one was *ever* there.

I was floating in a sea of nothing.

Everything was so…*white*. So…empty. So not real.

I started to feel like I wasn't actually *there*…that I was slowly disappearing, sinking into the white.

It kept happening.

Every time it happened, I ruthlessly pulled myself back.

I DIDN'T KNOW how long I sat there. It may have been hours; it may have been days. At last, footsteps approached.

I jumped. I'd been dreaming of the white walls collapsing and burying me.

It was time to ask an important question. "Who am I? I am…Leliel. Wife of Rick. Former Grim Reaper."

This time I remembered. Next time, I might not.

More time floated by.

I asked myself again: "Who am I? I am Leliel. Wife of Rick. Former Grim Reaper."

At some point, I thought I heard footsteps. I also thought I was about to be eaten by the white. That the very walls would close on me, and I would cease to exist—

"Who am I?"

Who *was* I?

"Leliel. Wife of…of Rick. Former…something—oh. Grim Reaper."

It was getting harder to remember.

Harder to not imagine those white walls—

Harder to keep myself from freaking out—

Footsteps again. Were they real?

Mercy strode in. I let out a breath of relief.

"How are you, Leliel?" Mercy asked softly. She, too, was wearing white now. Even her hair, which I could have sworn was black, was now white.

She held up a white tray. On it was white rice on a white plate. A small piece of white bread—the crust cut off, because it wasn't white—sat on the edge. "Dinner! *Bon Appetit*!" She left me for a few minutes and came back rolling what looked like a hospital food tray. And it, too, was white. She set the tray on it with a flourish.

She undid the restraints on my left arm. "Can't have you eating like a dog. That wouldn't be VIP treatment now, would it? Ta-ta."

And then she was gone.

She hadn't given me a fork or spoon.

But I realized I was hungry, so I scooped it up with my fingers and ate it. All of it. I felt the white entering my bloodstream, becoming part of me.

I was sure that at some point I'd turn as white as snow.

And that should have bothered me more than it did.

Everything felt so…unreal. Like I was here, but not. I was *really* in a white room in the Underworld. His Highness might do something like this.

"Who am I?" I asked through clenched teeth. "Who…Leliel. I am Leliel."

I could not remember anything but white. My memories…were of all white things, white rooms.

Had I been living in this room forever?

Had I only *thought* I'd had a life outside these walls? There was something else I was missing. Something really important.

I couldn't hear anything. No footsteps. No voices.

Was this it? How I'd spend the rest of my life?

Surely I had a life outside of here…didn't I?

I made a mental note to ask Mercy or Officer Carlos—

Wait.

Officer Carlos. She was important, too. But damned if I could remember *how*.

There were too many holes in my memory.

Hours or days passed.

I kept asking myself who I was. Just to keep myself from forgetting. Over and over again, infinitely, it felt like.

Mercy kept serving me white food on a white plate on a white tray.

"Leliel, Leliel, Leliel," I murmured as I chewed my rice. "Wife of Rick. Former Grim Reaper." I raised my voice. "I. Am. Leliel. Wife. Of. Rick." I put more rice in my mouth. "Former. Grim. Reaper. I will *not* forget."

I WAS LONELY, surrounded by white. Was I floating on a cloud, or in some kind of torture room? I had to get away—

The door flew open.

Mercy and Officer Carlos walked in.

"It is time," Officer Carlos said, "for the next phase to begin."

Mercy stopped in front of me. "What is your name?"

Panic was a knife to my insides. *Who* was I? "Leliel." The name made my stomach flutter and my mouth go dry. "I'm...Rick's wife. And your prisoner?"

Officer Carlos grinned. "Yes, you are. But if you cooperate, we will let you go. How does that sound?"

"Scary. I am used to the white."

Mercy chuckled. "All things that are different are scary, hmm?"

I nodded.

"So, here's what you will do." Officer Carlos held up the white notebook. "You will write what we tell you in this." She held up a white pen. "You will use this pen."

She handed both to me.

I was startled to realize that my left hand had been free this entire time. I'd forgotten. And not once had I thought about trying to escape.

"This is your journal," Officer Carlos said. "You will write your final message to the world."

A feeling of calm acceptance washed over me. This was what I needed to do. What needed to happen.

I sat with the journal in my lap, left hand gripping the pen, poised above the book.

"Are you ready?" Officer Carlos asked.

It sounded like Officer Carlos was speaking with a different voice. It didn't make any sense.

"Who are you? Why does it sound like you have two different voices?" I asked.

Officer Carlos smiled wolfishly. It was unnerving. "I am Samantha Rhodes. And you, my dear, will give me life." Her voice was distinctly different from Officer Carlos's.

I just stared at her. "Huh?" How could that be?

"Open the book," Samantha said.

My hand—damn it!—moved, without my control, toward the book. Deep down, I did not want to do this. I stared at my hand, willing it to *stop*, and it wouldn't.

Hellfire.

I gritted my teeth and tried to force my muscles to move. And they wouldn't.

"I... can't..." I said as my fingers opened the book. I tried to clench my hand into a fist, but it was useless. "I can't!"

"You won't be able to resist," Mercy said with a smile.

My blood ran cold. "I—" I jerked back into my chair, and a tugging feeling overwhelmed me.

"Shall we proceed?" Samantha asked.

Tears filled my eyes. "Hell no!" I took a breath. "I am Leliel, I am Leliel, I am Leliel…"

I dropped the pen.

"What are you doing?" Samantha asked, her eyes boring into me.

"I am trying not to forget."

Samantha frowned. "You aren't supposed to be as lucid as you are. Mercy, what happened?"

Mercy came to where I was sitting, looking at me as if I were a specimen under a microscope. "She has an extraordinary sense of self. She has not allowed herself to forget."

"What does that mean?" Samantha asked, her voice quivering.

"It means," Mercy said, "that she will be harder to control."

Samantha scowled. "Wonderful. Let's continue." To me, she said, "Pick up the pen again."

"No," I whispered as my fingers grasped the pen. I tried to open my hand, pry my damn fingers off the damn pen with will alone, but it just wasn't happening. "Rick..."

"Rick is already dead," Mercy said.

I dropped the pen again, my heart lurching. "No. He…can't be."

Mercy looked me right in the eyes. "Yes, Leliel. You took too long to acclimatize, and even so, you are making it so hard to control you. So we killed him."

My heart lurched. "No…please…"

"Yes," Samantha said. "And you friend is very close to death, too."

"David…"

"Yes, him too."

I couldn't believe it. Rick and I were bonded, so…wouldn't I feel his death? "This…is a trick."

"You didn't feel it because we blocked it from your senses," Mercy said. "We needed the element of surprise. Now will you cooperate? You have nothing to lose."

Was it true?

Anger boiled in my veins. I was helpless, defenseless, and they could have been lying. Or telling the truth. No way to know for sure. Hellfire.

"Fine," I said through clenched teeth.

"Good girl," Mercy murmured. "Now, continue."

Samantha picked up the pen and handed it to me. She felt evil, oily, like Professor—what was her name? The professor…who…the professor—

"Get moving. You're stalling," Mercy said.

I yelped as my fingers clenched the pen too tight. "This hurts!"

"You're getting distracted." Samantha's face hovered in front of me, and I closed my eyes.

"Why does it matter? You're the one controlling my hand!"

"I want you to see and feel everything to its fullest," Samantha explained, oh so patiently. "And you can't when you're distracted."

It felt as if my fingers were being clamped together, stretched to their breaking point. I swallowed down a scream.

"Now write what I say," Samantha continued, grinning evilly. My fingers clamped even tighter. This time, I couldn't hold back the scream. It cut through the silence, through air thick with tension. "Focus." Her breath tickled my ear. "Write this. 'I am so sorry, but I cannot go on like this.'"

"No," I snapped, focusing on not letting my hand—damn it, it set the tip of the pen onto the white page and began to scrawl the words. I watched in horror as it wrote the sentence with no interference from me—even though I was screaming inside. I was screaming and no one could hear me.

"I. Want. To. See. Him," I said through clenched teeth. "I want proof that he's dead."

Samantha and Mercy exchanged a look. Samantha nodded.

"Okay, we'll show you him in his room. Mercy, turn on the feed, please."

Mercy ran off to do that, and Samantha glared at me.

I...didn't like that look. "Why... are you looking at me like that?"

"So sentimental," she said. "I was like that once. And it turned out to be my greatest downfall. Love can get you killed. Or worse." She brought her hand down to her abdomen and sighed. "Continue!" She pinched the nape of my neck. It felt like I was home, back a long time ago, getting taught at school and being punished for not listening... "'The loss of my Reaper powers has been too much for me to bear—'"

"No one's…going to believe…" She was insane if she thought it mattered. That anyone would think it mattered *that* much, enough to burn myself to death.

Samantha was suddenly in my face, and I was up close and personal with her eyes. They were two empty pits. Lovely. "But you *do* care, don't you? Deep down."

I hesitated. Did I care? Did it matter?

Well...my stomach twisted. I did miss it on some level, even though it was a loveless, lonely existence.

I shrugged. "I guess. Reaping souls is the only thing I know how to do." Tears filled my eyes, against my will, but it wasn't the compulsion. This whole time I'd been wanting to be like everyone else, a true wife to Rick who cooked and cleaned and didn't burn casseroles, an independent woman who could get herself anywhere she needed to go…a woman who knew the value of money…was I doomed to failure because reaping souls was all I knew? Would I ever be normal?

I didn't want to cry in front of this bitch. She'd just use it against me. I blinked a few times, took a deep breath, and prepared to fight.

Again.

The screen flared to life.

And there was Rick, looking like he was sleeping peacefully. Ironically, he was also in a white room.

"Is he alive or dead? I can't tell." When I searched inward for our bond, I couldn't feel it.

"He's gone," Samantha said.

Something inside me snapped. "How could you do such a horrible thing? He didn't deserve to die!"

He was too young. And Love…she'd be devastated…

Our little family. No more.

Tears filled my eyes again, and it felt as if my heart was breaking.

Samantha's eyes narrowed. "Okay, write this down. 'The loss of my Reaper powers has left me without a purpose and—'"

"No!" I focused all of my energy on making my hand stop moving the pen. The words blurred and drifted in my vision, and all I could think of was that Rick, if he'd been alive, would have known the truth. And now he was gone.

My hand continued to scrawl the words on the page. *Scratch, scratch.* The sound was about to give me a nervous twitch.

"It's a perfect reason to die, don't you think?" Mercy asked.

"Yes, that's it!" Samantha smiled. "Write this! 'I wish to return to the Underworld where I can be of use to'—what's his name?"

"His Highness," I muttered, watching the pen scratch against the page.

"Doesn't he have a name?" Mercy asked. She was just standing there, watching the show. Anger made me clench my teeth.

"We've always called him 'His Highness.' He's the supreme ruler of the Underworld, and there's no one else, so there's no point in worrying about a name."

"Tsk, tsk, someone's irritable." Mercy came to me, wrinkling her nose. "You should try to be more cheerful. You may be home before you know it."

"Soon, my dear, soon," Samantha said softly.

Mercy said, "We should say something about Rick's death. Let's see… 'Losing Rick has broken my heart. Leliel.'"

Tears ran down my face. "I won't write that."

"You don't have a choice, dear," Samantha said with a grin. "Haven't you realized that by now?"

I wrote it.

"Have you finished yet?" Samantha asked me.

I flicked my gaze to her. "Yep." I leaned forward as far as I could go. "I promise you this. I am not going quietly or willingly. You will have to force me, and even then...I will stop you. I don't know how, but I will. And then you and Mercy will go down. Preferably in flame. Fitting, don't you think?"

"Shut up," Samantha snapped. "We're not dying by fire. *You are.*"

I had to keep her talking. "Why are you so angry?"

"Angry?" Samantha's face twisted, became ugly. "You're asking me why *I* am angry?" She looked at Mercy. "Can you believe it?"

"For real?" Mercy asked.

Samantha faced me again. "I am angry because Fred burned me to death while Shelby and Mark laughed and my baby died," Samantha said through clenched teeth. Her eyes glistened with tears. "My life and my baby's life were stolen away from me because of some stupid coven thing. Because of Pamela and her obsession with power. I wish I had never joined." She wiped her cheeks with sharp motions. "But I was in too deep. I couldn't just get out. Not when I was close to having it all."

Fred had murdered her?

"Fred killed you?" I asked. "Is that what you're saying?"

"Yes," Samantha snapped. "And I killed him—and the others—for revenge."

"Oh," I said. "Why did they do that?"

Samantha started pacing. "Freddie didn't like that I was pregnant. Said I'd ruin his life, his future. So he wanted to get rid of it. And me." She sighed.

"That's awful," I said. "But revenge is never the answer."

Samantha's hands curled into fists. "It is for me. Now we can change things. Leliel, you will give me more power. More power than I ever had while I was alive. And Mercy will bring me back to life."

That was wasn't going to happen on my watch. "I will fight you with every breath I take."

"Try it, sister," Samantha said with a laugh. "You can't fight me when you're tied to a chair!"

"I'll find a way," I said. "Your power is about to go up in flames."

Samantha glared at me. "You don't understand. Power is everything, especially at the college. Doors would open up to me that never would have otherwise. I could have my pick of High Priests." She cast a longing glance at the screen. "It's a damn shame he isn't a witch. He is a fine specimen."

Wait a sec. She'd used *present tense*. Maybe it was a mistake but...could Rick actually be alive?

My heart raced. I hoped I was right.

I smiled. "He is, isn't he? But he's a plain old human being. Works in a garage. Likes coffee and cookies."

Samantha made a disgusted look. "Whatever." She seemed to compose herself, smoothing her shirt and fussing with her hair. "It's time we continue. No more distractions!"

Mercy came up to me and held her hand out. "The journal, please."

I closed it, feeling as if my fate was already sealed. I was going to die. Unless I could make something happen.

"Here you go." I handed it to Mercy. She thumbed through it and gave Samantha a thumbs-up gesture. "Next is the lighter fluid," Samantha said.

And it hit me.

I was about to die.

Just like in my vision.

Chapter 19

"You know, you could just let this all go," I said. "I know you want revenge but look at all the horrible things you had to do just to accomplish it. And will you truly be happy afterward?" I licked my dry lips. Somehow, I doubted she'd *ever* be happy. "And what about your child?"

"My child will be a Reaper," Samantha said, touching her abdomen again. "That's where you come in, Leliel."

"No child should have to bear the pain I've had to bear," I said. "It was a horrible, lonely life. Best to leave her human. Give her the best life you can give her."

Samantha rolled her eyes at me. "Yes, but she'll have power over the living *and* the dead. She'll be unstoppable. Naturally, I will guide her to do the right things."

She suddenly appeared to have two bodies. One was a ghost. Samantha? So…all this time, the people who'd had second bodies were being controlled by Samantha? The guy in the police station? The guy in the car?

What about Mrs. Allison? Had she been compelled by Mercy or Samantha? My head throbbed as I tried desperately to puzzle it all out.

"You've been controlling people, haven't you?" I asked. "I've been seeing people with two bodies for awhile now. And I haven't been able to figure it out. Until now."

Samantha scoffed. "You have such a vivid imagination. Controlling people, how crazy."

"You might as well admit it," Mercy suggested, glancing at me. "She's going to die anyway. Give her a moment of victory."

Samantha shrugged. "Sure, why not?" Her eyes met mine. "Yes, I was controlling people. It was so *much* fun. They'd do anything while under my control. Like that mother who snapped." She laughed. "And you actually believed it! And the guy in the car! You were so easy to fool, Leliel. I had expected more from you."

Rage grew within me as I thought about what she'd done. Controlling people. Making people burn themselves to death. That poor child. Growing up with Samantha as a mother.

I had to stop her. Not just for us, but for her child, and for the coven.

Something had to be done…what, I wasn't quite sure.

Mercy went to a cabinet and pulled out a few plastic containers. They looked like the lighter fluid in my vision.

She grinned at me. "Nothing but the best for our Reaper Girl." She handed Samantha one.

"Don't. Call. Me. That," I snapped.

"You need to understand…you will always be a Reaper," Mercy said. "Your powers are part of your soul."

"I. Am. Not. A. Reaper!"

Just then something cold and wet hit me. And a pungent smell.

Lighter fluid.

My stomach twisted. This was it.

I was going to die.

Samantha uncurled my hand and placed a lighter in it. "Whenever you are ready, Reaper Girl."

My hand moved on its own. It held the lighter up and one finger got ready to light it.

I tried so hard to stop it.

But I couldn't. I freaking couldn't—

A *snick* as I lit it.

As I felt the burning kiss of flame, I cried out Rick's name.

SOMETIMES I think the mind tries to keep you from feeling horrific pain, especially when it is for the second or third time. So at first I felt kind of numb.

Death had its claws in me tight. I could feel everything inside me slowly shut down, my body losing life. I was taken back to that day so long ago when I'd died the first time. It felt as if my entire body were being flayed at once. I couldn't think past it. My vision blurred and I fought to stay conscious.

Pain…searing me. My soul…being torn from me.

Nothing could save me. I was cast adrift on a sea, a sea that tried to pull me under with every breath.

I was hurting, my brain was shutting down, and I wished I could have told Rick that I loved him one last time.

The pain made me weak. Distantly, I remembered something about stopping, dropping, and rolling. My vision was growing hazy, and I was so hot, and there was smoke everywhere. Every nerve ending singed, bringing a pain I couldn't even describe, except that it was all-encompassing, horrible, and searing.

My back bowed with the pain, my skin feeling as if it were melting. I was losing consciousness…

The absence of feeling was a pain all its own.

Memories flashed by: my childhood; my first kiss of fire and death; reaping souls, so damn many; meeting Rick when I accidently reaped his soul…and everything that came after: our small wedding on the beach, Love, me moving into his apartment with nothing but the clothes on my back; our first week together, how wonderful and perfect and lovely. How it was not at all how I imagined love could be, but in a totally good way.

I was dying.

I was about to lose all of that.

I didn't want to let it go.

I needed to live. Somehow.

But how?

Racking my brain, I tried to think of some way not to die.

And came up empty.

I was running out of time. To live. To save Rick and David. If they were still alive.

And it was getting harder and harder to think through the pain—

I closed my eyes and let the fire take me.

"Leliel!" a voice cried. A familiar voice.

I opened my eyes.

And saw my living room. In our apartment. What was I doing there? And Love was there, too, but she looked translucent...like a ghost kitty.

"Leliel!" Rick ran into the room, and he, too, was translucent.

Did this mean that he was dead? That Love was dead? Was I dead?

I looked down. I was translucent as well.

Hellfire.

My heart damn near shattered.

"Leliel!" Rick grabbed my shoulders. He could somehow do that without his hands going through me. Neat trick. "Listen to me. I don't have much time. I need you to focus."

"Rick, are we dead?" I asked, looking into his eyes. Or what were supposed to be his eyes.

"No, not yet. We're sort of hovering between life and death. You have to use your powers to reap Samantha's soul."

"What powers?" I asked.

"Your Reaping powers," Rick said slowly. "I believe you still have them."

David walked into the room, also translucent. "Hi…what are we doing here?"

Rick glanced at him. "Long story. Just roll with it."

"I don't have any powers," I said. Just for fun, I searched within myself…and found a whole lot of nothing. "They are gone. His Highness took them away."

"No. You still have them. I'm sure of it." Rick was *really* looking at me now. Like he was trying to see inside me. He'd be disappointed. "You've been seeing visions. You saw a portal to the Underworld…"

"You're wrong," I said. "Face it. We're all dead."

"I refuse to believe that," Rick said.

Okay, now I was getting irritated. "Why? Rick, I'm human."

Rick squeezed my shoulders, and I could have sworn I felt his love warming me from the inside. "That's because you're still a Reaper. Look inside yourself. Go deep. You can do this. I believe in you."

"I believe in you, too," David said. "Even though I have *no* idea what you two are talking about."

Maybe it wouldn't hurt to look. One more time. "Okay."

"Excellent," Rick said.

I closed my eyes and searched. And searched. I looked *everywhere.* In every corner of my mind, every place in my soul.

And…I caught the faintest glimmer of something. I tried to grab it, bring it closer to the forefront of my mind, but it slipped through my fingers like sand.

I opened my eyes. "You're right. There's something there. But I can't touch it."

"Maybe it's blocked," Rick said. He rubbed my shoulders, and the tension I was feeling began to drain away.

"Maybe. But we have to be fast. My body is dying."

"What's—" David started.

Pain took me to my knees. The carpet dug into my skin. I took a deep breath and let it out. I had to get this figured out, and fast.

I glanced at Rick. "Help me." I held out my hand.

He took it and kissed my knuckles. "What's happening?"

"I'm feeling it here. The fire," I said, gritting my teeth.

"I can't let you die!" Rick cried. "Fight it!"

David walked over to us. "Can I help?"

"Yes. Hold her other hand," Rick said. "I suspect that she needs all the energy and love she can get."

I nodded, hurting too much to say anything.

Closing my eyes, I held on to both of them as tightly as I could without breaking their bones. That would be horrifically unproductive.

I searched again. And again. And again.

Death came quickly. And I knew the precise moment when it happened.

I let go of their hands.

And I fell into darkness.

I WAS NOWHERE and everywhere all at once. In the distance, I could hear the flames…but I didn't feel the pain of being burnt anymore.

Maybe it was all over.

I blinked.

A hooded figure was walking toward me. I couldn't see a face, and my heart rate spiked. Was it His Highness? Why would he be here? I was dead, right?

I wasn't sure I wanted the answer to that question.

As the figure came closer, I busied myself with a system check. I could feel my body. I could take my pulse, so blood was being pumped. I could see, and possibly hear—I wasn't hearing anything at the moment, though. I could feel pain. Yeah. A little post-death advice: don't pinch yourself multiple times. It actually freaking hurts.

I wasn't warm or cold. My feet were bare. I was wearing the same clothes I'd died in.

No burns at all.

My skin was as smooth as silk.

So…

The figure stopped in front of me and inclined its head. "Greetings, Leliel."

"Greetings. To what do I owe the pleasure of this unexpected meeting?"

I still wasn't seeing a face, but the voice was definitely male. He didn't give off His Highness vibes, though. So maybe a servant? A representative? Like His Highness would actually deign to come in person to this weird non-place and talk to me.

"I have come to make you an offer," the representative said. "His Highness asked me to speak with you."

So, yeah, a rep. "Okay. But first…am I actually dead?"

"Not yet," he said. "You're close. We've got about five minutes before—"

"Right," I said quickly. "Lay it on me."

"You realize—at least we hoped you realized—that you retained some of your Reaper powers."

So Rick had been right. That was...good. Maybe. Depending on this offer.

"Yes." I wanted to know more, but I was about to die.

"His Highness would like you to formally swear fealty to him and become a Reaper in full again."

I blinked at him. "No, I can't. I like being human."

"Then you will die," the representative said.

"But I don't want to die," I protested. We were wasting time.

The representative sighed, his shoulders slumping. "Why must you make everything so difficult? Accept His Highness's deal, and you may live. Simple. And we're down to two minutes."

My head spun. So this was what this was about. He wanted me back as a Reaper, even though our previous deal had been to let me be human. If I didn't agree, I'd die. I'd become one of many wandering souls in the Underworld, untethered and without purpose.

That wasn't going to work.

If I died, I'd lose my family. The life I'd built. I'd never see Rick or Love again.

"Will I get to stay on Earth with my family?" I asked. Agreeing to be a Reaper would be meaningless if I had to return to the Underworld.

"His Highness prefers not," the representative said. "Reapers live in the Underworld, as you recall."

"Let me live on Earth with my family and you have a deal."

"No, that's not—"

"That is the *only* way I'm going to do this. I live with my family on Earth or I die."

"His Highness says no. Time's almost up."

"Then I am dead," I said. It was gamble I hoped would pay off.

"His Highness says he wants you as a Reaper and not dead," the representative said with a sigh. "So, he will make an exception this one time."

I smiled. The choice was easy now.

"Just one more thing," I said. "His Highness and I had a deal. I was to be human. What about that?"

"If you want to live, you must sacrifice something," the representative said. "One and a half minutes."

"Okay, fine, I'll do it," I said.

"Swear fealty."

Crap. Could I speak fast enough? Time to see. "I swear fealty to His Highness, King of the Underworld. I am his humble servant. Long may he reign."

"It is done."

I WOKE TO THE sound of people talking.

"I swear, her chest is moving."

"It can't be. She's *dead*. You're imagining things."

"I don't know, Sam. My sensing says she's still alive."

"Well, I guess it doesn't matter now. She probably won't be the same. I took a lot out of her. Almost everything. Including her Reaper powers."

That piqued my interest.

I cracked open one eye.

"Her eye opened!"

"Sure, sure. Wait—it *is* open. Leliel, can you hear me?"

I opened the other one. Blurry shapes in front of me resolved into three human shapes. "Wha—"

"It's alllliiiiive!" cried one of the women. I wrinkled my nose. I remembered that that had something to do with a monster. A scary monster.

My vision normalized. Three women stood around me, blocking my view of the rest of the room. It was still white, though, and my heart lurched.

No more white, please.

There was something important about this. I had to remember—oh wait. I was trying to find my Reaper powers when—

"What should we do with her?" one of the women asked the others. "I don't understand why she's not dead!"

"She won't be a problem anymore," another woman said. She had long, brown hair and green eyes. And she was pregnant, so she had to be Samantha. "I have my ways of disposing of pesky people."

I assumed I was a "pesky person." How sweet.

I had to reap her soul before she "disposed" of me, assuming I still could. If I she was still alive when I reaped her soul, she'd become a Reanimate—invisible to the world, cursed to wander forever, never able to rest.

Which was worse than anything else I could ever do to her.

I stood, a bit shakily. The three women backed up. "What have you done?" I asked. My hands caught my eye, and it dawned on me that I wasn't burnt. My face and hair didn't feel burnt, either.

Samantha glared at me. "I killed you. But you don't seem to be able to die. Or get burnt."

"How are you walking and talking right now? And not burnt!" Mercy said. She turned to Samantha. "I thought we figured this out. That it would be foolproof."

I smiled. "I thought I was dead, too. Guess we were both wrong."

"I'll just kill you again," Samantha said. "We'll use magic this time. I'd wanted so badly for you to feel as I did, dying by fire, but clearly it's not going to work."

"Are you sure it'll work now?" Mercy asked, her eyes narrowed. "I know of a few spells we could use to accelerate the burning process."

"That sounds good," Samantha said.

I didn't care, because it was very likely that I'd come back.

Which meant…I must have Reaper powers after all.

I thought about the six victims, and myself. How horrible dying by fire was, and how much they had all suffered. For what? For Samantha to get revenge on those who'd killed her? I got that, I really did. Maybe if I'd been different I'd feel the same. But killing people was never the answer.

And yet…I should probably kill her. Just so she wouldn't become a Reanimate. I had mercy, unlike her.

"How do you want to do it?" Officer Carlos asked. She still had a double body, which meant that Samantha was still controlling her.

"Fire, of course!" Mercy said. "I think we have some lighter fluid left."

A plan formed in my mind. It was going to be tough, but I only had one shot. And I doubted His Highness would allow me to make another deal.

This was it.

I needed something to kindle the flames. Something really flammable.

My cloak! As much as I loved it, it'd be perfect for my plan.

But where was it?

The three women were still talking, paying little attention to me. I slipped away and started looking for my cloak.

It was a small room. It had to be in here.

What if it wasn't?

I refused to let myself think that way. It was here, and I needed to find it. Fast.

Walking along the perimeter of the room, I lifted every white sheet-turned-curtain. Something told me it was near, but hidden, because they wanted everything to be white. I was almost to the other side when Mercy caught me.

"What are you doing? You can't leave—"

"It's okay. If she leaves, she'll never be able to save her husband and friend," Samantha said with an evil grin. "I won't be calling you with instructions on how to find them. So your best bet would be to stay."

So they were alive!

"Stay and die, you mean?" I asked, stalling for time. I lifted up another sheet. Nothing. I moved toward the desk.

"Whatever. Your call, Reaper Girl."

I was in front of the desk drawers now. There were three on each side. I opened each in turn. Nothing, nothing, nothing.

Hellfire. Maybe it was gone.

No. It was here.

I opened the first drawer on the opposite side. No cloak.

"What are you doing?" Officer Carlos asked.

I shrugged. "Wasting time. Waiting for you to get your acts together and kill me."

"No way would you just *wait* for it," Mercy chimed in, her eyes narrowed. "You've got something planned."

Second drawer. Nothing. "And what if I do? You've got magic. Magic trumps Reaper powers every time."

"Maybe," she replied, drawing out the word. "Sam, we have a problem..."

Third drawer. A ball of black cloth sat inside. I reached out and touched it, my heart fluttering.

It was my cloak!

I grabbed it and shut the drawer. The three women were headed toward me.

Hanging onto my cloak with a death grip, I headed for them, a smile on my face.

We met in the middle of the room.

"I'm ready to die," I said, glancing at Samantha. "I'd like you to do the honors."

"What the hell?" Mercy asked. "What is that in your hand?"

I tried to look and sound casual. "My Reaper cloak. I'd like to be wearing it when I die. I'm very sentimental."

"You're obviously not in your right mind," Officer Carlos said, her eyes wide with fear.

I crooked my index finger at Samantha. "Come here. Look into my eyes while you do it."

Samantha glanced at Officer Carlos and Mercy and shrugged. They shrugged, too, as if to say they had no idea what to do.

Excellent.

Samantha stepped forward.

I did two things at once. I threw the cloak onto Samantha, hoping the fabric covered her eyes, effectively blinding her. And I pushed the other two women as hard as I could with my free hand.

So they'd hopefully fall and take some time to regroup.

Samantha screamed, clawing at the fabric. "Noooooo! Noooo!"

"You bitch," Mercy snapped from her place on the floor. She tried to untangle herself from Officer Carlos.

I focused on finding the lighter. It had to be around here somewhere.

Officer Carlos was standing. I had to hurry.

My chair! It had to be near my chair!

I headed in that direction, keeping the officer in the corner of my eye. Mercy was still struggling. Maybe she was injured?

That worked.

I didn't see the lighter underneath my chair.

Samantha was still screaming, and the cloak covered her head and was twisted around her shoulders now. She was trying to move, but the fabric still blinded her.

Someone tackled me from behind, and we hit the floor hard, pain flaring in my hip and wrist. Damn!

"You're not going to hurt her!" Officer Carlos screamed, so loud my ears hurt. I tried to stand, but the officer kept grabbing my arms. And shoulders.

I got one hand free and felt around on the floor for the lighter. Horribly inefficient, but I had to do *something*. Where the hell was it?

Officer Carlos straddled me on my back and pummeled my shoulders with her fists. Hellfire. It felt like being hit by a boulder. Several boulders. She was strong!

Samantha was able to get my cloak untwisted, but she was still blind.

Mercy hobbled toward me. "Stop! I will force you if you don't!"

Yeah, now I really had to move. She could use magic on me—

What was that golden thing over there? By the door?

Hellfire.

I'd never make it. And as soon as they figured out what I was doing, they'd grab it before I could.

This was *not* over. I just had to find a way to get out from underneath Officer Carlos and somehow not let on to Mercy what I was doing. Although she was moving rather slowly…

I jerked sharply to the side. Officer Carlos fell, hitting the floor with an awful-sounding *crack*. She didn't get up.

One down, one to go.

I stood and headed for the lighter, my shoulders burning.

"I know what you're doing," Mercy said as she hobbled toward me. "It won't work."

I was almost there. "Really? Samantha's made of flesh and blood, right? She can burn." I bent over and grabbed it. I spun around. Mercy was right in front of me.

How did she—

She slammed her fist into my stomach.

I dropped the lighter.

As I fell, I saw Samantha with most of my cloak off of her.

Hellfire.

I hit the floor hard, the air leaving my lungs all at once.

The room spun.

I reached out my hand, hanging on to consciousness as everything swam around me. I had to finish this.

"Do you really think," Mercy said, looking down at me with a smirk, "that you can best me?"

"No," I rasped, still feeling for the lighter. I had to keep her occupied. "Did you…hurt yourself?"

"Twisted my ankle." She shrugged. Maybe. It was hard to tell with everything going in and out of focus. "What's it to you?"

I kept searching. It had to be nearby. "Curious." *Think of something, anything!* "They won't go easy on you, Mercy. Best to turn yourself in."

My fingers touched steel. I grabbed the lighter and hid it in my palm.

"Turn myself in? Are you stupid? Why would I do that?"

"Would be better." I sat up and pushed her with everything I had.

Mercy fell backward and the room spun again.

I could see Samantha still fighting with my cloak.

Vertigo stopped all ideas of standing. I fixed my eyes on my cloak—a target—and crawled toward it. Ignoring the pain in my stomach and shoulders, the hard floor on my knees and elbows, the panic that was rising up my throat every second I fought to get to Samantha.

"You dumb bitch!" Samantha screamed, and my cloak fluttered to the floor.

No. No, no, no!

I crawled faster, gritting my teeth.

"You can't kill me!" Samantha said. "I'm immortal."

"Really?" I said roughly. My tongue felt like sandpaper.

I kept crawling.

"The spell not only brought me back to life, but it gave me the ability to suffer any wound and not die."

What, she was bragging now? How special.

At long last, I made it.

With much difficulty, I stood. She blurred in and out, and the room pitched forward. As I fell, again, I grabbed the edge of my cloak.

I looked up at Samantha. "Prove it." I lit the cloak and threw it at her.

It hit her, and the flame grew. Smoke filled the room as the fire devoured her.

She screamed incoherently.

Just how immortal was she?

I said a prayer for forgiveness. It was an awful way to die. But being a Reanimate was far, far worse. She would probably thank me.

Okay. Maybe not.

Mercy had somehow managed to get here, and frantically tried to put out the flames. Maybe she was doing it with magic, because she had nothing to put the flames out with. Every once in a while, she'd shoot me a dirty look or two. I just smiled.

I moved a bit closer. "I am giving you…mercy," I said as Samantha shrieked and flailed. "If I reap your soul now, you'll wish that you were dead and you would live forever in a truly horrible state. But I have to kill you first so you'll go to the Underworld. You'll be whole. So. Stop. Fighting. It. Mercy, stop!"

I was running out of energy. Apparently dying and coming back to life took a lot out of a girl. Who knew?

Mercy tried doing whatever she was doing, but after Samantha stopped screaming, she gave up, watching as the flames took more and more of Samantha. She'd stopped giving me dirty looks but didn't once look at me.

I tried to feel pity, but all I could do was think about how she'd hurt so many people, including me.

Silence descended as the flames lessened. Samantha was a burnt, blackened mass.

It didn't look like a human body anymore.

"Is she dead? Oh, no. What have I done?" Mercy held her head in her hands, her face in a grimace.

"Well, you've been involved in a horrible thing, and you're probably going to jail for it," I said. "Unless you can convince a judge that you were not in your right mind. But wait. No evidence." I gave her a serene smile. "Hope your magic works better in jail than it does here."

Officer Carlos walked over to me slowly, as if she were in pain. "What happened? What am I doing here? And did you just kill this woman?"

I looked at what used to be Samantha. "I am about to reap her soul."

Officer Carlos's eyes widened. "I...don't understand."

"You *can't*," Mercy pleaded. "Please..."

I made a dismissive gesture. "Just let me work. I am giving her mercy. She doesn't deserve it, but I am a merciful person. Unlike her." I knelt down and glanced back up at Officer Carlos. "This is going to look really weird. Just bear with me, okay? It only takes a few seconds." Without waiting for her answer, I bent down.

And kissed the least burnt part of the mass. I tasted ashes, this time for real.

Her soul, warm and sweet, filled my mouth. It felt like singing, like joy, like chocolate and roller coasters and making love with Rick all at once.

I didn't understand how such a horrible person could have such a beautiful soul.

It just went to show that there was the potential for good in all of us.

I stood. Officer Carlos was staring at me. "You…kissed *that*? And something went into your mouth? Am I hallucinating?"

I shook my head grimly. "No. You saw her soul." I pointed at Mercy, who shrank back. "I think you should arrest her. Accessory to murder, I think. I'm not up on all the terminology. But she was definitely part of it."

Officer Carlos's eyes narrowed. "I'm not…sure."

"Attempted murder?" I asked. "Something!"

"I can try." She pulled out handcuffs from her belt. Slowly. "Mercy—what's your last name?"

Mercy looked as if she were headed to her own execution. She wouldn't even look us in the eyes. "Hillington."

"Mercy Hillington, you are under arrest for attempted murder. Anything you say can and will be used in a court of law…"

One tear dripped down Mercy's cheek.

"Hey," I said softly after Officer Carlos was done. "It could be worse. You could be dead." I glanced at the burnt mass and wished she hadn't done what she'd done.

I glanced at Mercy. "Mind telling me where I can find my husband and friend?"

At first, it looked like Mercy wasn't going to tell me, but then she let out an exaggerated sigh. "Okay, *fine*. There's a conference room upstairs."

"Okay." My eyes narrowed when she didn't say anything else. "And?"

Now she *really* looked put out. "There's..." She glanced at Officer Carlos, who arched a brow in question. "There's a fire up there. If you don't go *right now*, they will both die."

Hellfire! I took off running, not even knowing the direction I needed to go. My heart raced, my throat seized up, my head spun, and I was terrified I was going to be too late.

That Rick and David would be burnt and dead when I got there.

But...

White walls.

All around me. Collapsing on me—

Think, Leliel, think! They were upstairs—

More white.

I slid to the ground and curled up. I couldn't make myself freaking *move*—

A stray thought...

I am Leliel. Wife of Rick. Grim Reaper.

And...Rick needed me, damn it! And David!

Slowly, I stood.

And ran.

Chapter 20

IT SEEMED LIKE forever before I made it to Rick and David. I was sure I was late, that I'd failed them. The fire was everywhere, smoke made me cough, and I wasn't sure *where* the room was—

I got down, remembering that smoke inhalation could be dangerous. I'd already died from fire twice, so it didn't really scare me anymore. But losing Rick and David?

I couldn't breathe through my fear.

"Rick! David!" I cried.

Where was the freaking room? Here? I bumped into a wall. There? No, that was a door.

I couldn't see anything through the flames and smoke.

"Leliel!"

It was Rick! I could hear him!

"Rick! I'm here! Keep talking!" I spun around, trying to figure out where his voice was coming from—

Everything spun around me, and I stumbled. But didn't fall, thankfully.

"Baby, I'm here! Room two forty-five! We're trying to find our way out!"

Room two forty-five?

I went to the nearest door and looked for the number through the smoke…two forty-one.

So he was just down the hall!

I coughed and coughed and coughed. My lungs felt like they were on fire and I ran into something—

Hands clamped on my wrists. "Leliel?"

"Rick!" I groped around for him and finally embraced him, feeling his warmth, sinking into him—

"We need to move," David said from somewhere. "Link hands!"

I took hold of Rick's hand, and I assumed that Rick linked with David. "Are we ready?"

"I was born ready," Rick said.

And little by little, we made our way downstairs and out the door, where firefighters were congregating.

Someone had called 911.

Paramedics approached us and offered to check us out.

I was just glad to be alive. That Rick and David weren't dead.

That I'd made it. I wasn't too late.

That was all that mattered, now.

"So glad you're okay," Rick said. "I don't know what I would have done if you'd died."

I glanced up at him. "How did you—"

"Best I can tell, whatever magic was holding us in an unconscious state was released somehow," Rick said. "Although I am a bit confused. David told me that I was unconscious from a bomb exploding near me."

David shrugged. "I had to tell him."

I looked at Rick. "You were in a coma after the bomb at Ms. Chandler's house exploded near you. Do you remember any of that?"

Rick shook his head. "No, I don't. I'm sorry I wasn't there to help."

"No, you don't have to apologize. I managed," I said with a smile. "Although I missed you terribly."

Officer Carlos approached, clearing her throat. "Glad you all made it out alive. I can't believe…Samantha…"

Rick turned to me. "What happened?"

"Samantha was the mastermind," I said. I explained what I'd learned, and Rick's jaw dropped. I finished with, "And I took take care of her. The same thing she did to the others."

"Awesome. But revenge and a baby? Never would have thought that would be enough to hurt people the way she did."

"I should get going," Officer Carlos said. "See that police car over there? Mercy's in there, and she's getting restless."

Chapter 21

SO MERCY WAS in prison, awaiting arraignment. Officer Carlos was allowed to come back to work but was given mandatory therapy. Because having someone control your every thought and action was deemed traumatizing.

I could honestly see why, having been compelled myself.

My first time back at the apartment, I had a serious issue.

We walked in, and—

"Oh no," I whispered, grabbing Rick's hand. "The walls are white!" I had completely forgotten.

I felt as if I were back in the school, feeling like the white would consume me—

I went to my knees, covering my eyes. "I can't—I have to go—"

"Leliel? It's okay. You're home. You're not going to be hurt anymore," Rick said, taking my hands in his and helping me stand. "You're with me now. I will keep you safe."

I nodded, putting my head on his chest, breathing in his smell of oil and earthiness. "Can we paint them?"

"I'm not sure that's allowed," Rick said. "Usually when you rent a place like this, you can't do anything permanent."

"We can paint them white again if we ever want to move out," I said, pulling Rick closer. Hell, I never got tired of this. Love wove her way between our legs, meowing mournfully.

"I can't stand looking at them."

"Can you talk about it yet?" Rick ran his fingertips down my cheek, and I shivered. "Only if you can. I don't want you going through any more pain."

I withdrew and looked him in the eyes. If I focused on his eyes, I wouldn't see the white. "It was horrible. Everything was white. At one point, I believed the walls were going to collapse and bury me. And I couldn't hear anything. It sure made me feel unbalanced." My hands clenched into fists. "I kept forgetting who I was."

"I'm so sorry."

"Thanks. I decided to say my name every single time I started to forget. I think the objective was to turn me into a super obedient slave. Fortunately, I didn't let that happen."

"Because you are really strong. And to be burnt again..." Rick pulled me close again. "I'm sorry I wasn't there to protect you."

"You were in a coma. I can give you a pass. You did visit me, though, while I was dying."

Rick's jaw dropped. "I did?"

I nodded. "You were the one that made me realize I still had Reaper powers. Without that, I never would have made it back."

"Wow. I don't really—yeah, you know, I *do* remember flashes of something. I just assumed it was a dream."

"It wasn't. You saved us all," I said, smiling. We kissed, one of those sweet, semi-chaste kisses that promised more. When we separated, I said, "How do you feel about me being a Reaper again? Or, rather, being a Reaper when we thought I was human?"

Rick led me to the sofa, and we both sat down. Thankfully, it wasn't white. I tried not to look at the walls.

Love jumped up and got onto my lap, purring away. I petted her, and she licked my fingers.

He took my hands in his. "I really don't care. I mean, I'm happy for you, but you're still you. And…this is gonna sound crazy, but I'm glad that you won't die. I was so worried about everything, stupid stuff that I thought would kill you and take you away from me…"

"I get it. But you're going to die at some point." My eyes filled with tears. "What we need to do is have the best life we can possibly have. And then, well…" I shrugged. "I may go back to the Underworld or something…"

"Will I see you again? After I…die?" Rick asked. He squeezed my hands, so hard, as if he didn't want to ever let go.

"I'll try to see you somehow." Honestly, I wasn't sure I could do that, but no use in saying that now. I had many years to research it. Maybe talk to His Highness. He might be merciful this go around. "Anyway, that's what saved me from burning to death. And," I added as something occurred to me, "that is also why I was able to be compelled. I believed I was human. I never once thought to check inside. To search for my powers."

"I had a feeling all along, especially after you saw the portal. But I didn't want to push. And then I apparently *had* to push because...I seem to remember you emphatically denying the existence of any powers."

"I did. I refused to believe it. I wanted to be human," I said. "But that's not in the cards for me, I guess."

"We need to celebrate. How about some margaritas, tacos, and flan?" Rick stood and led me to the kitchen.

"I would love that." I pulled him close, savoring his warmth and his *life*. "But can we start with dessert, then have tacos?"

Rick kissed me, and I forgot how to breathe. Good thing I was immortal. "Absolutely."

"NOW, DO YOU WANT to press charges against Ms. Chandler?" I asked Rick the next morning. We were sharing leftover flan and drinking coffee. Love had milk, naturally.

Rick nodded. "Absolutely. She should pay for what she's done."

So we went to the police station, which was starting to feel like home. We saw David, who personally took care of our paperwork.

"So, how you doing?" David asked, looking concerned. "What an ordeal."

"It wasn't pleasant," I admitted. "But Samantha can do no damage any longer, so it's a win."

"And how are you?" Rick asked.

David took a breath, then released it. "Hanging in there. Trying to believe that magic exists. It's a bit weird." He lowered his voice. "I also heard from Juanita that you did something…?"

I felt my face flush. It was weird talking openly about this. "Yeah. Long story. Basically? She's dead." I shrugged.

"I will pretend I did not hear that," the detective said. He stapled some papers together. "You're all set. I'll keep you posted on everything."

I smiled. "Great, thank you. You've been a big help."

"So have you two. Solving the case was no small feat. You should be proud of yourselves."

Rick turned a nice shade of red. "Thanks. Just wanted to see justice done."

Okay, this was getting awkward. "Well…we'll see you around?"

"Absolutely. Maybe we can get together and have drinks sometime."

"Sure. Sounds like fun," I said. We waved our goodbyes and Rick and I left.

"HOW ABOUT THIS?" Rick asked.

We were at the law school, with the sun shining and a light breeze rustling my hair. Students were everywhere, talking, studying, joking around. There were students of all ages, so I didn't feel so bad. Although I doubted any of them were three hundred years old.

Through some more sleuthing, we found out that the law program was going to be closed, restructured, and reopened at some point in the future. The current students would attend a satellite school somewhere in Amsburg until then. And the school would be hiring new professors to replace the ones that were fired over this.

"Leliel?"

I jolted out of my daze. "I'm sorry?"

Rick pointed at something in the course catalog we were looking at. "It's creative, right?"

"Photography?"

"Yeah. I've always thought it would be cool to do."

I shrugged. It just didn't sing to me. I figured my future career path would announce itself. It would feel right, a part of me that I never knew I had. "I don't know."

Rick flipped through a few more pages. "English?"

"What?"

"You could learn how to write. Become a novelist," Rick said, his eyes dancing in the sunlight. He was so beautiful like that.

"I'm not much of a storyteller."

"But you have a unique perspective on life," Rick pointed out.

"How long before I am outed as a—" I stopped myself, then lowered my voice. "Special kind of person."

Rick took my hand in his. "You are very special, Mrs. Ashton."

I leaned into him, resting my head on his chest, listening to his heartbeat. "This is too complicated."

"Wait a sec." Rick closed the catalog. "I'm such an idiot. Law enforcement!"

My eyes widened. "What do you mean?"

"I'm not suggesting you become a cop," Rick said. "Because I'd worry myself into a heart attack. But maybe something else? Like a CSI, or a paralegal?" He thumbed through the catalog again. "Look here. They are two-year programs. You'd work with lawyers. And made really good money, too. CSIs look more complicated."

Did the idea of being a paralegal sing to me?

Not really.

"Where would the money for school come from? We've just revamped our budget, and we're on track…"

Rick nodded. "Yeah, you're right."

I smiled as an idea hit me. "Let's go into business together. We can be private investigators. We can keep doing what we just did."

Rick grinned. "That sounds pretty cool. If we can handle the stress."

"We can handle anything, right?"

Rick took my hands in his. "Together, we can do anything, partner."

I chuckled. "You got it."

So Ashton Investigations was born.

From the ashes we rose, stronger than ever.

ABOUT THE AUTHOR

Erin Zarro is an indie novelist and poet living in Michigan. She's married to her Prince Charming, and she has a feline child named Hailey who she's convinced is part vampire. She loves all things scary and spooky, and is on a mission to scare herself, as nothing lately has scared her. She writes in the genres of sci-fi, fantasy, and horror. Her first published novel, Fey Touched, is a blend of sci-fi and fantasy. She is currently working on a nonfiction book and is trying to stay out of trouble. Mostly. Her website is at http://www.erinzarro.com.

Turtleduck Press is a small independent publishing company that endeavors to bring less commercial but quality works to the public. For more information, go to http://www.turtleduckpress.com.

A NOTE FROM THE AUTHOR

If you enjoyed this book, please consider leaving a review. Independent authors like myself depend on reviews to bring more visibility to our work.

And if you'd like to hear about new releases, news, and giveaways, you can sign up for my newsletter at http://eepurl.com/bjsKaL. I only email you when there's something to say. I promise not to spam you.

ACKNOWLEDGEMENTS

I'd like to give a huge thank you to the following people without whom this book would not exist:

My wonderful family, for encouraging me and believing in me.

My wonderful husband, my #1 fan.

My fellow Turtleduck Press co-conspirators: Kit, KD, and Siri. You always have my back and have been the reason why I've been moving forward with my writing career. And for the Under Her Protection anthology, in which Leliel and Rick were born.

For Fran, Tom, and Cathy: you have been a gift that I treasure daily. You've encouraged me, helped me grow as a writer, and have been the most amazing friends. Thank you for your presence in my life.

For my friends at The Spork Room: We've been friends forever, and you've celebrated my accomplishments and held my hand when I needed moral support. You've given me the wings I needed to fly.

To my Absolute Write friends: Thank you for everything. You have supported me and helped me. I appreciate you more than I can say.

For SM Reine, one of my oldest friends: You inspire me every day.

Molly Phipps: For your amazing cover art skills. You've saved me from making my own covers and embarrassing myself. □

For Blue Öyster Cult: "Don't Fear the Reaper" was the theme song for both Reaper Girl and this book. Rock on.

Printed in Great Britain
by Amazon

53363397R00199